Time Benders
Wild West Adventure

Daniel J Kelly

First edition published 2022

Prologue

Let Me Tell You About Max

Max Russell Walsh was born in 1978.

As an only child he spent most of time reading books about quantum physics, metaphysics, and quantum mechanics. As most children do!

He was mainly a loner through high school. He was too geeky for the cool gang, and too cool for the geeks.

He went to college to study physics, he lasted two days before dropping out. There was nothing they could teach him.

He decided to study chemistry instead. That's where he met Joe Brown.

Now it is said that opposites attract, and that was definitely true in Max, and Joe's case.

Max is a tall skinny white guy. He has green eyes, and long brown hair down to his shoulders. He has a wild shaggy beard. He looks like a stereotypical mad scientist.

Joe is a short black guy of Jamaican descent. He has a wide muscular build. He has short black afro hair, brown eyes, and is usually clean shaven.

They got partnered together in their chemistry class.

Now I shall begin with their first conversation.

So Max, and Joe have just been paired up, and are standing together behind their desk with a rack of test tubes in front of them.

“Alright man, I’m Joe,” said Joe.

“Max” replied Max.

“So why are you doing chemistry?” Asked Joe.

“I though it may be of some use when carrying out my physics experiments” replied Max.

“I see, you aint must of a conversationalist, are you?”

“No, not really. I talk more when I’m stoned”

“You smoke ganja?” Joe asked surprised.

“Yep, it helps me concentrate”

“Wicked bro, I’m doing chemistry because one day I hope to develop a strain of weed that can’t be detected by drug tests”

“If someone developed a strain of weed that couldn’t be detected by drug tests, or sniffer dogs, would that make some money?”

“Yeah man, serious money”

“OK, I think we can work together then”

“What seriously, you think you can do it?”

“Won’t know till we try; I’ve got fifty plants on the go at the moment”

“Fifty plants! Where?”

“In the loft of course”

“Do you have your own place?”

“No man I’m 17, I still live with my parents”

“Don’t your parents mind you growing fifty plants in the loft”

“My parents are alcoholics, they don’t know what day it is most of the time, let alone what’s in the loft”

“Oh, I see”

“Here is my address, come round later Joe” said Max handing Joe a piece of paper.

After two years of painstaking research, and smoking more weed that any sane person should within a two year period, they did it.

By altering the genetic properties of THC, they developed a strain of weed that couldn't be detected by drugs tests, and couldn't be sensed by sniffer dogs.

They called it secret garden.

They sold the formula to some shady underworld figures for two million pounds.

Max brought an old warehouse near docklands in East London, and started his experiments. Joe became his assistant, and his first ever friend.

On Friday 25th March 2016.

Max, and Joe arrived at the National Physics laboratory in Teddington.

They carried a large crate between them.

They entered the demonstration room.

There were around thirty scientists sat in the room watching. Mostly men, but some women, all dressed in their white coats.

Max, and Joe stood at the front of the room, behind a large table.

"Thank you very much for having us here today. I have been working on this experiment for nearly twenty years," said Max.

Max looked at Joe.

Joe opened the crate, and lifted out a strange contraption which he placed on the desk.

The contraption was a square loop of metal, with a metal ball floating in the middle, and a large metal ring around the metal ball. The loop of metal had wires coming off of it which connected to a dual plug socket.

“Right basically, I have used magnetic force to suspend the ball, and ring. I will now spin the ring around the ball, and it will generate electricity, but it will not stop spinning as I have cracked perpetual motion,” said Max.

There was a collective gasp from the audience.

Max spun the ring. It started spinning really fast around the ball.

He looked at Joe.

Joe passed Max a large lamp.

Max plugged the lamp into the electrical socket, and switched it on. A bright red bulb lit up.

The audience applauded.

Joe past Max a small fan heater.

Max plugged it in, and turned it on.

The audience stood up, and gave them thundering applause.

Max beamed a huge smile at the audience.

He turned, and shook hands with Joe.

“We’ve done it Joe; we’ve bloody done it” Max said happily.

“Max, there is smoke coming out of the box,” said Joe.

Max turned around, and looked at the perpetual motion device.

Smoke was starting to come off the ball as it heated up.

“Can you turn it off?” Asked Joe.

“Damn, I knew I forgotten something” said Max anxiously.

“I guess you mean the off switch,” said Joe.

Suddenly the table caught fire.

The fire alarm went off, and everyone starting rushing out the building.

Water started rushing down from the sprinklers.

What was supposed to be a momentous day for Max, and Joe turned into a nightmare.

The water that flooded through the National Physics laboratory caused over £100,000 worth of damage.

The National Physics laboratory took a restraining order out against Max, and Joe. They were not allowed within half a mile of the lab.

They were also barred from all scientific institutions in the UK.

Max started smoking more weed to calm his nerves. In his paranoid mind he decided that MI5 where after him. Trying to get his brain. He decided to move to America.

Joe decided to go with Max, he felt he needed looking after. Especially as Max decided he wanted them to sneak into America in a van full of weed, scientific equipment, and a small arsenal.

So, using their shady underworld contacts they relocated to a quiet part of Texas, a couple of miles away from the city of Sherman.

They had to spend two weeks in a shipping container in order to sneak into America. Max spent most of their money on the voyage.

Chapter 1
Accidental Bending

Max, and Joe had been living in Texas for three months. Max had purchased a small wooden shack, and a little piece of land off a farmer. They lived near the city of Sherman. Their shack was close to the crossroads of the 56, and route 289.

In the past three months they had made a few changes to the shack. They had added partitions to turn the shack into three rooms. An open plan living room, and kitchen. A bedroom, and a bathroom. The shack was completely wooden from floor to ceiling.
The bedroom had two single beds in it, and a large woolly red rug on the floor.
The living room area had a three-seater sofa, wooden coffee table, forty-five-inch plasma TV, and a desk with Max's laptop on it. There was a large faux Persian rug on the floor under the coffee table, and by the sofa.
The kitchen had a worktop, a couple of cupboards, a sink, an electric oven, a fridge/freezer, a washing machine, and microwave.

Their water supply came from a borehole out the back in their garden area. Water was pulled up with an electric pump, it then went through a homemade water treatment unit that Max had built. He had used a fly screen as a sand filter, and a piece of perspex with tiny holes in it, as a bacterial filter, and finally he fitted an ultraviolet lamp to kill any bacteria that got through the screen.

Their power source was solar panels on the roof. This meant that during the day they had plenty of power. At night-time they had to use a battery back up to run the TV, and the fridge.

Out the back they had made a small garden area by installing a fence. They had hammered logs into the ground, and run chicken wire round to create their rustic fence.
In their back yard they had a large polythene tent for their cannabis plants. Their two, six-hundred-watt sodium lamps, and ventilation fans also had a large battery back up in case the solar panels where not enough, and for low light periods.

There was a cow, a goat, and six chickens in their garden as well. They had built a small hut for the chickens, and a small barn for the cow, and goat.

A wooden garage sat at the side of the shack, for their van.

Joe nearly always got a surprise when Max would go out in his van, and then come back with various items. Especially when he came back with a cow, and a goat.

“What’s with the cow, and the goat?” Joe had asked.

“Milk, cheddar cheese, and feta cheese of course” replied Max.

And when he came back with chickens.

“I didn’t figure you to be someone who kept chickens,” said Joe.

“No, but I like eggs” replied Max.

When he came back from a scrapyard after buying fifteen windscreens.

“What an earth do you need fifteen windscreens for?” Joe asked.

“I’m gonna make a green house in the garden, all weather fruit, and vegetable growing” replied Max.

“Wow, that’s actually a good idea”

“Aren’t all my ideas good?”

“Do you want me to answer that question?”

“No.
Ooh I’ll tell you something funny though. The scrapyard I found was called Stinky’s scrapyard”

“Seriously” said Joe laughing.

When Max came back with a van full of lead tiles, nails, and a ladder, then covered the roof in lead. Joe realised his friend still had some issues.

“Max my friend, may I ask why you have covered the roof in tiles?”

“They’re lead tiles” replied Max.

“And why do we need lead tiles on the roof?”

“So, aliens can’t beam us out of the shack at night”

“I see”

So, after three months they had settled into their new surroundings.

That afternoon Joe was sat on the sofa watching CNN. Max was sat by his desk fiddling with something.

“Right, I think I’ve done it,” said Max.

Joe looked over at Max.

“Done what?” He asked.

“I think I’ve solved our power problems; we should be able to flush the toilet at night now” replied Max.

“It’s not another perpetual motion device, is it?”

“No mate, I learnt my lesson there, perpetual motions is hard to switch off. This device uses a magnetic loop, and a white crystal cut into a pyramid shape. The magnetic loop draws energy from subspace through the crystal basically”

“And is it safe?”

“Probably. I have encased it in a lead box to contain the electromagnetic radiation, and I have fitted a small surge detector on it. If there is a power overload it will shut down, and send a message to my phone”

“So, it’s not gonna burn our shack down then?”

“I am almost, quite fairly certain it won’t”

Max went to the kitchen where their fuse box was located. He shut the feed off from the solar panels. He connected his box, and activated the switch, so the fuse box would draw power from it.

He walked back into the living room.

“OK I have now fitted the new power supply. I have isolated the fridge, and the grow tent outside for now, just while we test it. The battery backups supplying power to them will last for seventy-two hours so plenty of time,” said Max.

“Well, the TV seems brighter,” said Joe.

Max walked into the kitchen, and ran the hot water. It heated up very fast. He dried his hands, and walked back into the living room.

“Holy Einstein. I think it works,” said Max smiling.

“And it hasn’t caught fire yet” said Joe also smiling.

“Well Joe, I think this calls for a celebration”

“What did you have in mind, getting more stoned than usual?”

"No Joe. How about dinner at McDonald's, and then we find a bar?"

"Seriously Max?"

"Yes Joe, seriously"

"And you're not worried about MI5 or aliens trying to kidnap you?"

"Well, I'll take my Berettas with me as I usually do, but tonight is about you, and me having a good time. The government, and the aliens be dammed"

Max, and Joe usually dressed casually in shorts, and t-shirts. Tonight though, they dressed in suits, and shirts. No ties though. They didn't want to overdo it.

They made the one mile walk to Sherman along the 56.

They found the main street through the city know as Texoma Parkway.

They went to McDonald's for dinner. They were the smartest dressed people in there.

After they finished at McDonald's they walked along Texoma Parkway looking for a bar. They walked into Applebee's Grill & Bar. The place was very lively.

They walked over to the bar, and ordered some drinks. Two bottles of Fat Tire Amber Ale.

“I wish they did pints” said Max as they picked up their bottles.

“Come with me” said Joe as he started walking away.

Max followed Joe to a table where two women where sat.

“Hello ladies. I’m Joe, and this is my friend Max. Would you object to us sitting with you?” Asked Joe.

“Not at all honey, sit down” said the one on the left in her Texas accent.

Joe sat down, and Max followed.

“I’m Sandy, and this is Linda” said the one on the left sat opposite Joe.

Sandy was white with long brown hair, and hazel-coloured eyes. She looked like she was in her thirties.

“Hi” said Linda.

Linda was oriental with long black hair, and brown eyes. She also looked like she was in her thirties.

Both women where slim and toned like they worked out.

“So, what do you ladies do for work?” Asked Joe.

Max just sat with a nervous smile on his face. Taking to women, taking to people in general was not something he enjoyed.

“We teach at Austin College. I’m a drama teacher,” said Sandy.

“Being friends with this guy gives me a lot of drama” said Joe pointing to Max.

“I teach physics,” said Linda.

Max stared at Linda wide eyed.

“I’m, I’m a physicist” he stuttered excitedly.

“Oh, you can speak” said Linda looking at him.

“Yeah, but he only speaks science” said Joe smiling.

“He’s right, I’m a tiny bit obsessed with my experiments, but we’re out tonight as my new power source hasn’t blown up” said Max.

“Well, that is good sign,” said Linda.

“Yes, I used a magnetic loop to draw subspace energy from a crystal,” said Max.

“Wow, that is fascinating,” said Linda.

“You actually understand what he is talking about?” Asked Joe.

“Oh yeah, she is miss science. You should marry this guy honey,” said Sandy.

“Sandy please, we’ve only just met” said Linda blushing.

“It would seem like we have a physical attraction, I mean a physics attraction,” laughed Max.

“I agree. I’d love to see your lab sometime” said Linda smiling.

“Our lab is quite rustic,” said Joe.

“Do you live in a barn?” Asked Sandy.

“No, we live in a wooden shack with a lead tiled roof,” said Joe.

“And we’ve got a cow, a goat, and six chickens,” said Max.

“By the way are you guys Australian?” Asked Sandy.

“No, we’re English,” said Max.

“Oh, how exotic,” said Linda.

“If you say so,” said Max.

“So, what are you guys doing in Texas?” Sandy asked.

“Well, my friend blew up the National Physics laboratory in England, and convinced himself the government wanted to steal his brain, so I guess we’re hiding”. Replied Joe.

"May I just clarify something please. I did not blow up the National Physics laboratory, I set fire to it," said Max.

"How did you set fire to the laboratory?" Asked Linda.

"OK so, I invented a perpetual motion power supply. It worked, but you see the problem with perpetual motion is once you've activated it, it can't be stopped, so the device overloaded, and caught fire," said Max.

"You cracked perpetual motion?" Said Linda amazed.

"Yes, I suppose I did," said Max.

"I think I do want to marry you one day, but today, how about we just exchange phone numbers," said Linda.

"Yeah, good idea, you guys seem OK, a bit weird but you're cute," said Sandy.

They all got out their phones.

"We're actually all good looking, because we have symmetrical faces," said Max.

"Max don't ruin the moment please" said Joe.

"What's wrong with symmetry?" Asked Max.

"I like symmetry," said Linda.

"Max, marry that girl," said Joe.

They both wobbled home after a great night out. They both had a new contact on their phones. It was nice to have someone on their phones that wasn't each of them, or their family members, or shady underworld contacts.

They stumbled into their humble shack.

"Joe, you left the TV on" said Max drunkenly.

"You left your laptop on," said Joe.

"At least the shack hasn't burn down," said Max.

They both fell on the floor laughing.

After they finished laughing, they turned the TV, and the laptop off.

They each visited the bathroom, it was nice to have a flushing toilet, and hot water at night-time now.

They lay in their single beds on each side of their tiny bedroom with three feet of space between each bed.

"I'm very proud of you Maxwell," said Joe.

"Why is that Joseph?"

"You did well tonight, you managed to get a girls phone number"

"Yes, I did. I was quite content not to die as a virgin, but having a girl's phone number on me own tefelone, that isn't related to me is quite satisfying" Max slurred drunkenly.

"Have you only had sex once Max, with that drunk hippy girl?"

"No Joe, I've done it twice. Remember Shaz?"

"Shaz, the big black muma, you didn't, did you?"

"Yeah, I did, or rather she did me"

"Ha, I bet she ate you alive"

"Well, I did pull a muscle in my back, took me three weeks to recover"

They both started laughing.

Soon they were both fast asleep snoring away.

"Max, Max" said Joe gently shaking him.

"What Joe"? Said Max sleepily.

"I've just been to the toilet"

“Did you just wake me up just to tell me you’ve been to the toilet?”

“No. The power is off. The water isn’t running, and the TV won’t work, or the lights, we’ve got no power”

“Oh shit”

Max sat up.

“Is the shack on fire?” He asked.

“No” replied Joe.

“I guess this power supply is safer then”

Max reached onto the floor, and picked up his phone.

“Ah yes” he said looking at his phone.

“What?” Asked Joe.

“Right, there was a power overload last night, and the device shut down just like I designed it to. I can’t seem to get a signal on my phone though”

Joe picked up his phone.

“I can’t get a signal either, but you did something to our phones, so they pick up satellites, maybe there are no satellites near at the moment” he said.

"Joe, there are always satellites orbiting the Earth. Thousands of them. Yesterday I could pick up fourteen satellites, today nothing," said Max.

"What are you going to do about the power?"

"I will fix it, after I've peed" said Max running off to the bathroom.

Max came out the bathroom in his boxer shorts. He walked to the kitchen, and picked up his box.

He opened the lid, and moved the magnetic loop back into position. He closed the lid, and put the box back.

He walked into the bathroom, and flushed the toilet, then he washed his hands with hot water.

He walked out into the living room where Joe was.

"Power is back, you can wash your hands" he said.

"Cheers Max," said Joe.

Whilst Joe was in the bathroom Max fired up his laptop.

Joe came back into the living room.

"So, have you worked out what went wrong with the power?" He asked.

"We've got bigger problems at the moment," said Max.

“What?”

“I can’t get any signals at all on my laptop, we have no internet”

Joe turned the TV on.

A blue screen came up with a message saying there was no signal. It was the same on every channel.

“TVs stopped working as well,” said Joe.

“What the fuck is going on?” Said Max in a grumpy tone.

Joe walked into the kitchen, and looked out the window into their back garden.

“Max, come, and look at this” he called.

“What” said Max strolling into the kitchen.

“Look out the window,” said Joe.

Max looked out.

“Some bugger has stolen our Cow, and Goat” he said.

“They’ve also stolen the barn, and most of our fence. The chickens look like they’re shaking with fright, and the electric pylon over yonder has disappeared,” said Joe.

“Hang on a minute. Last night something stole our cow, goat, barn, and fence, and stole an electric pylon, and steel cables, and our power supply overloaded”

“Do you think you know what happened Max?”

“It’s obvious isn’t it. It was aliens”

“Aliens, are you serious?”

“Of course, and if it wasn’t for the lead tiles, they would have taken us too”

“What the hell would aliens want with a cow, a goat, a barn, part of a fence, and an electric pylon?”

“Well, I don’t know. They’re aliens aren’t they; they do strange alien things. Maybe they got angry with us because they couldn’t abduct us, so the stole our cow, goat, barn, and fence”

“And what about the electric pylon?”

“Well maybe they though that belonged to us, have you got a better theory?”

“Sadly no, I haven’t”

“Any way aliens are the least of our worries now. We need to get a phone signal”

“Why are you so desperate to get a phone signal”

“Joe, for the first time in my life, I have the chance to get a girlfriend, to have sex with someone more than once. To live a semi normal life, so I need to call to Linda tonight, so we need a phone signal. Come on let’s go to town”

“Do you think we should get dressed first?”

“Fine, just hurry up”

“I’ll make you some hot chocolate”

“Oh, thank you Joe, you know I get cranky when my body runs out of sugar”

Half an hour later, they were ready to leave.

They both wore blue jeans, and white trainers. Joe had a brown jacket on, and Max had a red jacket.

They headed to the 56, to start walking into Sherman.

“The god damn road has disappeared” yelled Joe confused.

“That’s settles it, it’s definitely aliens,” said Max.

“What would aliens want with tarmac?”

“No idea, maybe they eat it”

They headed towards Sherman.

As they got close, they noticed the city had changed. It seemed to have shrunk.

“Don’t tell me Max, aliens stole Sherman, and replaced it with a bunch of big sheds,” said Joe.

“Well what other explanation is there?” Said Max.

“Maybe we took a wrong turn”

“It’s damn straight road. We head to the 56, and we walk in a straight line for a mile, then we reach the outskirts of the city. We did it yesterday”

“Well, I don’t think this is Sherman”

They walked over to the small town. It was a collection of wooden buildings lined up on either side of dirt track. It looked like something from a western film.

There was a sign at the entrance to the town.

Sherman
Built 1846

Pop 204

“What does pop mean?” Asked Joe.

“Population” said Max.

“204, that’s not many”

"No, it's not, yesterday Sherman was a city with around forty thousand people in it. This is definitely aliens messing with us"

"Let's see if we can find someone to ask"

They walked into town.

They headed over to a man standing outside the sheriff's office. He was short, and plump. In his forties. He wore leather boots, brown chaps, a blue shirt, a black leather waistcoat, and a brown Stetson hat. He was wearing a star shaped badge, and had two revolvers stuffed into his belt. He had brown hair, blue eyes, and a bushy beard.

"Hi Sheriff" called Max.

"I'm the deputy" he replied in a rustic Texan accent.

He turned, and looked at them.

"Hey, no niggers aloud in this town" he said angrily.

"You can't talk to my friend like that, you stupid hick" said Max shocked.

"And nigger loving Australians aren't allowed here either," said the deputy.

"Did the 1964 equal rights bill pass you by sir?" Said Max.

"I can't understand you crazy Australian"

“I’m not Australian, I am English”

“Oh, that makes sense. A god damn limey. Git outta here now both of you”

The sheriff walked out of his office.

He was a tall man with piercing blue eyes, grey hair, and a large busy moustache. He wore a black Stetson hat, a white shirt, brown waistcoat, brown chaps, and snakeskin boots. He looked like he was in his sixties. He had two long barrelled silver revolvers in his belt.

“What’s all this hollering about?” He said in a firm voice.

“Sheriff there’s a god damn nigger, and a limey in our town,” said the deputy.

“Now, now boys. We don’t want no trouble in this town, so how about you turn around, and mosey on out of here,” said the sheriff.

“You can’t stop someone entering a town because of the colour of their skin” said Max annoyed.

“Look you niggers have got your freedom now. This is nice town, we don’t want trouble, now get out of town, I won’t ask you nicely again boys”

The sheriff put his hand on his gun.

“Fine, we know where we’re not wanted,” said Max.

“What kind of moccasins are you wearing?” Asked the deputy.

“They’re called trainers” said Max as they started walking away.

“You limey’s sure are strange” the deputy called after them as they walked away.

Back at the shack.

They sat in the living room drinking coke, and smoking a joint.

“Man, I’m so sorry about that Joe,” said Max.

“It’s not your fault Max man, I’m used to shit like that any way,” said Joe.

“It’s not right man, it shouldn’t happen in the twenty first century”

“Yeah Max, but those guys didn’t look like they were from the twenty first century”

“No, that whole town looked like it was from the past”

“Don’t tell me Max, have aliens sent us back in time?”

“Hang on a minute,” said Max thinking.

“You’ve got your thinking face on Maxie”

“Maybe just maybe”

“What have you just realised Max, you got that look on your face?”

“Well in theory it could be possible that when the power supply overloaded it sent out a massive wave of electromagnetic energy, bent the fabric time, and sent us back in time”

Max got his phone out, and tapped away on the screen “right the power supply discharged forty gigawatts of energy, fuck that’s a lot, I suppose that could be enough to bend time”

“So, what does that mean?”

“We need better shielding on the box, the lead lining is not good enough”

“No, I mean, what does it mean for us, are we stuck in the past?”

“Well, let’s not jump to conclusions, that is very unscientific. We need to deal with facts, first we need to find out if we are back in time, then establish what year it is”

“OK, and if it turns out we are back in time, can you get us back to our own time?”

“That’s a very good question Joe. I’d need to have a think about it”

“Oh fuck, we’re lost in time!”

Chapter 2
Excuse Me, What Year is it?

Max came out of the bedroom dressed in his black suit, and shiny shoes. He had no tie on. He had his two Berettas in shoulder holsters, concealed under his jacket.

“Right, I’m going back to town to find out what year it is, best I go alone. I think,” said Max.

“Are you crazy Max. What if the sheriff shoots you?” Joe asked worried.

“Joe, don’t worry, I thought of that, I have a kevlar vest on under my shirt”

“What if he shoots you in the head?”

“I’ll duck. You know I’ve been studying martial arts for like eleven years now”

“Yeah, I know, in case you get attacked by ninjas”

“Exactly, you never know when a gang of ninjas might attack you, that’s why I brought a samurai sword along”

“You have a samurai sword hidden under your jacket?” Asked Joe.

“No, I meant when we travelled to America, I brought a samurai sword, and a handful of guns” replied Max.

“Doesn’t hurt to be prepared I supposed. What guns have you brought along?”

“Right, I’ve got my two Berettas, I also brought two Browning HP pistols for you to carry around. I’ve got an M16 assault rifle, an American AK47 with grenade launcher, two Skorpion sub-machine guns, an RPG launcher, and a mini-Gatling gun. And of course, a few crates of ammo.”

“Fucking hell. Are you preparing for war, or something?”

“Well, if the government, or aliens come for me I won’t go down without a fight. Oh yeah also I’m building a laser rifle. I need diamonds for that, I brought some at Hatton Gardens. I’m taking a large two carat diamond with me to get some cash for us”

“I thought we still had some cash?” Joe said looking concerned.

“We do, but if we are indeed back in time, then twenty first century cash will look strange”

“OK then, well good luck”

Max headed off to town.

Twenty-five minutes later he arrived, and entered the small rustic town of Sherman.

The sheriff was outside his office smoking a cigar.

He saw Max, and wondered over to him.

"I thought I made myself clear to you earlier limey" he yelled annoyed.

"I think we got off to a bad start earlier sheriff. I'm Max Walsh, I am a scientific explorer from England. My servant Joe was with me earlier, I met him in the Caribbean on my travels. We are not troublemakers, we are in fact perfect gentleman. We have recently moved here. We are good Christian men, and I promise we will cause you no trouble," said Max.

"Well now, I suppose I can allow you to come into town, but the nigger, no way, for his own safety as much as anything. There are plenty of folk here who are still pissed about the recent civil war, and seeing a nigger in town walking around free kinda rubs it in their faces. It's the north's fault imposing the damn reconstruction on us"

"OK thank you sheriff. I will keep my servant at home then"

"You do that, but I warn you, if you do cause any trouble, I won't hesitate to haul your arse into jail"

"Very good sheriff. Now can I ask a couple of questions please?"

"Sure. Fire away sir"

"Well, I have been travelling for many years, and I don't even know what the date is"

“It’s May twelve”

“And what year is it?”

“Jesus, you have been travelling for a long time. It’s the year of our Lord 1870”

“Excellent, thank you sheriff. Last question. I have no money, and I would like to trade a diamond for some dollars, where can I go?”

“Go to the First Bank of Texas, other end of town”

“Thank you very much sheriff”

“You’re welcome, sir, now remember what I said, NO trouble!”

“Of course, sheriff”

Max walked down to the other end of town, and entered the First Bank of Texas. Part of the building was made from stone, and the rest wood.

Obviously, the vault is in the stone part thought Max.

He walked in, and wondered over to the female cashier. She was wearing a frilly red dress covering her whole body, and a black bonnet. She had a pretty face, blue eyes, and long brown hair. She looked like she was in her early twenties.
She sat behind a desk with no screens in front of it. It looked strange nothing like a modern bank.

“Howdy sir, how can I help you?” She asked.

“Hello madam. I would like to trade a shiny diamond for some cash please,” said Max.

“Hold on a minute please sir”

She turned to look over at a man in suit who sat behind a desk in the corner.

“Randy, there’s an Australian man here who wants to trade a diamond for cash” she called.

Randy stood up. He was a tall slim man with short grey hair, and a large moustache. He had brown eyes, and looked around fifty.

“Come over here son” he called beckoning Max.

Max walked over to his desk.

“Sit down son” Randy said.

Max sat down.

“Hi I’m Max Walsh”

“Howdy Max Walsh, I’m Randy Bulmer”

They shook hands.

“Well let me see this diamond then please Max”

Max pulled the diamond out of his pocket, and put it on the table.

Randy pulled a magnifying glass out of his desk draw, and examined the diamond. He picked it up, and bit it, then slammed it on the desk, making a dent in the wood.

“Ooh wee, that is some sparkler, and a genuine diamond, where do you get it from son?”

“Hatton Gardens in London”

“Oh my, a diamond all the way from London. I’ll give you twenty bucks for it”

“Twenty bucks that’s a two-carat diamond from London”

“OK son, twenty-one bucks but that is my final offer”

“OK then, I accept” said Max sheepishly.

Randy pulled some money out of his desk. He gave Max a ten-dollar bill, a five-dollar bill. A three-dollar coin, and three one-dollar coins.

Max left the bank, and wondered off to the Sherman saloon, and hotel.

He walked through the double swinging saloon doors.
Around twelve men sat around the bar area.
Everyone in the place gave him a funny look.

He wondered over to the bar.

The barman was a short guy with long blonde hair, and a bushy beard. He had green eyes, and looked about forty. He wore a long white apron.

“Well don’t you look fancy boy. Are you from the East?” He asked.

“Actually, I’m from England,” said Max.

“Oh, a limey. Better than a Northern spy I suppose, what are you having?”

“What have you got?”

“Whiskey”

“I guess I’ll have a whiskey then”

The barman poured a whiskey for Max, and placed it in front of him.

“Fourteen cents” the barman said.

“Wow” said Max, and handed him a one dollar coin.

The barman took the coin, and counted out eighty-six cents in change for Max.

Max picked up the whiskey, and took a sip. His mouth started burning. It was the strongest drink he's ever had in his life. He went bright red, and coughed a bit.

"This limey's never tried Texas whiskey" called the barman.

Everyone in the saloon started laughing.

Max picked up the glass, and downed it.

"Another please" he said placing the glass down.

The barman poured another, and Max gave him fourteen cents.

A lady came over to Max. She was gorgeous. She had a long frilly blue dress on. She had long brown curly hair, and big blue eyes. She was short, and looked like she was in her twenties.

She stood next to Max, and stroked his arm.

"I bet you've travelled a long way sweetie pie, and you need to relax" she said in a soft voice.

"Yes, I have travelled a very long way. I'm Max"

"Hi Max. I'm Madeline, and you can spend an hour with me for just a dollar if you like"

Max picked up his drink, and downed it.

"I'm all yours Madeline" he said excitedly.

Max stumbled into the shack, and kicked his shoes off.

Joe was sat on the sofa listening to Bob Marley whilst smoking a joint.

Max stumbled over, and fell onto the sofa.

"You took your time mate, want some" Joe said holding out the joint.

"No thanks bro" said Max drunkenly.

"Shit man, turning down Ganja. How pissed are you man?"

"The whiskey here is fucking strong, it's like drinking a fire. But worse than that, worse than that man, they spell whiskey with an e"

"They spell whisky with an e?"

"Yeah bro, I feel like gunning them all down just for that, the fucking heathens"

"So, what took you so long did you pass out?"

"No, I had sex. With a women man"

"A women man?"

“Yeah bro”

“So where did you meet this lucky lady then?”

“In the Sherman saloon, and hotel”

“Oh, I see, how much did that cost you?”

“One dollar for an hour, and I gave her a one-dollar tip, and she was very grateful, and she loved the way I talked, and how nice I smelled”

“One dollar for an hour, fucking hell, how much did you get for the diamond?”

“Twenty-one bucks”

“What’s that in modern terms?”

“Do I look like a fucking economist to you? Probably about three hundred dollars, or three thousand, or something”

“So, what did she look like?”

“Lovely, I think I’m in love with her, Madeline is her name”

“OK nice, did you find out what year it is?”

“Oh yeah I forgot about that, its 1870”

“1870! So, what does that mean?”

“Houses don’t have electricity yet”

“No, I mean for us, what does it mean for us, can you get us back to our time?”

“Hmm well, let me think about that for a minute”

“What now when you’re this pissed?”

“I have some of my best ideas when I’m inebriated”

“That explains a lot”

“OK so let’s examine the facts. We’ve gone back in time one hundred, and forty-six years”

“And what does that tell you?”

“We are currently minus one hundred, and eight”

Max started laughing.

“Max, get serious please”

“OK tomorrow I shall go into town, and get Madeline, and we’ll ride off into the sunset together”

“What? Max, we’re talking about time travel”

“Oh, are we? Oh yes. So, I think what happened is the crystal power supply overloaded, and sent a massive electromagnetic shock wave out which bent the time space continuum. So, imagine a straight line, we are at one end, and 1870 is at the other end, if the line gets bent then we move closer to 1870"

"I see, so what does that tell you?"

"That we bent time, so we are benders"

Max started laughing.

"Max please, this is serious"

"Lighten up bro, it's possible to get back. We just need to reverse the process. So instead of discharging a massive electromagnetic shock wave, we need to absorb one"

"So, you know how to do that then?"

"No, I don't, I still don't know how electromagnetic energy actually bent time"

"So, what you're saying is we're stuck here"

"No not really, what I'm saying is we're stuck here until I can work out how to get us home"

"And how long will that take?"

"How long is a piece of string my friend"

"Like that is it?"

"Ooh I just realised why the power supply overloaded"

“Why?”

“It’s the crystal, once you start drawing power from subspace it keeps coming, so if there is nothing drawing power the power has nowhere to go, and it just builds up until it overloads. So, I will connect the fridge, and the grow tent to the power supply then we will always be drawing power”

“Now does working out how long it took the power supply to overload help you at all?”

“Yeah, but doing fiddly working out will have to wait for the morning when I’m sober”

“Good, because I don’t like it here”

“Oh, Joey boy, I’ll look after you mate. Think of the opportunity we have here, to explore the old west”

“Yeah, and get shot”

“We are more that capable of defending ourselves, although we must remember causality. No, we must respect causality probably”

“What’s causality?”

“Messing up the timeline. Now for example if we killed a guy who was gonna have children, grandchildren, and great grandchildren, and so on. We would have wiped out that line. If one of the people we wiped out invented the vaccine for tuberculosis then millions of people could die because of that, see what I mean?"

"I think so"

"Well, let us consider Sir Isaac Newton, my God, and his laws of physics. So, in nature every action has an equal reaction. So, if a plant needs a bug to care for it, then that bug will be available. Let's say we wiped out all those bugs, then that plant would be become extinct. So, our actions in the past will have reactions in the future, if we are not careful, we could go back to world where shrimp don't exist, or where all human life has been wiped out. We have a great responsibility"

"So, what you're saying is, is someone wants to shoot us, we have to let them because of causality?"

"Hell no, if someone tries to shoot us, we pop the bitch first, causality be dammed"

"You are a very confusing man"

"We just need to be careful that's all, now I'm off to pee, and then bed"

"Don't forget to do that thing with the power supply"

"Oh yeah, we don't want to go back another hundred, and forty-six years, you'd have to be my slave then"

Max woke up in the morning feeling very hung over. He looked over, and saw Joe sitting on his bed dressed, and looking at him.

“Hello Joe” Max mumbled sleepily.

“How are you, Max?” Asked Joe.

“I feel awful, that whiskey they have is lethal, I reckon that if you drink it every day for a year or two your liver would probably melt”

“Well, you did snore really loud last night”

“Oh, sorry mate “

“That’s OK, I got some sleep. Did you mean what you said last night before bed?”

“What did I say last night before bed, I don’t remember?”

“You wanted me to drive you into town, while you sat in the back of the van, and you were gonna open the side door, and gun everyone down with the mini-Gatling gun, and then you were gonna pick up Madeline, and we would drive off into the sunset”

“I really said that?”

“Yes, you did”

“Fuck I was pissed”

“Yes, you were”

“And I slept with a prostitute?”

“That’s what you told me”

Max reached under his bed, and grabbed a large sports bag.

“What’s in the bag Max?”

“This is my emergency medical kit”

“Why do you need that?”

“I slept with a prostitute, I’m worried I might have caught something, like syphilis, so I’m gonna inject strong antibiotics, and antivirals into my groin”

“Well, I think I’ll leave the room then”

“Yes, please do, I have to pull my pants down”

“Alright I’m gone”

Joe hurried out the room.

Joe walked into the kitchen, and switched the kettle on. He got two mugs ready with coffee, milk, and sugar.

Once Joe had made the coffees he went to the living room, and placed them on the coffee table. He sat on the sofa.

Max came out the bedroom wearing his dressing gown. He was walking funny. He went to the bathroom.

He came out a few minutes later, and sat down on the sofa next to Joe.

“Made you a coffee mate,” said Joe.

“Cheers mate” said Max picking up his mug.

“So got any plans for today?”

“Yeah, I’m a bit worried about the grow tent out the back, it’s very exposed. I thought I’d go to town, and buy some wood to put around it”

“And how do you plan to transport the wood home?”

“In the van of course”

“Don’t you think the van might look out of place in 1870?”

“Yes, I do, but I’m not using a bloody horse, and cart to transport things”

“How do you think people in the town would react to seeing a van?”

“That’s a fine question Joe, I’ll make a scientist out of you yet. It would be a good experiment to see how people in 1870 would react to a Ford Transit van”

“Suppose they thought you were the devil, and started shooting at you?”

“That would be a highly likely outcome, however, the van is armoured, and I have superior weapons”

“And what about causality?”

“Oh fuck. How do you know about causality?”

“You told me about it last night, you also said we could get home it you reversed the process that brought us back in time”

“That would be the logical way. Unfortunately, I don’t know how to reverse the process, but I will think about it”

“Come on Max, you’re the smartest guy I know”

“I’m aware of that Joe. But Isaac Newton, and Einstein weren’t able to crack time travel, and they were a damn sight smarter than me”

“So, what are your plans for today?”

“Get stoned, and see if I have a good idea”

Chapter 3
Mr & Mrs Woods

Max walked over to Joe who was sat on the sofa. Max was carrying a bundle of papers.

Max sat down, and placed the papers on the coffee table. He put two pairs of scissors down. One in front of Joe, and the other pair in front of himself.

“What’s this? You been printing money?” Asked Joe.

“Yes Joe. I scanned the ten-dollar bill I had into the computer, and I used duplex printing onto the bonded paper I had. Now we just need to cut all the notes out,” said Max.

“What do you mean bonded paper?”

“It’s the paper they use at the US Federal Reserve to print money”

“How did you get hold of that?”

“I brought it off Ebay”

Max had gone to town earlier, and brought a couple of axes from the hardware store.

He also brought two black Stetson hats from the tanners, to help them blend in.

It was now 1am, and they both set off in the van.

They were both dressed in black suits with no ties on, shiny black shoes, and their new hats.

They travelled north a few miles over the bumpy terrain, and found a small copse with several white oaks.

They both jumped out, and began chopping trees down.

After working hard for over two hours, they had chopped down two trees, and stripped them of their branches.

“This is bloody hard work, and damn slow with hand tools” moaned Max.

“Why didn’t you buy a chainsaw Max?”

“Haha, very funny Joe”

They loaded the two logs into the back of the van.

They were just about to jump in the van, and head home when they heard footsteps.

Two people came running over.

A man, and women. The man was tall with long brown hair. He was dressed in a white smock with bare feet. The women was short with long blonde hair. She was dressed in a white night gown, and also had bare feet.

“Oh, please help us” said the women panting.

“They burnt our house down, and now they’re after us” said the man also panting.

“Woe there calm down people it’s OK. Who is after you?” Said Max.

“The Callaghan brother’s gang. My brother gave a statement to the sheriff after he saw them rob a stagecoach that he was riding in. Now they’re trying to find my brother,” said the man.

Max drew his two Berettas.

“Don’t worry good people, I will protect you. I’m Max Walsh by the way, and this is my servant Joe,” said Max.

“Hi Max, and Joe, I’m Tobias Woods, and this is my wife Emily,” said Tobias.

They heard the sound of horses galloping.

Four mean looking outlaw types rode up to them.

“Now Tobias you will tell where your brother lives, or we will kill your wife” said one of the outlaws.

Max stepped forward holding a Beretta in each hand, cocked, and ready to fire.

“These people are under my protection now, boys,” said Max.

“What are you, an Australian?” Said the outlaw.

“No, I’m English” said Max annoyed.

The outlaws started laughing.

“A God damn limey, oh I’m so scared”

What the outlaws didn’t know was that Max was a sharpshooter. He had been practising shooting guns for many years, just in case the government or aliens ever attacked him.

“Now boys. I will give you a chance. Kindly fuck off, and I won’t kill you” said Max menacingly.

“Line this Limey’s belly with lead boys” said the head outlaw.

Max quickly fired four shots with one of his Berettas.

The four outlaws fell from their horses with blood pouring from their heads. Their horses ran off.

“My gosh. I have never seen anyone shoot that fast,” said Emily.

“Me neither,” said Tobias.

“I am a scientist from England. I made these guns myself,” said Max.

“Well, gosh, you must be so smart,” said Tobias.

“Yes, I suppose I am,” said Max smiling.

“And what is this big white box here?” Asked Emily looking at the van.

“This is another one of my inventions, I call it a horseless carriage. It uses a small steam engine similar to what a railway locomotive uses” replied Max.

“You mean that thing moves” said Tobias intrigued.

“Yes, it does, now would you like us to transport you to the town, and you could stay at the Sherman saloon, and hotel?” Said Max.

“It won’t be open now, its mighty late,” said Tobias.

“Well, I guess you can stay with us tonight then, we have some camping mattresses so you can sleep on the floor,” said Max.

“Why thank you Max, that’s mighty kind of you,” said Tobias.

“We’ve only got three seats so Emily you will have to sit on Tobias lap,” said Max.

“I’m not sure I can sit on my husband’s lap in front of people” said Emily embarrassed.

“Yeah, can we sit in the back of the carriage?” Asked Tobias.

“Not really there are two logs in the back. Look you don’t need to be embarrassed in front of us, we are English explorers, and we’ve seen everything,” said Max.

“OK I suppose it would be OK just this once,” said Tobias.

They all climbed into the van.

Max sat in the driver seat with Joe next to him. Next to Joe, Tobias sat with Emily on his lap.

Max started the engine.

“It’s mighty quiet,” said Emily.

Max set off over the bumpy ground.

“It’s so smooth,” said Tobias.

After a few minutes they reached the shack.

Max parked in the wooden garage.

They got out, and Max unlocked the front door. They all walked inside.

Max turned on the living room light.

“Oh my. How did you light that bright lantern?” Asked Emily.

"Look Tobias, Emily. My work is very secretive, so I would appreciate it if you didn't tell anyone about this place, or my horseless carriage," said Max.

"After what you did for us Max, that is no problem. We wont tell a soul about your weird inventions" said Tobias.

"Would anyone like a drink?" Asked Joe.

"My, you don't sound like a Negro man," said Emily.

"He was born in England. He's not really my servant, he is my friend, and faithful companion," said Max.

"Oh, things sure are different in England," said Tobias.

"Thank you for the offer, I think we'd just like to go to sleep" said Emily looking at Joe.

"Fetch the camping mattresses Joe," said Max.

"Excuse me Maxwell, you just said I'm not your servant, so you get them" said Joe defiantly.

"OK fine," said Max.

Max walked into the kitchen, and fetched two rolled up camping mattresses out of a cupboard.

He walked back into the living room, and pushed the coffee table back against the sofa. He unrolled the mattresses out, and laid them on the floor.

"I like your rug," said Emily.

"Thanks, it's a faux Persian rug," said Max.

"And what is the box with glass screen?" Said Tobias pointing to the TV.

"That's another one of my inventions it doesn't work at the moment," said Max.

"Oh, I see, well we go to sleep now if that's OK," said Tobias.

"I have no blankets for you I'm afraid, I'll leave the heating on in the living room tonight," said Max.

"We'll be fine, its mighty warm in here," said Emily.

Max opened the bathroom door, and turned on the light. He opened the bedroom door, and turned on the light. He turned the light off in the living room.

"OK, see you in the morning," said Max.

"Thank you so much Max, you saved our lives, we are forever in your debt," said Tobias.

Max woke up. He though he heard a knock on the door. Joe was snoring away fast asleep.

He heard the knock again. He climbed out of bed, and grabbed his dressing gown off the hook on the door. He slipped his gown on, and opened the door.

Emily was stood in front of him.

“Hello Emily” he said sleepily.

“I’m mighty sorry to wake you Max, but I really need to use your outhouse, where is it?” She spoke.

“We don’t have an outhouse,” said Max.

“But I really need to pass liquid”

“Oh, I see, you want the bathroom”

Max walked past Emily, and opened the bathroom door. He switched the light on, and motioned for Emily to come in.

Emily walked into the bathroom, and looked around amazed.

“What is this place?” She said confused.

Max put the toilet seat down.

“Right, I have put the seat down for you. Now you sit down here, and pass liquid into the bowl. Then you grab a piece of thin paper from here to wipe yourself, then push this metal handle down, and the bowl will clean itself. Once you finished here, you come here to the wash basin, and turn this tap like so”

Max turned the hot tap, and water came out.

“Then you can wash your hands, there soap there, and there is a towel hanging down here. Did you get all that?”

“I think so”

“Right, I’ll leave you in peace then”

Max left the bathroom, and shut the door.

He walked into the kitchen, and looked out the window. The sun had just come up. He heard the toilet flush. Then he heard the electric water heater below the sink clicking as it activated.

Looks like she remembered everything he though.

He heard the door open, he turned around to face the bathroom.

Emily walked out, and came over to him.

“Are you a sorcerer Max?” She asked.

“No, I’m a scientist. Some of the stuff I do will seem like magic to you” replied Max.

“Well, the water came out the faucet, I’ve seen running water before, but I couldn’t hear the steam pump when your water runs, and to my amazement the water got hot, how on earth do you get hot running water?”

“Just think of me as a sorcerer Emily, but a good one”

“I’m going back to sleep if that’s OK?”

“Sure Emily, sleep as long as you like, I’m going back to bed myself”

Max went back into the bedroom, and shut the door.

Later.

Emily took great delight showing Tobias the bathroom, especially the magic hot water tap.

They all sat in the living room drinking coffee. Emily, and Tobias sat on the sofa with Max, and Joe sat on Max’s office chair.

“We are mighty grateful to you both for saving us last night, and we are forever in your debt,” said Tobias.

“It’s no problem. Glad we could help,” said Max.

“And Joe, it’s a pleasure to meet you sir, I just want you to know we never agreed with the slave trade,” said Tobias.

“Thank you, that’s very kind of you to say,” said Joe.

“But we are in a small minority, most folk around here would probably shoot you if they saw you,” said Emily.

“Yeah, I know, I can’t go into town,” said Joe.

"We'll talk to the sheriff, and tell him what you both did for us," said Tobias.

"Oh, it's gonna be so embarrassing going to town in our night clothes," said Emily.

"No choice dear, we lost everything last night," said Tobias.

"You're wrong actually, you didn't lose everything, you are both still alive, and I will go out soon, and buy you clothes, then I will walk to town with you," said Max.

"Oh no we can't ask you to do that," said Tobias.

"You didn't ask me, I offered," said Max.

Max came back from town carrying two large paper boxes with two pairs of leather boots on top.

Tobias, and Emily were delighted. Tobias had a new pair of brown trousers, a white shirt, and black leather boots. Emily had a blue frilly gown, and red leather boots.

They all bid goodbye to Joe, and set off to town. Max was wearing his black suit with no tie, shiny shoes, and his Stetson hat.

Max pulled a joint out of his inside jacket pocket, and lit it up.

"Oh, you're a tobacco smoker I see," said Tobias.

“Yes, I suppose I am. Do you smoke?” Said Max.

“No, we never got into it, don’t really like the smell,” said Tobias.

“Your tobacco has a very sweet smell though Max,” said Emily.

“I picked this tobacco up in Jamaica,” said Max.

“Where’s that?” Asked Tobias.

“In the Caribbean, south of Florida, near Cuba, and Mexico,” said Max.

“My, you do get around don’t you,” said Emily.

“That’s my job, I’m a scientific explorer, so I have to travel around, and learn things,” said Max.

Soon they reached town. They went to the sheriff’s office.

Inside the sheriff’s office there were three small wooden desks on one side, and two cells surrounded by stone walls on the over side.

The sheriff sat behind one desk, and the deputy was sat behind the other desk.

“Tobias, Emily, and Max the limey, what can I do for you?” Said the sheriff standing up.

"Oh sheriff, last night Emily, and me was attacked by the Callaghan brother's gang. They burnt our house down, and they would have surely killed us if this man, and his friend hadn't saved us," said Tobias.

"I'm sorry to hear that, Tobias. Every law man, and soldier in Texas is on the lookout for the Callaghan brothers. Now how did this limey save you exactly?" Asked the sheriff.

"He killed the Callaghan brothers gang single handed," said Emily.

The deputy started laughing.

"Hush now Ned," said the sheriff.

"I'm sorry sheriff, but do you really believe this limey could take on the Callaghan brothers?" Asked the deputy.

"If Tobias, and Emily Woods say so, then yes I do, you know these people very well, and they are not liars" said the sheriff firmly.

"Yes of course, sorry sheriff," said the deputy.

"Now how on earth did you manage to take on the Callaghan brother's gang?" The sheriff asked Max.

"Sheriff, I travel around the world with just my friend Joe. If I couldn't take care of myself, I wouldn't be here now," said Max.

"Well, I must say I'm mighty impressed with you limey," said the sheriff.

"Now sheriff we lost all our possessions, and our home last night. What shall we do?" Said Tobias.

"Well, I think I could spare five bucks, have you got any money Ned?" Said the sheriff.

"I could spare like a dollar," said Ned.

Max pulled out some cash, and counted out a bit.

He handed the money to Tobias.

"Here that's a hundred bucks, stay in the hotel until you get back on your feet, and if you need any more you know where to find me," said Max.

Tobias started crying.

"I can't" he blubbered.

"What my husband is trying to say is, you done so much for us Max Walsh, and we can't except that much money from you," said Emily.

"Look it's not a problem, I'm happy to help, I have enough money," said Max.

Emily started crying. She put her hand on Max's shoulder.

“You are a true gentleman, and a saint” she said weeping.

Tobias shook Max’s hand.

“We are forever in your debt Max Walsh. Thank you so much,” said Tobias.

“Now where in the hell did you get all that money from limey?” Asked Ned.

“From science Ned,” said Max.

“That’s deputy Ned to you, and I never knew science paid so well”

A tall slim man walked in. He had short brown hair, a huge moustache, and bright blue eyes. He wore black leather boots, brown trousers, a white shirt, and a waistcoat with a star shaped badge on it. He looked like he was in his early thirties.

“Well, howdy deputy Handsome,” said Ned.

“Very funny deputy ugly,” said the man.

“Deputy Hanson, this is Max Walsh” said the sheriff pointing to Max.

Deputy Hanson strolled over, and shook Max’s hand.

“Nice to meet you Max Walsh, I’m Davie Hanson,” said Davie.

“Nice to meet you deputy Hanson,” said Max.

“You must be the limey that my sister keeps talking about,” said Davie.

“Yeah, that’s him,” said Ned.

“Who’s your sister?” Asked Max.

“Madeline, she’s a pleasure girl at the saloon,” said Davie.

“She’s your sister?” Said Max surprised.

“Yes, she is”

“And you don’t mind her working there?”

“Sure, I do, but my Daddy owed big John money, and he had to give him Madeline or we’d all be killed”

“And that’s legal”

“Of course, it is limey. If you owe money, and you can’t pay, you have to find another way to pay,” said Ned.

“Why didn’t your dad just kill big John?” Said Max.

“Cos that would be illegal,” said Davie.

“But if big John killed you all that would be legal?” Said Max.

“Yes, cos my Daddy owed big John money,” said Davie.

“Strange laws,” said Max.

“Anyway, are you gonna go, and say hi to my sister?”

“I’m not sure if I can face sticking a needle in my groin again so soon”

“Sticking a needle in your groin, what the hell do you do with these girls?” Said the sheriff.

“Yeah, I’ve never been offered that service,” said Ned.

“OK Davie, tell her I’ll come see her tomorrow, I’m a bit worn out today, had a busy night,” said Max.

Max was walking back home. He was just leaving the town when he heard a gunshot, and felt like someone punched him in the back.

He spun round, and saw a short young looking cow boy was stood behind him, with a smoking revolver in his hand.

“Did you just shoot me?” Asked Max.

“Oh, sorry mister, I thought you was someone else,” said the cowboy.

“No harm done kid, trying shooting people in the front from now on”

“OK mister, how come you aint bleeding?”

“The power of Kevlar kid”

“I had an idea on the walk home” said Max entering the shack.

“What, how to get us home?” Asked Joe who was sat on the sofa.

Max sat next to Joe.

“No, how to use the van during the day,” said Max.

“Have you worked out how to make it invisible?”

“No silly, I know how to make something invisible, but I don’t have the necessary equipment. No, I thought we could camouflage the van”

“Camouflage it as what?”

“A big shrub”

“A big shrub, were you smoking on the walk back?”

“Yes of course. But I noticed all the bushes and shrubs around as I was walking, that’s when I had my idea”

“How would you see out the windscreen”

“We don’t cover the whole van until we’ve parked up”

“Why don’t you make it look like a mini train?”

“I thought of that, we haven’t got any paint”

“Why do you wanna drive the van during the day anyway?”

“In case you haven’t noticed, we are getting low on milk, cheese, and meat, also beer, but I haven’t found anywhere in town that sells beer”

“And you really won’t use a horse, and cart?”

“Do you know something Joe, I am probably the smartest guy in the world at the moment, so no I am not using a fucking horse, and cart”

Chapter 4
Madeline Hanson

The next afternoon Max walked into town. He went to the Sherman saloon, and hotel.

He walked in, and got funny looks from most of people in the bar. He was dressed in his suit, with shiny shoes, and his Stetson on.

He walked over to the bar where a lady in a red frilly dress was sat. She had long blonde hair, and blue eyes. She looked around forty years old.

“Howdy sugar, wanna buy me a drink” she said.

“Sure, why not, two whiskeys please,” said Max.

The barman placed two glasses down, and poured some whiskey into them.

“Twenty-eight cents please” he said.

Max handed him a one-dollar coin. The barman counted out some change, and handed it to Max.

“Thank you darling. By the way are you that limey called Max?” She asked.

“Yes, I’m Max Walsh, pleasure to meet you madam” said Max holding out his hand.

The lady shook his hand.

“Nice to meet you Max, I’m Betty Sue. Madeline has been talking about you, I think she wants to marry you,” said Betty Sue.

“Oh wow, that’s nice to hear. Where is Madeline?” Asked Max.

“She is upstairs at the moment being fucked by farmer Tom”

“Oh, I see” said Max a bit lost for words.

“So would not mind marrying a whore?”

“Well, if she didn’t mind a couple of needles in her groin then no I wouldn’t mind”

“Needles in the groin! You limey’s sure are strange”

“It’s a medical thing”

“Oh, are you a doctor?”

“In a way yes”

“Oh, that’s good, I’ve got an itchy rash on my left buttock”

“How often do you bathe?”

“Once a week, I can’t afford to go to the bath house more than that”

“Well, when you have a rash, you need to wash it everyday”

“Damn, well I can’t afford that, it cost two dollars to have a bath”

“But you get a dollar for every hour you work”

“No honey, big John gets a dollar for every hour we work, we get ten bucks a week allowance”

Max pulled out some money, and handed two ten dollar bills to Betty Sue.

“Here there’s twenty bucks, now bathe every day for a week, and the rash will go,” said Max.

“My goodness. No wonder Madeline wants to marry you, you really are a kind gentlemen, and quite rich it seems”

“She doesn’t just want to Marry me for my money, does she?”

“Oh no honey, she said you were the most polite, and kind gentleman she has ever met, and that you smelled great, and you do smell great”

“Thank you, I won’t smell great when the deodorant runs out”

“You limey’s sure do talk funny”

“Hi Max” said Madeline excitedly walking up behind him.

“Hello Madeline” said Max turning around.

Madeline sat at the bar next to Max.

“He really is a gentleman, and he is a doctor as well,” said Betty Sue.

“Really you are a doctor,” said Madeline.

“Yes, I am,” said Max.

“He told me how to get rid of my rash,” said Betty Sue.

“Are you gonna buy Madeline a drink mister” said the barman as he walked over.

“Sure, why not whiskey for Madeline please,” said Max.

“I could do with another one,” said Betty Sue.

“Make that two whiskeys,” said Max.

“Are you not having one?” Asked Madeline.

“No, I’m fine at the moment, I like my liver intact,” said Max.

The barman poured two glasses of whiskey.

The ladies picked up their glasses, and downed them.

“So Max, you wanna spend an hour with me?” Said Madeline.

“Yes, I do,” said Max.

“Oh goodie” said Madeline excitedly.

They walked off together.

“Have fun you two” said Betty Sue smiling.

Max went upstairs with Madeline, and into her room. Her room had an oak framed double bed, and an oak chest of draws. There was a brown rug on the wooden floor, and the walls had red wallpaper on them.

They sat on the bed.

“I don’t like charging you Max, but I gotta ask for a dollar before we start,” said Madeline.

“That’s fine,” said Max.

Max handed her a ten-dollar bill.

“I need to pop down to the bar to get some change,” said Madeline.

“No, that’s all for you,” said Max.

“Ten bucks, are you after something weird, do you wanna stick it up my arse?”

“Tempting offer, but I actually just want to talk to you”

“What, you could have just brought me a couple of drinks if you wanted to talk”

“I wanted to talk in private”

“Well, it’s your money so talk away, you’ve paid for ten hours”

“Are you happy here?”

“What do you mean?”

“Are you happy with your life?”

“Not really, but who is these days?”

“OK let me ask it a different way. If you had a choice, what would you do with your life?”

“Well, if it was up to me, I would like to marry you, and have your children”

“Wow, I’m flattered. OK how about we date for a bit, then get married”

“What do you mean date?”

“Courting”

“Oh, I see. Max I would love to court with you, and you know I don’t mind fucking before marriage”

“Yes, I figured as much, so let’s do it then”

“Oh, that would be nice, but big John owns me, and he wouldn’t let me court someone, let alone get married”

“I could buy you off big John, I’ve got some money”

“Big John wouldn’t sell me; he likes me too much. I’m his best girl, and he likes to fuck me as well. One time this rich prospector from California offered him a thousand dollars for me, and he turned it down”

“Would he accept ten thousand dollars?”

“You would pay ten thousand dollars for me?”

“Yes, I would”

“You really love me then”

“I guess I do”

“Big John wouldn’t take any money, he wouldn’t even accept a million dollars, but no one has a million dollars, do they?”

“No, I haven’t got enough bonded paper”

“You sure do talk funny”

“Yes, I do, but I’m serious now. I will talk to big John, and if we can’t strike a deal, I will come, and rescue you one night”

“Do you know why they call him big John?”

“I suspect it because he is fat”

“No, he is over seven feet tall, and he is wide, and he is the strongest man in the whole of Texas”

“Well, that doesn’t scare me”

“Well, you are either very brave or very stupid”

“I’d say I’m a bit of both”

“You are lovely Max, but big John has a whole crew, he sits with them in the bar every night. If you picked a fight with big John, you end up fighting seven people”

“No problem I’ll bring an M16”

“I don’t know what the hell an M16 is, but I don’t think it would help you”

“It sounds like you don’t want me to rescue you”

“I would love you to rescue me, but I don’t want you risking your life for me”

“Well Madeline, I am an English gentleman, and I would do anything for love, I’d run right into hell, and back. I would do anything for love I’d never lie to you, and that’s a fact”

“That is the sweetest thing anyone has ever said to me” said Madeline teary eyed.

Thank you, Meatloaf, and Jim Steinman, thought Max.

Ten minutes later they were downstairs in the bar. Madeline took Max over to a large table at the back of the bar where two men where sat, a skinny fellow, and a giant.

“Big John, this man would like to talk to you,” said Madeline.

The giant stood up. He was tall, wide, and mean looking. He looked around fifty. He had short black hair, a huge black moustache, and brown eyes. He wore black trousers, big black leather boots, a white shirt with red braces, and a huge Stetson. He had a red belt with two long barrelled revolvers in holsters.

“Hello, I’m Max Walsh” said Max holding out his hand.

Big John grabbed Max’s hand with a vice like grip.

“Big John, how can I help you, Max?” He said with a deep booming voice.

“Well sir, I was wondering if I could buy Madeline off you for ten thousand dollars” said Max nervously.

“She aint for sale” big John replied.

“One hundred thousand dollars” offered Max.

“Are you deaf boy? I said she aint for sale. Ask me one more time, and I will fill your belly with lead” said big John menacingly.

“OK, I’m sorry big John, I didn’t mean to offend you, can I buy you a drink?” Asked Max.

"Sure, you can get me, and my buddy a bottle each" said John.

Max walked over to the bar.

"Three bottles of whiskey please" he said.

"That will cost you six dollars sir," said the barman.

Max handed him a ten-dollar bill.

"Oh, we don't get folks in her with ten-dollar bills much," said the barman.

He placed three bottles down, and handed Max his change.

"And can I have an empty glass please?" Asked Max.

"Sure" said the barman handing him a glass.

Max walked back to big John's table, and placed two bottles down.

"Here you go" he said.

"Well thank you good sir, you are welcome here anytime" said big John smiling.

Max smiled, and walked over to Madeline.

He put a glass down on a table, and poured some whiskey in it. He handed the glass to Madeline.

“Here you go” he said.

“Aw thank you Max, you really are kind” she said taking the glass “sorry about big John” she whispered.

“Tomorrow night I’m gonna rescue you Madeline” he whispered.

“Please don’t risk your life for me Max, I can’t believe you offered a hundred thousand, you are a very special man” whispered Madeline.

“Thank you, Madeline, you are special to me, and big John is the one who just risked his life by refusing my offer.

Max left the saloon carrying the bottle of whiskey, and went to the sheriff’s office.

He walked in. The sheriff wasn’t there. Ned, and Davie were sat at their desks.

“Howdy Max,” said Davie.

“Can I have a word with you in private please Davie?” Asked Max.

Davie got up, and strolled over to Max.

“Sure buddy, let’s go outside” said Davie.

They walked outside together.

“What’s up Max?”

“I have just spoken to your sister, and she doesn’t want to work for big John anymore”

“I don’t think any of the girls there actually want to work for big John”

“Well, let go in together, and get her out”

“Max, my sister is big Joe’s property, if we take her that would be stealing”

“What if big Joe was dead”

“Then I guess she would be free. Now you aint thinking about killing him are you Max, you would hang for that”

“I offered big John one hundred thousand dollars for her, and he turned me down”

“A hundred thousand dollars, seriously. Are you in love with my sister?”

“I believe I am”

“Gosh Max, a hundred thousand dollars, Jesus. Well, if big John won’t take your money there is nothing else you can do”

“Well, it would seem to me that I can’t use money, and I can’t use the law, then I’m left with one option, my M16”

“M16 is that some legal document or something”

“It is certainly an enforcement tool”

“Well, I wish you the best Max, but I don’t think a lawyer can help you with this”

Max strolled into the shack. Joe was in the kitchen.

“Just making coffee, want one?” Said Joe.

“Yes, please mate, and then we have to talk,” said Max.

Max kicked off his shoes, and sat on the sofa. He placed the bottle of whiskey down on the coffee table.

Joe walked in, and placed the mugs on the coffee table. He sat down next to Max.

“You look like you’re in a very serious mood,” said Joe.

“I am,” said Max.

“Just rolled this” said Joe picking up a joint.

Joe sparked up the joint, and had a few tokes, then passed it to Max. Max two a few big tokes, and passed it back.

“Thanks bro, I needed that,” said Max.

“What’s up mate?” Asked Joe.

“I’ve been thinking”

“That’s a bit dangerous, isn’t it?”

“Yes, can be, however this time I thought we should think about moving somewhere that is more accepting of black people”

“Is that your way of telling me we are stuck in 1870?”

“No mate, it will take me a long time to figure out how to get us back, and there is a small chance we may be stuck, so it would be fairer on you if we moved”

“OK that’s nice, when shall we move?”

“Tomorrow night”

“Tomorrow night! Are you serious man?”

“I’m deadly serious”

“What did you do?”

“I got myself a girlfriend”

“Are you taking about that whore Madeline?”

“I rather you didn’t refer to my girlfriend as a whore”

“I’ll take that as a yes then, so you actually wanna move because of her?”

“No, it’s actually for all of us, for our safety”

“What have you done?”

“Nothing yet”

“Yet? What are you planning?”

“I’m planning on going to rescue her tomorrow night”

“And did you think about me at all when you made this crazy plan?”

“Of course, I did, you are the getaway driver”

“Maxwell Walsh, I love you like a brother, but you have fucking lost it. You want to drive the van in town, and grab this girl, and drive off into the moonlight?”

“Not quite, I need you to be near the town in the van with the engine running, and I’ll deal with the seven guys who will try, and stop me getting Madeline, and then we can drive off into the moonlight”

“I’m dreading the answer to this question. How do you plan on dealing with these seven guys?”

“With an M16”

“You go on about causality, and now you wanna gun down seven men with an M16”

"When you are doing something for love, causality has to take a back seat"

"You really love her that much, that you would be willing to risk the whole damn timeline?"

"Yes, I do"

"OK mate, I'll help you then"

"Really?" Said Max surprised.

"Yeah mate, it's about time you got a girlfriend"

"Yeah, I'll second that mate, by the way that whiskey on the table is for you to try mate"

Joe picked up the whiskey, and took a sip.

"Fucking hell mate" he said gasping.

"Strong aint it?" Said Max.

"Fucking lethal, I aint drinking anymore"

"No problem, it will make a good fire lighter"

The next day Max, and Joe were up bright, and early. They had a lot of packing to do.

They harvested the cannabis plants in the grow tent, and hung them outside to fast dry in the sun. Not ideal but time was against then. The grow tent, and equipment was packed up into a box. That went into the back of the van.

Max disconnected the pump on their bore hole. He dug all the underground steel pipe work, and boxed that up. He put that in the van.

It took both of them to lift the washing machine into the van, it was bloody heavy. They strapped it in place.

Joe lifted the fridge into the van while Max disconnected the power supply box, and fuse box. Max rigged the fridge up to the fuse box, and power supply so power would continue to be drawn through the crystal to prevent another overload. They strapped the fridge, and power supply down.

They boxed up the cooking utensils, plates, glasses, cups, and cutlery. That went into the van.

They packed there bedding up into a box, along with their camping mattresses.

The emergency medical bag was placed in the van. Followed by their clothes in a bin liner.

Max boxed up the water heater, and the microwave, and placed that in the van.

He packed up his laptop, and bag of scientific equipment, crystals, and diamonds. That was put in the van.

Lastly the bags of guns, and ammo was placed into the van.

“It’s a shame we can’t take those logs with us we cut down,” said Joe.

“Oh, that reminds me, the axes, we can cut down more trees then, we’ll need wood to build another home,” said Max.

“I put the whiskey in the front, we may need a drink after tonight”

“Good thinking Joe. Killing people is not nice, I still feel a big sick from gunning those men down the other night. I don’t know what is happening to me, I don’t let emotion rule me, I am a man of logic, and reason”

“Logic, and reason. What would logic, and reason say about gunning seven men down so you can date an ex-prostitute?”

“Well thankfully logic, and reason can’t talk!”

Evening came, and Max, and Joe were sat in the van. Joe was in the driver seat.

“OK, I’m ready, I’ve got my M16 locked, and loaded, and two spare clips” said Max holding his rifle.

“Two spare clips, you only going up against seven people, and you’re taking one hundred, and fifty bullets with you,” said Joe.

"It doesn't hurt to be prepared, have you got the two Browning pistols?"

"I've got one Browning pistol, and one spare clip on me"
"Maybe you should have the AK as well just in case"

"Max, I have never fired a gun in my life. You have shown me how to use the Browning, that's enough for me, I am not using a fucking AK47"

"Fine Joe, if you wanna play fast, and loose with your own safety then that's up to you"

Joe fired up the engine, and they set off for town.

It took five minutes on the bumpy track to reach town.

Joe parked up behind the general store at the end of town.

Max climbed out the van. He was wearing a long trench coat with the M16 hidden underneath.

He strolled into the Sherman saloon, and hotel.

He spotted Madeline sitting by the bar. He looked over to the rear where big John was sat with five mean looking guys. The rest of bar was half full of customers.

He walked over to Madeline.

"Hi Madeline" he said.

"Oh, hi Max, good to see you, wanna spend some time with me?" She spoke.

"Yes, I would like to spend the rest of my life with you please"

"I would love that too, but it's not possible"

"If I kill big John, will you come away with me"

"Max please don't risk your life"

"Answer my question please"

"Yes, I would follow you to the end of the world"

"Enjoy the show Madeline, I'll be back"

Max walked over, and stood close to big John's table.

He pulled out his M16, and held it ready.

"Big John, your reign of terror ends tonight" he said confidently.

Big John, and all his cronies jumped up, and faced Max.

"What the hell do you want limey?" Boomed big John angrily.

"You know what I want big John, one hundred thousand dollars, take the deal, and you get to live," said Max.

"Boys let's kill the fucking limey," said big John.

They all reached for their guns.

Max pulled the trigger, and the sound of automatic gun fire echoed around the saloon.

Big John, and his cronies fell to floor as the hail of bullets slammed into them. Blood poured from their wounds, as the rapid fire cut them to shreds.

The customers in the bar dived onto the floor. Women started screaming.

Max emptied the clip into big John, and his boys. He ejected the clip. He reached for another clip, and went to slam it into the rifle when there was a loud bang. Max felt pellets striking his back.

He turned around, and saw the barman with a smoking double barrelled shotgun.

“Shooting someone in the back, that’s pretty fucking low,” said Max.

“What the fuck are you?” Said the barman shocked.

Max pulled out a Beretta, and took aim.

“I’m an English scientist” he said.

He put a hole in the barman head.

He holstered his Beretta, and shoved another clip into the M16.

A crowd of people gathered on the upstairs hall overlooking the bar.

Max strolled over to Madeline.

"Would you do me the honour of being my girl?"

"Oh Max, yes, I can't believe you did that for me, I am yours forever" said Madeline overwhelmed.

"WHAT THE HELL'S GOING ON" yelled Betty Sue from above.

"BIG JOHN IS DEAD, WE'RE FREE" yelled Madeline.

Six ladies came charging down the stairs cheering.

Max took Madeline's hand, and led her out of the saloon. In his other hand he held the M16 ready to shoot.

They began walking through town. Madeline was lost for words, but inside she felt happier than she had ever been.
Ned, and Davie burst out the sheriff office.

They stopped, and looked at Max, and Madeline.

"What in tarnation has been going on at the saloon limey, there is a woman in the office who said some guy shot the place up with some magic gun that spits out bullets?" Said Ned.

"Ned, why don't you go, and check the saloon, and I will talk to Max, and my sister," said Davie.

“OK fine,” said Ned.

Ned wondered off.

Davie walked up to Max, and Madeline.

“Oh Davie, Max saved me from big John, I am going to go off with him now, and we will get married one day,” said Madeline.

“That’s great news, what happened in the saloon?” Asked Davie.

Max held up the M16.

“I used this magic gun to kill big John, and his associates” he said.

“That think can spit bullets?” Said Davie.

“It can fire ten bullets a second,” said Max.

“No way. No rifle can fire ten bullets in a second,” said Davie.

“Oh Davie, you should have seen him in action he blew the hell out of big John, and his boys, and he was shot by both barrels of a shotgun, and the pellets just bounced off him,” said Madeline.

“Well, if that true, you better get out of here fast, Ned will be back soon gunning for you,” said Davie.

“Yes, we need to run,” said Max.

“Goodbye brother I love you” said Madeline embracing Davie.

“Bye sister I love you too, you take care of her now Max,” said Davie.

“I will, with pleasure,” said Max.

They started walking off.

“STOP THEM” yelled Ned from outside the saloon.

“JOE” yelled Max.

The Transit van came screaming into town with its head lights on.

Madeline froze with fear. Davie, and Ned looked on in shock.

“Don’t worry, come with me” said Max pulling Madeline’s hand.

He dragged her over to the van, and opened the door. He pushed Madeline into the van, and climbed in after her. He shut the door behind him.

“Have a seat Madeline,” said Joe.

“What an earth is going on?” Said Madeline confused.

"Don't worry you're safe now. This is my friend Joe," said Max.

Max gently pulled Madeline down into her seat.

"Oh my, this is a comfy seat. Hello Joe, I didn't know Max had a nigger as a friend" she said.

"Madeline, I would appreciate it if you didn't refer to Joe as a nigger," said Max.

"What should I refer to him as then?" She asked.

"Call him Joe, he is my best friend," said Max.

"Well, howdy Joe, nice to meet you" she said.

"Nice to meet you too Madeline," said Joe.

"You don't sound like a nig, I mean a Joe," said Madeline.

"I was born in England same as Max," said Joe.

"You have coloured men in England?" Said Madeline.

"Yes, we do, we also have coloured women," said Max.

Ned came running over panting. He pointed his gun at Max.

"Now you step out of the, whatever it is that you are sat in" said Ned.

“Sorry Deputy, can’t do that,” said Max.

“I will shoot,” said Ned.

“Go ahead,” said Max.

Ned fired a shot, it bounced off the windscreen.

“What the hell?” Said Ned confused.

“Armoured glass deputy, get us out of here Joe,” said Max.

Joe slammed the van into reverse, and they shot backwards. He spun the van around, and started racing forward out of town. They got out onto the bumpy track, and sped along, Joe switched the full beam lights on.

“I feel very confused. Firstly, where is the steam engine that powers this here carriage, and how do you get the lanterns at the front so bright?” Asked Madeline.

“Madeline, are we courting now?” Asked Max.

“Yes, I guess we are, but what is going on Max?”

“Right, I will tell the whole truth now. There is no steam engine in this carriage. There is an internal combustion engine which runs on diesel. I have also made a few modifications, there is a crystal battery pack which acts as a hybrid drive, and I have rerouted the exhaust manifold so the fuel is burned twice, that effectively makes the engine around 130% efficient, and means it can achieve around one hundred, and fifty miles to the gallon"

"I could not understand a single word of what you just said"

"Max talk plain English, not science," said Joe.

"OK sorry. Basically, we are from the future," said Max.

"What do you mean?" Said Madeline confused.

"OK I will simplify this. Right this year is 1870, and next year is 1871, right got that?"

"Yeah, I understand that"

"Well in one hundred years it will 1970, got that?"

"Yes, I got that"

"Well, we are both from the year 2016"

"Is this some kind of weird limey joke?"

Max lent forward, and switched the entertainment system on. The screen lit up. The radio made no sound, and said there was no signal. Max pressed the CD button, and Dire Straits Sultans of Swing started playing.

"What in tarnation. There are words appearing magically, and where is that sound coming from," said Madeline.

“This song actually came out the year I was born 1978,” said Max.

“So, you aint joking you really are from the future” said Madeline shocked.

“Yes, we really are. This gun I have is called an M16 assault rifle, you won’t be able to buy this for over a hundred years. This carriage we’re in is called a van. The internal combustion engine will be invented in around sixteen years. It will replace steam engines, eventually”

“So why did you come back in time?”

“It was an accident, but now I’ve met you, I’m glad we had the accident”

“Aw Max”

Madeline learned over, and they started kissing passionately.

“Guys could you save the smoochy stuff for when I’m not around?” Said Joe.

“Sorry Joe” Max, and Madeline replied together.

“We need to find Joe a girl, where are all the coloured girls hiding?” Said Max.

“Guess you could try East,” said Madeline.

“What direction are we heading in Max?” Asked Joe.

“Joseph, do I look like a compass to you?”

“Fine, you could have just said you don’t know smart arse. So, what is the plan then?”

“I’d say drive for an hour, and then we’ll set up camp, and have something to eat, and something to smoke as well”

Chapter 5
Out in the Open

Max, Joe, and Madeline sat by a roaring campfire in the wilderness smoking a joint.

“This tobacco tastes really strange, nice, and sweet,” said Madeline.

“Yes, it’s Jamaican tobacco,” said Max.

“Well, it’s making me feel lightheaded,” said Madeline.

“It’s good stuff, we grew this ourselves,” said Max.

Madeline started giggling.

“I’m so sorry, I don’t know what came over me,” said Madeline.

“Probably Max” said Joe laughing.

“Don’t be rude Joseph” said Max also laughing.

“I like this stuff you’re smoking,” said Madeline.

“I love you Madeline,” said Max.

“Aw Max, I love you too,” said Madeline.

“Get a room you two,” said Joe annoyed.

“In case you hadn’t noticed Joe, we are in the middle of nowhere, there are no rooms,” said Max.

“Are we wanted men now?” Asked Joe.

“I suppose so, wanted dead or alive,” said Max smirking.

“Oh, you certainly will be, there will pictures of you handed out all other Texas,” said Madeline.

“Don’t worry Joe, we just need to get out of Texas then we’ll be fine,” said Max.

“So, we won’t have loads of people after us?” Said Joe.

“No of course we won’t,” said Max.

“Actually, big John’s brother is a Texas ranger, and he has a friend who is a Major in the Union army. So, there will be lots of people after us” said Madeline laughing. “I’m sorry, I don’t know why I find that funny!”

“Oh great, so what do we do if a thousand soldiers turn up wanting to kill us?” Said Joe.

“I doubt that would happen, but if it did, we have RPGs, and a mini gun” said Max.

“So have you stopped caring about causality then Max?” Asked Joe.

“What is causality?” Asked Madeline.

"Well, it basically means if we change things in the past, it could affect the future," said Max.

"What do you mean change things?" Madeline asked.

"Like if Max killed eleven people, and married you," said Joe.

"Joe, the eleven people I killed where bad guys, they were bound to die eventually, and marrying Madeline won't change the future, it will change my future only, and make me very happy," said Max.

"Well, you're the scientist apparently," said Joe.

"Yes, I am, and actually come to think of it, I might like to stay in this time, Madeline, and I can get married live on a ranch, and have some kids," said Max.

"And what about me?" Said Joe.

"I'll send you back to 2016 if I can mate," said Max.

"Oh, I can't wait to get married, and have children," said Madeline.

"How many kids do you want Madeline?" Asked Joe.

"Six" said Madeline.

"Six"! Said Max chocking with shock.

"Yeah, is that not enough?" Said Madeline.

“Why six?” Asked Max.

“Well, some of them will die unfortunately, so we need a few” said Madeline.

“OK, if I could guarantee none of our children would die, how many would you like to have?”

“Six”

“Still six?”

“Yeah, I always wanted six children, ever since I was little, I can’t believe my dream is gonna come true” said Madeline smiling.

“Six it is then”

Joe laughed.

“OK Joe, I will come back to 2016 with you then,” said Max.

“Oh OK, what made you change your mind?” Said Joe.

“I’m not raising six kids in the old west, I need to have hospitals, midwives, and childcare,” said Max.

“I feel hungry,” said Madeline.

“You’ve got the munchies my dear, hang on a minute,” said Max.

Max got up, and walked over to the van. He opened the side door near where the fridge was. He opened the fridge, and took out three chocolate bars.

He came back to the campfire.

“Here you go” he said passing Madeline a Mars bar.

He passed one to Joe.

“Cheers mate,” said Joe.

“What do I do with this?” Asked Madeline confused.

“Oh sorry,” said Max.

He took the bar off her, and opened the top. He passed it back to her.

“You eat the chocolate inside” he said.

Madeline took a bite.

“Oh my God, I have never tasted anything so delicious in my life” she said smiling.

“From now on darling, you will only have the best things in life,” said Max.

“Aw Max, you are the greatest man I have ever met in my life,” said Madeline.

"Just don't start having sex next to me, when we're in bed," said Joe.

"Oh, we wouldn't do that," said Madeline.

"No, we wouldn't, no sex until Madeline has had her shots," said Max.

"You wanna shoot me Max?" Said Madeline.

"No dear. That's a medical term. It means injections, future medicine to get rid of anything you may have caught off one of the men you slept with," said Max.

"Oh, I see," said Madeline.

"Yes, it will just be a tiny prick," said Max.

"Tiny prick, don't sell yourself short Max" said Joe laughing.

"Very funny Joe, I am perfectly happy with the size of my willy thank you" said Max annoyed.

"So, Madeline how many men have you slept with?" Asked Joe.

"Why would you ask that Joseph?" Squealed Max annoyed.

"To annoy you mate. So how many Madeline?" Said Joe.

"Well, over a hundred I guess, I was whore for seven years," said Madeline.

"Does that bother you, Max?" Said Joe.

"Not at all Joe, we all have a past, remember Sian the ladyboy?" Said Max smiling.

"Ah come on Max, you know I was wasted that night" said Joe blushing.

"So, you say Joe, so you say," said Max.

"I think its bedtime now," said Joe.

"It's mighty cold tonight," said Madeline.

"You can snuggle up with me under my duvet," said Max.

"What's a duvet?" Asked Madeline.

"A future blanket that keeps you nice, and warm," said Max.

Max woke up in the morning the sun was low in the sky. He turned over, and noticed Madeline was not there.

He jumped out of his camp bed.

"MADELINE" he yelled.

Joe jumped up.

"What's up mate?" He said sleepily.

“Madeline’s gone” Max said.

Madeline came running out of a small copse. She rushed over.

“What wrong Max, I heard you hollering?” She spoke.

“I didn’t know where you were” Max said relieved.

“I had to pee,” said Madeline.

“Well, you should have woken me, I would have come with you”

“I’m a big girl Max, I can pee on my own, and there is no one around”

“Yes, I know, but you have to watch out for rattlesnakes out here”

“Did you say rattlesnakes?” Said Joe worried.

“Yes, I believe there are rattlesnakes native to Texas,” said Max.

“And we slept outside,” said Joe.

“Well, there wasn’t enough room to sleep in the van,” said Max.

“We need to find shelter, I am not sleeping outside again,” said Joe.

“OK, we’ll head west for half a day, and then we’ll look for shelter”

“And which way is west, Mr I am not a compass?”

“Well considering the sun rises in the east I would say it’s the opposite direction to where the sun is now”

“Good plan smart arse, I need to pee now”

“Thank you for that info, Joe, I also need to pee in case you were wondering”

After a few minutes Joe, and Max came back from peeing.

“Just thought of something Joe, did we bring any toilet paper?” Asked Max.

“No mate, we ran out yesterday,” said Joe.

“Madeline, can I ask you a delicate question please?” Said Max.

“Of course, Max, you can ask me anything you like” replied Madeline.

“Well, when you go to the outhouse, and you need to wipe your bottom, what do you use?”

“You mean what do we use to clean the shit off our arses?”

“Yes, that’s right”

“We use a piece of corn; we always keep some corn in the outhouse”

“Not the worst answer you could have given, but I’d still prefer to use toilet paper”

After a mug of coffee each. Which impressed Madeline, she had never seen coffee made so fast, and never seen a magical electric kettle before. They decided to move on.

“Are you sure about driving the van during day Max?” Asked Joe.

“No choice mate, we can’t just sit out in the open waiting for a gang of Texas rangers, or the Union army to stumble across us,” said Max.

“Good point, but what if someone sees us?”

“I guess they will have a good story to tell people, let’s go”

They climbed into the van. Max was in the driver’s seat, Joe was by the passenger window, and Madeline sat in the middle.

They headed off west not knowing where they were going.

“How will we know when we’re out of Texas?” Said Joe.

“I was kinda of hoping they would have a sign,” said Max.

“I’d love to help you boys, but I have never been outside of Sherman,” said Madeline.

"Fantastic, I can show the whole world Madeline," said Max smiling.

"Oh, thank you Max, you are the best" said Madeline also smiling.

"You planning on booking an around the world cruise when we get back?" Said Joe.

"Actually, I was thinking about showing her Google maps," said Max.

"What are going to do about the water situation wise one, we have half a jug left in the fridge?"

"I'm sure we'll find a river soon enough then we'll stock up"

"We can't drink river water though"

"Sure, you can, we get our water from the Red River sometimes when the well runs dry" said Madeline.

"Don't worry Joe, we'll boil the water first," said Max.

"Why do you need to boil the water?" Asked Madeline.

"To get rid of microbiological organisms," said Max.

"I really don't understand your strange talk sometimes," said Madeline.

"Very tiny things you cannot see with your eyes, river water is full of them. Legionella, E-coli, Cholera, and Cryptosporidium to name a few. They make you sick," said Max.

"Do people not get sick in the future?"

"Yes, we have future illnesses, but the illnesses that effect you these days we can cure"

"We can't cure cancer," said Joe.

"Yes, we can my friend it is just illegal to cure cancer in western country because corporations own the government, and curing cancer means pharmaceutical companies can't make money treating it. I don't think they had cancer in the 19th century, I think it was invented in the 20th," said Max.

"You serious believe the government or some corporation invented cancer?"

"Yes Joe, companies have made billions if not trillions out of cancer, so yeah they invented it, probably got it from the grey aliens, the evil bastards"

"The future sounds quite scary," said Madeline.

"The world is a scary place Madeline, but there is also great beauty in it, just look in the mirror," said Max.

"Aw Max, you say the sweetest things" said Madeline smiling.

"When did you turn into Mr romance Max?" Asked Joe.

"When I fell in love Joe," said Max.

"Shit look at that" said Joe pointing.

Max looked where Joe was pointing. There was a stagecoach being attacked by native Americans.

"Right Joe, drive by time, open your window, and shoot the native Americans as we pass them," said Max.

"Max, just because I'm black doesn't make me a fucking expert on drive by shootings" said Joe annoyed.

"Fine I'll do it then," said Max.

Max headed towards the stagecoach. He drew one of his Berettas, and eased the hammer back. He pressed the window button, and the window rolled down.

"That is magic" said Madeline watching the window roll down.

"It's not magic darling, it's called electricity" said Max.

He pulled out alongside the native Americans on their horses. He fired a shot, and hit on of the natives in the arm. The native Americans turned, and saw the van driving alongside them. They steered their horses away, and fled in fear.

"I thought you liked head shots Max," said Joe.

"I didn't want to kill him, it's not the native Americans fault, if it wasn't for the white man, they wouldn't have to rob stagecoaches. The white man has a lot to answer for," said Max.

"You are one strange white man Max," said Joe.

"It's not the white man's fault Max, the savages won't do as they're told," said Madeline.

"Madeline one day I will teach some real history," said Max.

The stagecoach stopped, and Max parked up near it.

Max jumped out, and rushed over.

"Is anyone hurt" he called.

"No, no, we are fine thanks to you pilgrim" said the coach driver.

The coach door opened, and Tobias, and Emily stepped out.

"I don't believe it, Max Walsh you saved us again" said Tobias shocked.

"We must stop bumping into each other like this," said Max.

"Well, we are mighty glad you did bump into us Max," said Emily.

The coach driver, and guard got down, and walked over.

The coach driver was a tall slim man with long grey hair, and a large grey moustache. He had grey eyes, and looked around sixty. He was wearing a black suit, and a black top hat.

The guard was a short stocky fellow with short brown hair, a bushy brown beard, and green eyes. He looked around thirty, and was wearing a blue suit, with a brown Stetson. He was carrying a Winchester rifle.

Joe, and Madeline walked over.

“There’s a god damn nigger” said the guard raising his Winchester.

Max drew both his Berettas, and aimed them at the guard.

“No, it’s OK Patrick, he works for this man who just saved us” said Tobias.

Patrick lowered his Winchester, and Max holstered his Berettas.

“My apologises sir, I didn’t know he was your servant,” said Patrick.

The coach driver approached Max, and held out his hand. Max shook his hand.

“Jesse Jones, I thank you for your assistant good sir,” said Jesse.

“Max Walsh, it was my pleasure to help” replied Max.

"That strange looking carriage you have, how does it move with no horses?" Asked Jesse.

"It has a miniature steam engine in the back like what a railway locomotive uses"

"Holy Mary, can I see that?"

"No, I'm very sorry, the back has to remain sealed to keep the boiler pressure up, if I open the back, and depressurize the boiler, it would take me an hour to repressurize it, and we are in a bit of hurry"

"Oh, I see I don't know about these fancy steam engines, are you a railway engineer?"

"No, I'm a scientific explorer, so I know how things work"

"Is that an Australian invention?"

"No, we're actually limey's"

Joe, and Madeline walked over to Tobias, and Emily. Patrick was stood close by just staring at Joe bemused.

"Hi Tobias, and Emily, how are you?" Asked Joe.

"We're good thank you Joe, how are you?" Said Tobias.

Max, and Jesse strolled over to them.

"Well, we actually fleeing town as Max caused some trouble," said Joe.

"Oh, I see," said Tobias.

"Did I see you in the saloon?" Emily asked Madeline.

"Yep, you sure did, I used to be a whore," said Madeline.

"Oh, I see, that's erm, erm, nice" said Emily lost for words.

"What sort of trouble are you fleeing from Max?" Asked Jesse.

"I killed big John, it was either him, and his six buddies or me," said Max.

"Are you shitting us limey?" Said Patrick stunned.

"No, he aint, he did it to rescue me, and we is gonna get married, and have six babies" said Madeline proudly.

Joe nudged Max, and whispered to him.

"Six babies' mate"

Max cringed.

"Do you know what you've done boy?" Asked Patrick.

"Let me guess, big John's brother is a Texas ranger, and he has a mate who is a Major in the Union army," said Max.

“Yeah boy, but thems the least of your worries. Big John’s uncle is the governor of Texas, he will hire thousands of men to hunt you down boy,” said Patrick.

“This situation just gets better, and better,” said Joe.

“It’s fine we’ll be out of Texas soon,” said Max.

“You might wanna get out the country boy, big John’s uncle will put a huge bounty on your head, every bounty hunter in the country will be after you,” said Patrick.

“We’ve got a bigger problem” said Joe pointing.

Everyone looked where Joe was pointing. Lined up in the distance on the hilltops, where thousands of native Americans on horses.

“Holy shit, it looks like the whole Cherokee has come out to fight,” said Jesse.

“What do think Max, mini gun?” Said Joe.

“No way mate, I’m not hurting any horses,” said Max.

“We’re about to get slaughtered, and you’re worried about fucking horses,” said Joe.

“Animals are innocent. I’ll see if I can scare them off,” said Max.

He walked over to the van, and opened the back. He learned inside, after a few minutes he emerged with a loaded RPG launcher.

“What in God’s name is he holding?” Said Jesse.

“Don’t worry this will scare them off,” said Joe.

Max aimed a few feet short of the line of natives. He wasn’t trying to hurt anyone, just scare them off.

He pulled the trigger. The rocket blasted out of the launcher, and whistled forward.

There was a huge explosion in front of the natives, causing a rockslide, and frighting the natives, and their horses. Horses reared up with fright. The natives brought the horses back under control, and gallop away in fear.

Max walked back to van, and put the launcher back. He walked back over to Madeline, Joe, Jesse, and Patrick.

“What the hell kind of gun is that?” Asked Patrick looking nervous.

“Something I made myself, it launches dynamite,” said Max.

“I aint never seen no dynamite that powerful before,” said Jesse.

“It’s Chinese dynamite,” said Max.

"Well, that can stay in China as far I'm concerned, we don't need weapons that powerful in America," said Jesse.

"Yes, I completely agree, shall we get moving, where are you heading by the way?" Asked Max.

"We're going to Jacksboro to stay with my sister," said Emily.

"How far is that?" Said Max.

"Bout another two hours ride west," said Jesse.

"OK then we shall accompany you there to make sure you arrive safely, we're heading west anyway," said Max.

They all set off west to Jacksboro. The van followed behind the stagecoach.

"Hew wee, I could sure use a drink after all that excitement," said Madeline.

"Joe, where is that bottle of whiskey?" Said Max from the driver's seat.

Joe opened the glove box, and pulled out the bottle, he popped the cork out, and passed it to Madeline. She grabbed the bottle, and took a few gulps.

"Ooh that's better" she said, "want some Max?"

"No thank you darling, I need to be clear headed to drive this van," said Max.

“Joe” she said passing him the bottle.

“Thanks, just a sip, I’m cracking up here” he said taking the bottle.

“You still look like you’re in one piece to me Joe,” said Madeline.

Joe laughed.

“It’s just one of our English expressions Madeline, he means he feels anxious,” said Max.

“Well, I’m not surprised. I sure did get a fright by that explosion, does everyone in the future have guns like that?” She asked.

“No darling, that gun is used is a weapon of war, so only soldiers have them,” said Max.

“They still have wars in the future?”

“Yes, they do, usually because big corporations want control of oil”

“I hate war, my older brother Linus got killed, and my daddy lost an arm in the civil war, that why daddy had to sell me, he couldn’t work, and couldn’t pay for food, and supplies; so he borrowed money off Big John, but couldn’t pay him back”

“Aw I’m so sorry to hear that, I would never let anything bad happen to you, I promise”

“And I believe you Max, I feel safe with you. Now tell me about the future wars”

“Maybe I shouldn’t tell you too much about the future”

“Damn it Max Walsh, you once told me you would never lie to me, so answer my damn question”

“Damn you Meatloaf! OK fine, future wars are terrible, more terrible than you can imagine. If you thought that explosion earlier was big, it was nothing compared to modern weapons. Weapons that can kill thousands of people, even hundreds of thousands of people in an instant”

“Well, I asked you to be honest, now I must be honest, I don’t think I can live in your time”

“I don’t live anywhere that war is going on, these wars happen on the other side of the world”

“So, I wouldn’t have to worry about getting blown sky heigh?”

“No darling, I told you I will always protect you from anything”

“You two better get a room tonight I can’t take any more of this gooey stuff,” said Joe.

After they said goodbye to the stagecoach, they headed west for a while, and came to a river.

Max got his pump, and homemade water treatment kit out of the van. He connected the electrics up to the crystal power supply.

Joe held the pump, so its hose was in the river. Max held the water treatment kit, and Madeline held the one-gallon bottles under the steam of water coming out the end of the water treatment kit.

Soon they had filled four, one-gallon bottles.

Madeline tried some of the water.

"Golly, this is the nicest water I've ever tasted" she said amazed.

"That's called clean water," said Max.

"It's starting to get dark Max," said Joe.

"OK pack up, and we'll move on," said Max.

They started packing the van up.

"I'm hungry," said Madeline.

Max looked in the fridge. There were three rashers of bacon, a small piece of cheese, and a Hershey's chocolate bar.

Max broke the cheese in half, and ate one piece, he gave the other piece to Joe. He gave the chocolate bar to Madeline.

“And that leaves a piece of bacon each for supper,” said Max.

“We need to get some more food, like soon mate,” said Joe.

“We’ll drive for another hour, and then we’ll set up camp, if we see anything moving, we’ll shoot it, and eat it. We’ve got plenty of water now, that’s the main thing,” said Max.

Chapter 6
Comanche's in Trouble

Joe was sat by the campfire frying some rattlesnake meat. Max had caught a rattlesnake earlier, and chopped its head off with a kitchen knife, then he skinned it, and removed the tiny bones.

Max, and Madeline came back from the van, and sat down by the campfire.

"My arse feels strange," said Madeline.

"What have you two been up to?" Asked Joe.

"He stuck it in my arse," said Madeline.

"You dirty boy Max, hope you washed your cock," said Joe.

"She's talking about the injections Joseph, get your mind out of the gutter," said Max.

They all started laughing.

"Is the snake ready yet?" Asked Max.

"I think so, but I never cooked rattlesnake before," said Joe.

Joe used a spatula to move the snake meat from the frying pan onto plates.

They sat, and ate the snake meat.

"Mm this quite nice," said Max.

"Yeah, it's a bit spicy," said Joe.

"That will be the venom," said Max.

"The venom" said Joe worried.

"Don't panic mate, the venom evaporates out during the cooking," said Max.

"I never knew you could eat snakes," said Madeline.

"You can eat any animal if you cook it properly said Max.

"Even people," said Madeline.

"Yes, but that is not very tasteful," said Max.

"I bet you taste great Max, I'd eat you" said Madeline smiling.

"Thanks, I think" said Max a bit confused.

That night Joe slept in the van, and Madeline, and Max slept together outside.
In the morning Joe climbed out the van, and had a big stretch. He wandered over to where Max, and Madeline were. They were still asleep together under the duvet. He notices their clothes where in two neat piles near them.

"Yo sleepy heads," said Joe.

Max opened his eyes.

“Alright Joe?” He said sleepily.

“Busy night?” Said Joe.

“What do you mean?”

“I know you two had sex last night, you weren’t quiet”

“Sorry mate, I never had sex with someone I’ve been in love with, so maybe we were a bit passionate”

“What you two talking about?” Asked Madeline sleepily.

“Joe says we were a bit noisy last night,” said Max.

“Oh my God, I’m so sorry, we just got carried away, and we spent the night together naked, I never thought I’d ever sleep naked” said Madeline embarrassed.

“You don’t need to be embarrassed Madeline, in the future people like getting naked,” said Max.

“They do” said Madeline shocked.

“Max certainly does, he likes to meditate naked when he is trying to work something out” said Joe smiling.

“It makes me feel close to nature, and the universe,” said Max.

“I’m sure it does” said Joe smiling.

“Joe, would you mind getting back in the van so we can get dressed?” Said Madeline.

“No problem, I have no desire to see Max’s skinny white arse,” said Joe.

“Some people like my skinny white arse I’ll have you know Joseph,” said Max.

Ten minutes later once everyone was dressed, they all sat together drinking coffee.

“I think we all need a shower,” said Max.

“I’d love a shower mate, but where are you going to find one out here,” said Joe.

“What’s is a shower?” Said Madeline.

“Just give me fifteen minutes, and I’ll show you,” said Max.

Max got up, and walked off to the van. They had set up camp close to a river.

“What is he up to?” Said Madeline.

“He does this all the time, he gets an idea, and just suddenly goes off, and does something,” said Joe.

Seventeen minutes later Max came back.

“Follow me” he said.

They followed Max down to the river.

Max had placed the pump by the river, with hose in the water. He had placed a rock on top of the pump to hold it in place. The water treatment unit was connected at an upwards angle, the pipe work coming out of the water treatment unit was leaning against a small tree that was growing on the riverbank. He had connected the water heater, then he had run a pipe up into the tree. He had punctured a few holes in a plastic bottle cap, and fixed it to the end of the pipe.

Max switched the pump on, and water started spaying out the end of the pipe, and cascading down by the tree.

“That’s a shower, we use it to wash,” said Max.

Joe went first while Max, and Madeline waited by the dead campfire. First Joe washed his clothes in the river, and put them on top of the van to dry. Then he had a nice shower, with the shower gel, shampoo, and condition they had from the future.

Afterwards Max, and Madeline washed their clothes, and then had great fun in the shower. Max enjoyed teaching Madeline how to wash properly, and Madeline enjoyed been shown.

Afterwards they all sat by the campfire which Joe had relit. They all had towels around their waists, and Madeline was wearing Max’s Hard Rock Cafe London t-shirt.

“I must say that was a great experience. I feel so clean, and I smell so nice, and I never know being naked could be so much fun. I’m so glad I met you Max,” said Madeline.

“Well, I’m glad you enjoyed it Madeline, and I’m glad I met you,” said Max.

“So, when you gonna marry me, Max?”

“When we’re somewhere safe, like 2016”

“Well don’t wait too long, if we’re having sex, I could get pregnant”

“Yes, I am well aware of that, did you ever get pregnant when you were a prostitute?”

“Yes, three times”

“And what happened?”

“I went to Dr Pretzel, and he sorted it out for me”

“Dr Pretzel that’s a funny name”

“He was German, he had a name I couldn’t pronounce, it sounded a bit like Pretzel, so I used to call him Dr Pretzel”

“Surprising you only got pregnant three times in seven years,” said Joe.

“I suppose, I’m not an expert on these things,” said Madeline.

“It’s that super strong whiskey, probably makes people infertile,” said Max.

“What is infertile?” Said Madeline.

“When you can’t get someone pregnant,” said Max.

“I was taught if you couldn’t get pregnant, then it was because you had upset God,” said Madeline.

“I’ll teach you basic biology one day Madeline,” said Max.

“Thank you Max,” said Madeline.

“Tell Madeline your theory about God Max” said Joe.

“Well, I believe God is a super advanced alien that controls the universe,” said Max.

“What is an alien?” Asked Madeline.

“A being from outer space,” said Max.

“You mean you have beings from outer space in the future”

“Yes, but the government hides them”

“Why would the government hide them?”

“Yes Max, explain to us why the government hides aliens,” said Joe.

“Well, they work together in secret to rule the world, and take control of all Earth humans,” said Max.

“The more I find out about the future the more I don’t like the sound of it,” said Madeline.

“Just focus on the good things in the future. Women can’t be owned by men, we have showers, we have chocolate bars, and you never need worry about the bad things as I can protect you from them,” said Max.

“Madeline what you need to understand about Max is he is a smart, and brilliant guy, but he worries about things that will never happen. Like aliens are really conspiring to take over the world,” said Joe.

“You’ll see my friend, you’ll see,” said Max.

They were driving in the van again. They had been travelling west for a few hours. Madeline was enjoying listen to music, until the next CD started playing.

“This music is so fast, and chaotic, I’m not sure if I like it,” said Madeline.

“This is Van Halen; you’ll get used to our weird future music soon enough,” said Max.

“Do you think we’re still in Texas” said Joe who was driving.

“Not sure mate, I haven’t seen any signs yet, and I think it may take a while to get outta of Texas considering we are averaging around thirty miles per hour,” said Max.

“I know, but this terrain is so bumpy, you just can’t go fast on it,” said Joe.

“I think we’re going quite fast,” said Madeline.

“Look at all that dust over there, something is going on,” said Max.

“Shall I head for the dust?” Asked Joe.

“Why not, something to do,” said Max.

The van veered to the left, and headed towards the dust.

As they got close, they could see a line of horses with men in blue uniforms on them. The dust was created by the hundreds of horses trotting. As they got closer, they could see a group of tepees. There was a line of native Americans on horses facing the men in blue uniforms.

“That’s the Union army,” said Madeline.

“The natives don’t stand a chance, there outnumbered, and the Union army has superior weapons. I can’t allow this, Joe head for the natives,” said Max.

“Sure mate, I’m with you on this,” said Joe.

“But they’re just a bunch of savages, why would you help them?” Asked Madeline.

“Madeline, they are not savages they are human beings fighting to maintain their way of life while the white man takes their lands from them, and forces them into tiny reservations, and even when in their reservations they are not safe. These people are the native inhabitants of America, and they do not deserve to be treated the way have been. Can you understand that?” Said Max passionately.

“Oh my, no one has every explain it to me like that, I was taught their all savages are just out to kill us all,” said Madeline.

“Well prepare to make friends with some native Americans,” said Max.

“We call them Indians,” said Madeline.

“Yeah, and that is stupid, they don’t come from Indian”

“What is Indian?”

“It’s a country on the continent of Asia”

The van got close to the natives, and Joe parked up.

Max jumped out, and walked towards the natives with his hands raised.

"I am here to help you; I am not like the other white men" he called.

A tall old man with a large feather headdress got off his horse, and walked over to Max. He looked about sixty. He had long grey hair, and brown eyes. He wore an animal skin loin cloth, and his head, and face were painted with red lines.

"Who are you?" He spoke.

"I am Max, and I can help you"

"I am Tʉoyobisesʉ Kwasinaboo, in your language that mean Chief Rattlesnake," said the Chief.

"I like that name, the rattlesnake is a mighty predator, and they taste nice too," said Max.

"You eat rattlesnakes?"

"Sorry has that offended you?"

"No, you just surprised me, you are not like other white men, white men usually fear rattlesnakes"

"I'm not like the other white, I don't agree what is happening to you, and I would like to help"

"Well, if you Australians can make five hundred Union soldiers disappear then I would love to see that"

"I'll be back in a minute" said Max annoyed.

Max ran back to the van.

“What’s going on mate” said Joe out the window.

“I’m fed up with everyone thinking we’re Australian, and I don’t give a shit about causality anymore mate, just sit tight, and enjoy the show,” said Max.

Max went to the back of the van, and grabbed a large heavy bag. He dragged it back to where the Chief was stood.

“What have you got there Max?” Asked the Chief.

“Do you believe in magic Chief?” Replied Max.

“Yes, the magic of nature, and the magic of the spirits of our ancestors watching over us”

“Well, there watching over you today, buy the way why are the Union army just lined up waiting”

“It’s what they do, they wait for some time to give us a chance to surrender”

Max crouched down, and unzipped the bag. He lifted out the mini-Gatling gun, which he could just about carry. He pulled out a nine yard belt, and loaded it into the mini gun. He took out the RPG launcher, and popped a grenade in the end.

He stood up, and held the RPG launcher up.

“Time for magic Chief” he said.

The Chief watching him intrigued.

“Sorry horses” Max said.

He aimed the launcher into the middle of the line of Union soldiers. They were lined up in three columns. One hundred, and fifty riders in each column.

Max pulled the trigger. The rocket blasted out of the gun, and whistled towards the Union army five hundred yards away.

A mighty explosion erupted. Body parts from men, and horses flew into the air. Blood rained down from the sky.

The riders close to the explosion who hadn’t been hit were thrown from their horses as the horses reared up in fright.

Max held up the mini-Gatling gun, and let rip.

The rest of Union army was cut to shreds in a hail of bullets as forty rounds per second were spat from the mini gun.

A minute later the nine-yard belt was spent, and the mini gun went silent.

Max turned around and looked at the Chief, another man was stood by him, dressed like the Chief but with a smaller headdress. He looked around forty.

“Tuhkwasi taiboo” said the man.

“My son thinks you are the devil,” said the Chief.

“I am, for killing those horses,” said Max sobbing.

“You cry for horses, but not for the man?” Asked the Chief.

“ahpʉ?” said the Chief’s son.

“pabo tailboo? Nabu̲si?aipʉ” replied the Chief.

Joe, and Madeline came rushing over.

“Oh Max, what’s wrong?” Asked Madeline throwing her arms around him.

“I killed loads of horses,” said Max.

“You also killed loads of men as well,” said Madeline.

“But the horses are innocent, they don’t kill native people, and drive them from their lands”

Joe walked over to the Chief, and his son.

“Hi, I’m Joe” he said holding out his hand.

The Chief turned to his son.

“pabo tailboo, tuhtaiboo? W, nai? bi, Nabusi?aipʉ ihka nʉe” he said.

“What are you saying?” Asked Joe.

The Chief turned to face him.

"Sorry, I was telling my son, that I have seen this in a dream. A white man, a black man, and a young lady," said the Chief.

Max, and Madeline came over.

"Tuhkwasi taiboo" said the Chief's son nervously.

"My son is convinced you are the devil Max," said the Chief.

"After killing all those horses, I think I am," said Max sobbing.

"Max, you saved my whole tribe, where did you get those weapons from, I have never seen such destructive devices?" Asked the Chief.

"We're time travellers, we are from the future, except for Madeline, I met her in Sherman," said Max.

"I see," said the Chief.

"You don't seem shocked by that," said Joe.

"I have heard many strange stories about beings from other planets, other dimensions, and other times. I am pleased to meet you Joe, and Madeline. I am Chief Rattlesnake," said the Chief.

"You seem very wise" said Madeline surprised.

"Let me guess you expected us to be primitive savages?" Said the Chief.

“I’m very sorry,” said Madeline.

“It’s not your fault Madeline, that’s the way the white man has portrayed us,” said the Chief.

“Yeah, the white man sure has a lot to answer for,” said Max.

“You certainly are not a white man from this time Max. Now you must stay with us tonight so we can help you,” said the Chief.

“Help us?” Said Max.

“With your quest,” said the Chief.

“Does that involve smoking the peace pipe?” Asked Max.

“It sure does”

“Yes, we accept your offer then, thank you”

“I’ll put the big guns back in the van, where can I park the van Chief?” Said Joe.

“The van?” Said the Chief confused.

“The horseless carriage,” said Max.

“Oh, just put it near the settlement, no one will touch it, they will be too scared,” said the Chief.

Madeline found out just how non savage the Comanche were. They made them all a nice meal. Buffalo meat, bread, and green beans.

The women brushed Madeline's hair, and made her a lovely feather headdress.

That evening they were all invited to the nasukoo?i kahni, or sweat house in English.

Inside the sweat house the Chief sat with his wife. His son, and his wife were there, and three other men were also there with their wives. The sweat house was a large teepee with a huge campfire in the middle, there were buffalo skins around the fire to sit on.

"Come in, and sit down, you sit here Max, then Madeline you next to Max, and Joe you take the last seat. It is a rare privilege for us to share this ceremony with a white man, and women, and a black man. Allow me to introduce everyone. This is my wife Isananaka, Howling coyote. This is my son Isawʉra, Crazy Bear, and his wife Hʉkiyani, carries a sunshade. This is my best warrior Paruwa Sʉmʉno, Ten elks, and his wife Topʉsana, Flower. This is our doctor Pua paatsoko, Medicine otter, and his wife Puhawi, Medicine woman, and this is our wise man Mukwoorʉ, Spirit talker, and his wife Hʉwʉni, Dawn. So now I have introduced everyone, we will begin. When the pipe is passed to you, you smoke it, and pass it to your left. There must be no talking while the pipe is being passed," said the Chief.

The doctor, and the wise man stared at Max with huge smiles on their faces.

Max, Madeline, and Joe got comfy on the soft buffalo skins.

The Chief picked up the peace pipe, and took a thin piece of wood. He placed the end of the wood in the fire, and once it caught alight, he used it to light the pipe.

The Chief took a big drag, and passed the pipe to Max.

Max took a big drag himself, and passed the pipe to Madeline.

Max blew out a huge plume of smoke, and instantly felt strange. The room seemed to be moving. His vision began to blur. He suddenly had the urge to lay down. He lay back on his buffalo skin, and passed out.

When Max woke up, he found himself in the middle of a forest.

He sat up, and looked around. He appeared to be alone.

He heard a twig snap behind him. He looked around, and saw a black panther strolling towards him.

He jumped up, and reached for a Beretta, only to discover he wasn't carrying them.

He readied himself to fight the panther with his hands.

"Hello Max" said the panther in a female voice.

"Did you just talk?" Said Max shocked.

"Hello Max, I'm Lusana your spirit animal," said Lusana.

"Hello Lusana, am I dreaming?"

"Of course, you are silly" said Lusanna laughing.

"Yes of course it's a dream, panthers don't talk in the real world"

"What is the real world, Max?"

"The conscious world, where people are awake"

"How do you know this isn't real world Max?"

"Oh, don't you get all metaphysical with me Lusanna, I am a physics master, yes this is the real world, and so is the conscious world. They are both real, one exists in my conscious mind, and the other in my subconscious mind"

"OK Maxwell if you're so smart then answer this question did you go back in time, or did you go into an alternate reality where time moves slower?"

"Damn it, I never thought about that. I'm so confused. If we have moved realities then that poses more challenges, and more questions, like do I even exist?"

"Calm down Max, I was just messing you with, you're back in time"

“I really am cracking up, first I discover I was capable of feeling emotions, and now I’m being wound up by a panther, just hurry up, and eat me please”

Lusanna started laughing.

“Oh Max, I can’t eat you, I am your spirit animal, we are the same being” she said.

“So, I’m talking to my spirit?”

“Yes Max”

“That’s really cool”

“Yes, it is, now I’m here to help you on your quest”

“My quest, oh to get married”

“Yes, and of course that big thing you need to do, go back to 2016”

“Yes, I am beginning to think it’s not possible”

“Maxwell Walsh! Are you really the sort of person who gives up?”

“No, I’m not, but part of me doesn’t want to go to 2016, I would have all the problems I had then”

“The government, aliens, and ninjas being after you?”

“Precisely”

“Max, all that stuff is in your head, the government doesn’t know about you, the aliens are not interested in you, and no gangs of ninjas have been ordered to kill you”

“But I thought”

“Try thinking when you’re not stoned Max, now what you must do is travel northeast to the town of Abilene”

“That’s it? Just travel northeast, and find the town of Abilene?”

“Yep, that’s it, now awake”

Max opened his eyes.
He sat up, and saw the wise man, and the doctor smiling at him. He looked around, and saw Madeline, and Joe starting to stir.

“So, what was your spirit animal Max?” Asked the Chief.

“A black panther,” said Max.

“tʉmahkupa? Said the Chief.

The wise man, and the doctor nodded with approval.

“The panther signifies strength, and determination,” said the Chief.

“Yep, that describes me,” said Max.

Madeline, and Joe were sat up now.

“What was your spirit animal Madeline?” Asked the Chief.

“A tiger, I have never seen a tiger before, but it spoke to me, and told me what he was, and told me to stick with you Max,” said Madeline.

“I am not familiar with a tiger,” said the Chief.

“Big cats, which come from Asia, bit like a lion, but they are orange with black strips,” said Max.

“Ah I see” said the Chief “pʉhʉ ku?”

The wise man, and the doctor nodded with approval.

“A lion, or a tiger is courageous, and fierce,” said the Chief.

“Oh, that doesn’t sound like me,” said Madeline.

“Yes, it does, you were held against your will for seven years, and you managed to survive, that took courage, and fierceness,” said Max.

“Aw thank you Max, you better hurry up, and marry me, I can’t wait any longer,” said Madeline.

“Max, do you want a job as a wise man?” Said the Chief.

“You couldn’t afford me Chief,” said Max smiling.

“So, Joe what was your spirit animal?” Asked the Chief.

“Erm, it was a rat,” said Joe.

“pia kahua” said the Chief.

All the Comanche in the sweat house started laughing.
Joe blushed.

“Don’t worry Joe. Rat is a very cleaver creature, very cunning, and very brave, and able to survive anywhere,” said the Chief.

“Yeah well, I managed to survive living with Max for twenty years,” said Joe.

“So, were you told to do anything by your spirit animals?” Said the Chief.

“Mine told me to travel northeast to the town of Abilene,” said Max.

“Mine told me to stick with Max,” said Madeline.

“Mine told me to stay with Max” said Joe.

“What are you going to do Chief?” Asked Max.

“We’re going to move our settlement to Mexico, we’ll be safer there. Thank you for making our move possible, I suspect we were destined to die yesterday, and you have given us a new chance of life,” said the Chief.

“My pleasure Chief, thank you for the peace pipe, that’s some powerful stuff,” said Max.

Chapter 7
Abilene

The Comanche were packing up their settlement ready to travel to Mexico.

Max, Madeline, and Joe bid farewell to the Chief, and set off in the van. Max was driving.

"Why do I always have to sit in the middle?" Asked Madeline.

"In case Joe, or I need to shoot out the windows for any reason," said Max.

"Oh, I see, fair enough," said Madeline.

They had been driving northeast roughly for a couple of hours when they reached a big river blocking their way. Max stopped the van, and jumped out.

He got the two axes out the back of the van. He handed an axe to Joe, who had just climbed out the van. Max pointed to some Cedar Elm trees by the river bank, they wandered over to them.

Max, and Joe quickly hacked away, and cut down a tree each, then stripped all the branches, so just the trunk remained.

They cut each end of their logs at an angle.

They dropped the logs over the river to make a bridge.

Max's log landed on the other side of the bank with a thud.

Joe's log landed, but bounced off the bank, and went into the river.

"Shit, Max, grab my log, and I'll go in the river," said Joe.

Max rushed over, and held Joe's log.

Joe climbed in the water, and lifted the log up, he manoeuvred into place, so it was resting on the opposite bank. Max let go of the log.

He started walking out of the river.

"OWWW" he screamed.

"What's up mate?" Asked Max.

"Something bit me" Joe said.

"Take my hand" said Max holding out his hand.

Joe grabbed Max's hand, and Max pulled him out of the river.

"Sit down mate," said Max.

Joe sat down on the riverbank.

"Where did it bite you?"

"Back of my left calf, just below the knee," said Joe.

Max pulled Joe's boots off.

“I need to take your trousers off mate” said Max.

“No problem, I feel a bit sick,” said Joe.

Max slipped Joe’s trousers off. He inspected the wound. There were two small pin hole marks on Joe’s calf.

“It’s a snake bite mate, stay very still,” said Max.

“Oh God, am I gonna die?” Asked Joe worried.

“Not on my watch mate. Wait here”

Max rushed over to the van, and opened up the back. He found his medical bag, and opened it up. He rooted through it, and found a snake bite kit.

“What’s happening?” Asked Madeline who was had come up behind Max.

“Joe got bitten by a Water Moccasin snake, also known as a Cottonmouth,” said Max.

“Oh my God, is he gonna die?” Asked Madeline worried.

“Not if I can help it” said Max confidently.

Max found the antivenom for Water Moccasins, and filled a syringe up.

He rushed over to Joe. Joe was throwing up by the river, and sweating.

“Max, I feel awful” said Joe in a croaky voice.

“Stop panicking mate, it’s all psychosomatic, the Water Moccasins venom will take several hours to kill you” said Max jabbing a needle in Joe’s leg.

“Is that gonna fix me?”

“Yes, but it will make you very sick I’m afraid. Now stay still, and I’ll fetch you some water”

Max rushed back over to the van.

“Is he alright?” Asked Madeline.

“Can you go, and talk to him please, and make sure he doesn’t move,” said Max.

“OK”

Madeline strolled over to Joe.

Max put the syringe in a yellow bag, with the empty antivenom bottle. He zipped up the medical bag, and closed the back of the van. He walked to the side door, and opened it. He took a one-gallon bottle of water out of the fridge, and found a glass. He filled the glass with water.

He walked over to Joe, and Madeline. They were both laughing.

“Here you go mate” he said passing the glass to Joe.

Joe guzzled down the water.

“What were you two laughing about?” Max asked.

“I was just telling Joe about the time a cowboy tried to rape me,” said Madeline.

“And that was funny?” Said Max confused.

“Yeah, cos he was so drunk he couldn’t get hard,” said Madeline.

“Have you ever been raped?”

“Yeah, loads of times, it always happens to whores”

“Right, we are going back to Sherman, and you are gonna point out all the men that raped you so I can beat them to death” said Max angrily.

“Oh Max, you are the sweetest man in the land, I just want to concentrate on the future from now on”

“OK, but from now on, no will ever hurt you again”

“You sweetie pie”

“When you’ve finished your lovey dovey talk, can you tell me how long I have to sit here with my trousers off?” Asked Joe.

“Get dressed mate, we just had to wait a few minutes, staying still ensures the venom doesn’t spread,” said Max.

Joe stood up, and wobbled a bit. Max held him, while he got his trousers on, and Max helped him put his boots on.

“Oh God, I feel terrible,” said Joe.

“That’s the antivenom mate, its powerful stuff,” said Max.

Max helped Joe walk back to Van.
They took their seats.

Max drove the van forward, and stopped by the riverbank. He got out, and rolled the logs into position so they were lined up with the wheels. He made sure the slanted bits they’d cut where in the right place so the van could drive up onto the logs.

He got into the van.

“Max, what holds the logs in place?” Asked Joe who was sweating heavily.

Max reached down, and turned the air-conditioning on.

“Oooh, that breeze is so cold,” said Madeline.

Max smiled, impressing Madeline made him feel good.

He slowly drove forward. The van slowly drove up onto the logs.

“The weight of the van holds the logs down,” said Max.

He slowly drove across the log bridge at around half a mile per hour. The logs creaked under the weight, and felt like they were bending as they reached the middle.

Soon they bumped off the logs at the other side of the riverbank, and all breathed a sigh of relief.

After three days they reached the outskirts of Abilene. Joe was feeling better now, he spent two days being sick, and not eating much.

Max parked the van in some bushes. They got out, and Joe, and Max fetched their shaving kits out of the back of the van. Max also grabbed a tape measure, and a pen, and notepad from his scientific equipment bag.

“Look what I’ve found” said Max holding up a pack of wet wipes.

“Nice one, no more wiping out arses on fucking leaves,” said Joe.

“And now we don’t have to use corn either,” said Max.

They covered the van in bits of bush, so it was hidden from view.

They walked into the town. It was a lively bustling place. Much busier than Sherman.

They walked into the Alamo saloon. The place was packed with cowboys, ladies in frilly dresses, and men in suits. It was noisy. Some people were gambling on a roulette wheel, and card games. Most people were getting drunk.

They walked over to the bar.

The barman came over to them. He was tall with green eyes, and black hair. He was clean shaven. He wore a long white apron.
"What can I get you folks?" He asked.

"What do you serve?" Asked Max noticing the bar had an array of drinks.

"Well, we have whiskey, beer, champagne, orange juice, and coffee" he said.

"Excellent. Can we have two beers, and a glass of champagne with a dash of orange juice please," said Max.

The barman got the drinks for them.

"That's a dollar, and a half please, the champagne is very expensive, it come from France you know" he said.

"Yes, I know, here you go" said Max passing him a three-dollar coin.

Max got the change, and they found the last free table at the back of the saloon.

“Oh, just a minute I forgot something,” said Max.

He rushed off to the bar.

“Typical Max, he gets an idea in his head, and just rushes off, you’ll have to get used to that Madeline,” said Joe.

“No, I won’t let him rush off, and leave me alone, especially when we have babies to care for,” said Madeline.

Max walked back over to the bar.

“Have you got rooms available?” Asked Max.

“What for an hour?” Asked the barman.

“No for three nights”

“Three nights, its two bucks a night here”

“OK two rooms for three nights please”

“That’s gonna be twelve dollars buddy”

“That’s fine”

Max pulled a ten, and a five-dollar bill, and handed it to the barman.

“You sure got plenty of cash to spare what do you do for work buddy?” Said the barman handing Max his change, and two large keys.

“I’m a scientific explorer” replied Max.

“Well, I have no idea what that is, but it must pay well”

“It’s OK”

Max walked back to the table, and sat down.

He placed a key in front of Joe.

“I got us a couple of rooms for three nights, thought we could do with a break from camping,” said Max.

“You star” said Joe smiling.

“Thank you Max, and what is this drink it’s delicious?” Said Madeline.

“It’s champagne with a dash of orange juice,” said Max.

Max drunk some of his beer.

“Mm not bad, quite a cheeky one” he said.

“I know it’s much better than I thought it would be,” said Joe.

“American hops are sweeter than British hops,” said Max.

“What is a hop?” Asked Madeline.

“It’s a plant used to make beer,” said Max.

"Do you know how to make beer?" Asked Madeline.

"Yes, you need hops, barley, water, and yeast, and whisky is even simpler grain wheat, water, and yeast," said Max.

"Max can make just about anything," said Joe.

"That's right, with the right ingredients, I could make gin, vodka, and tequila, oh, and moonshine, you only need potatoes for that," said Max.

"Gosh, you are so smart," said Madeline.

"Well, I don't like to boast," said Max.

"Ha, since when?" Laughed Joe.

"If you think about it Joseph, I'm actually one of the smartest people on the planet at the moment" said Max smugly.

Two men walked over to their table. One of the men was tall, and slim with short salt, and pepper hair, and a moustache. He had blue eyes. He was dressed in a suit. The other man had long frizzy brown hair, and a big moustache. He was slightly shorter, and had green eyes. He was dressed in brown chaps, and had a brown leather jacket on, and a big brown Stetson, he also wore a star shaped badge. Both men looked like there were in their fifties.

"Howdy folks, you new in town?" Asked the taller man.

Max stood up, which made Joe stand up, and then Madeline stood up.

“Good evening, sir, I am Max Walsh, this is my good lady Madeline, and this is my friend Joe”

“Well good evening to all, I am Mayor Joseph G McCoy, and this is Marshal William Hickok,” said Joe McCoy.

“Wild Bill Hickok” exclaimed Max excitedly.

“Some people call me that,” said Wild Bill.

“It’s an honour to meet you, I am a big fan,” said Max.

“Well, you are welcome to buy me a drink,” said Wild Bill.

“My pleasure,” said Max.

“Are you Australian?” Asked Joe McCoy.

“No, I’m a limey” said Max annoyed.

He walked off to the bar with Joe McCoy, and Wild Bill.

“Who is Wild Bill Hickok, and how does Max know him?” Asked Madeline.

“Not sure but I recognise that name, I think he is famous in the wild west,” said Joe.

Max came back, and sat down.

“I can’t believe I brought Wild Bill Hickok a drink” he said excitedly.

“Who was Wild Bill anyway?” Asked Joe.

“Not sure, but I know he was famous for something,” said Max.

“How about getting your lady another drink Max,” said Madeline.

“Oh yeah sure,” said Max.

“Stay I’ll get these; you have to stop abandoning your lady” said Joe.

Max handed Joe a dollar, and a half.

“Sorry Madeline I don’t mean to run off all the time I’m just overexcited,” said Max.

“Well Max, I can’t have you running off when we have babies to look after, and if we’re here for three days, can you make an honest woman of me, and marry me?” Said Madeline firmly.

Max took Madeline’s hand, and held it.

“From now on I will be with you all the time, apart from tomorrow when I have to buy something for you, and I want it to be a surprise,” said Max.

"OK Max, that would be acceptable, no running off, and leaving me, unless you need to get me a surprise gift. What are you getting me?"

"I can't tell you that, then it won't be a surprise"

Joe came back carrying three drinks, and put them down. He sat down.

"Thank you, Joe," said Max.

"Yes, thank you Joe," said Madeline.

They sat drinking their drinks.

A man came over to them. He was tall, and broad shouldered. He had short brown hair, and was clean shaven. He wore snake skins boots, blue jeans, and a red leather jacket with gold sequins on it. He had a big red leather belt, with two big red holsters, which also had gold sequins, and revolvers in them. He looked like he was in his forties. He was carrying a glass of beer.

"Howdy folks, you new in town?" He asked.

Max stood up.

"Sit down fellow, can I sit with you guys?" He spoke.

Max sat down.

"Sure, be my guest," said Max.

The man sat down.

“I’m Frank Mitchell”

“I’m Max, and this is my good lady Madeline, and this is my friend Joe”

“You sound English,” said Frank.

“I like you Frank, most people think I’m Australian,” said Max.

“Well, I’ve been around a bit,” said Frank.

“You look dressed to impress Frank,” said Joe.

“Dressed to impress, that is a fantastic expression, I like that, is that what you say in England?” Asked Frank.

“Yes, it is,” said Joe.

“You’re all smartly dressed I see,” said Frank.

“Well, my dress is a getting a bit tatty, I could do with some new clothes,” said Madeline.

“Aw you’re American my dear,” said Frank.

“Yes, I’m from Texas,” said Madeline.

“And are you from the England too friend?” Frank said to Joe.

“Yes, I’m also from England” replied Joe.

“I see, and where did you meet Madeline, Max?” Asked Frank.

“Sherman in Texas,” said Max.

“And were you there Joe?” Said Frank.

“No, I wasn’t allowed into town,” said Joe.

“No, they don’t like Negroes in Texas, or any southern states at the moment, there all pissed about reconstruction, they’re actually blaming the Negroes for it” said Frank.

“What is reconstruction?” Asked Max.

“The government is trying to give Negroes the same rights as white folk, it is driving the white folk in the south mad, I wouldn’t be surprised if there is another civil war,” said Frank.

“It takes the fucking piss” said Joe annoyed.

“I know, I’m with you friend, you shouldn’t judge a man by the colour of his skin, you judge him by his actions,” said Frank.

“I like you Frank, your smart,” said Max.

“Yeah, you are cool man,” said Joe.

“Cool, is that an English expression?” Said Frank.

“It sure is,” said Joe.

"You guys seem really out of place in this establishment," said Frank.

"We can look after ourselves, we travel all round the world, and this is nowhere near the worst place we've been," said Max.

"What is the worst place you've been, Texas maybe?" Said Frank smirking.

Max, and Joe laughed. Madeline looked annoyed.

"Sorry madam, no offence meant," said Frank.

"Well offence taken, I am a Texas girl," said Madeline.

"The worst place we've been is the Amazon jungle, we nearly died a few times there," said Max.

"My goodness, what is your job?" Asked Frank.

"I'm a scientific explorer, and Joe is my assistant, how about you Frank what do you do?" Said Max.

"I just enjoy myself," said Frank.

"Nice. Now do you know the town pretty well?" Asked Max.

"Yep, I've been here over a year," said Frank.

"Do you know if there is a jeweller?"

“A what?”

“Somewhere you can buy jewellery”

“Max this aint no big city in the east, it’s a western town, so no jewellery can be found here”

“Is there a black smith?”

“Yes, other end of town”

“Joe, you know that twenty-two carat gold necklace I brought you for your twenty first. Where is it?” Asked Max.

“I’m wearing it Max,” said Joe.

“I would never ask this if it wasn’t an emergency, can I steal it please, and I will buy you another when the chance befalls me?” Said Max.

Joe took off his necklace, and handed it to Max.

“If it’s an emergency then fine. But I want a gold necklace with diamonds on it, to replace it,” said Joe.

“Of course, mate, you have saved my honour, I’ll buy you a Cartier necklace, a manly one of course” said Max.

“Was that real gold he just passed you?” Asked Frank wide eyed.

“Well, it is ninety two percent gold,” said Max.

“Where in the hell did you get that?” Said Frank.

“London” said Max.

“Keep that under you hat brother,” said Frank.

“I’d rather keep it in my pocket,” said Max.

“I mean keep it hidden, there are folks in this town that would kill you for that,” said Frank.

“I’m getting mighty tired,” said Madeline.

“Yes, I think we’ll retire now,” said Max.

“Well, my office is just down the street, it says Frank Mitchell on the door. Come, and see me if you need anything, I’m kinda of a fixer, so I get things done,” said Frank.

“Thank you, Frank,” said Max.

Later, Max, and Madeline were in their room. Joe was next door. The room was quite simple. A large wooden bed taking up most of the room, and a desk with two large bowls of stagnant water on it, and a mirror on the wall.

“If it’s late at night, and you need to pee, just use the bowls Max, saves you going outside,” said Madeline.

“OK thanks, I’ll bear that in mind. I’m gonna have a shave now,” said Max.

“Oh good, I need to do my legs, they are getting hairy, and I left my razor back in Sherman,” said Madeline.

Max got out his Gillette Mac 3 razor.

“What is that?” Asked Madeline confused.

“That’s my razor,” said Max.

“That is not a razor”

“It’s a future razor, get you dress off, and I’ll show you how to use it”

“OK then”

Madeline slipped her dress off.

Max pulled a chair out from under the desk.

“Sit down” he said.

Madeline sat down. Max rubbed water over her legs, then he rubbed some shaving gel on her.

She giggled.

“That tickles Max, that stuff is so cold”

Max then ran the razor down her leg.

“See, you just run it up, and down your legs until the hair is gone. Do you like having armpit hair?”

“What’s wrong with armpit hair?”

Max took off his shirt, and lifted up his arm.

“You shave your arm pit hair?” She said surprised.

“We take personal hygiene more seriously in the future” he said.

“Well, if you want me to shave my arm pits then I will”

“No Madeline, don’t ever do anything you don’t want to do ever again, you have equal rights to me now, if you want hairy air pits then so be it, it is your choice”

“This is so weird, I’m not used to having rights, and being able to choose, what do women in the future do?”

“Well, most women, shave their legs, and arm pits, and they keep their pubic hair tidy”

“What is pubic hair?”

“Hair by your vagina”

“I am not putting a razor down there Max”

“I have an electric trimmer, watch”

Max took out his battery powered clippers, and trimmer his beard. After a few minutes he looked much smarter.

“That is magic,” said Madeline.

“It’s just science. I can’t wait to show you the future,” said Max.

Show me how to use that thingy, I want to look like a future lady, so do all ladies in the future shave their armpits, and keep trim down below?”

“Well, some women like to be hairy, they’re usually German’s”

Joe lay in bed unable to sleep. It wasn’t because of the grunting, panting, and vibrations coming through the thin wooden walls from next door. He was glad Max was happy. Max had dedicated his life to science. He never thought he’d see Max have a serious relationship, let alone get married. He guessed why Max wanted the chain, he was gonna find a way to make some wedding rings. The man was a genius, there was nothing he couldn’t do if he put his mind to it. Joe worried that once Max was married, he would take his mind off returning to 2106, and concentrate on his wife, and kids. But he knew Max well, Max wouldn’t be able to cope in this age, no internet, no TV, he knew Max was missing these things as much as him. No McDonald’s for fucks sake. Well at least science had helped Max find love. Joe wondered if he might meet someone soon, he felt ready to settle down, he was nearly forty after all.

Chapter 8
Six Gold Rings

The next morning Max, and Madeline were up, and dressed. There was knock on the door.

Max got up, and opened the door.

“Hi Joe, come in” he said.

Joe walking into their room.

“How are you both?” He asked.

“We’re good thanks, how are you mate?” Asked Max.

“Alright, a bit tired I didn’t sleep well last night. You look really smart by the way Max, trimmed your beard, and brushed your hair,” said Joe.

“Thanks Joe, why couldn’t sleep last night?”

“We didn’t keep you awake last night, did we? Max was a bit wild, he fucked me three times,” said Madeline.

“Yeah, sorry Joe, I was overexcited, I’ve never been in love before,” said Max.

“No, it wasn’t that I did hear you, but I’m pleased for you both. I’m getting anxious, I’m really worried we won’t be able to get home” said Joe.

Max walked forward, and put his hand on Joe's shoulder.

"Joe my friend, I promise you, I will get us home. I already have a theory. I think if I can make another crystal power unit, I can discharge them together, and bounce the electromagnetic waves off each other. I think that will work; I just need to get another crystal," said Max.

"Oh cool, where do you get crystals from?"

"I got mine from a hippy shop in London"

"No, I mean where do they come from?"

"Oh, caves I think, they grow in rocks"

"So, we just need to find a cave then?"

"Maybe, I'm going to see Frank today, I'll ask him, he said he was a fixer"

"I think I can guess what else you'll be doing today"

"Well keep that to yourself please, I want to surprise Madeline, and you just reminded me, I need to measure your finger"

"You wanna surprise me?" Said Madeline excitedly.

"Yes, I do," said Max.

"What are you doing?" Asked Madeline.

“I can’t tell you, or it won’t be a surprise,” said Max.

Max grabbed his tape measure which was on the desk. He quickly measured Joe’s finger, and scribbled a note on his notepad.

“He measured my finger last night, what are you up to?” Said Madeline.

“All will be revealed this evening my darling” said Max ripping out the paper from the notepad, and shoving it in his pocket.

“I need to use a toilet before we do anything today,” said Joe.

“Yes, me too, how about you Madeline, do you need to use the outhouse?” Said Max.

“I suppose I do,” said Madeline.

Max grabbed his shaving bag off the desk, and unzipped it. He took out the pack of wet wipes, and pulled out six wipes.

“Here two wipes each, so use the corn to wipe yourselves, and then freshen up with these” he said handing two wipes each to Madeline, and Joe.

Later on, Max, Madeline, and Joe were sat at a table in the bar drinking coffee.

"I have never felt so fresh, and clean after using the outhouse," said Madeline.

"Welcome to the future Madeline," said Max.

"So, if you have to go off, and do secret things, what can me, and Joe do today?" Asked Madeline.

"You two can go shopping if you like, get yourselves some nice clothes," said Max.

"But I have no money," said Madeline.

Max reached into his jacket, and pulled out some cash. He handed a bundle of notes to Madeline, and to Joe.

"There you go five hundred dollars each, knock yourselves out," said Max.

"Why do you want us to knock ourselves out Max?" Said Madeline.

Joe laughed.

"It just an expression Madeline, it means go wild, and have a great time," said Joe.

"I can't accept this money Max; you've done too much for me already" said Madeline.

"Madeline, where Joe, and I come from gentlemen enjoy buying things for their ladies," said Max.

Max walked into Frank's office. It was a small wooden room, with plain walls. There was a large mahogany desk with some papers on it. Frank sat behind it. There were two chairs in front of the desk.

"Howdy Max, have a seat," said Frank.

"Thank you, Frank," said Max sitting down.

"How can I help you, Max?"

"Well, I would like to get married"

"Oh, that is lovely news, so you wanna speak to preacher then?"

"Yes, do you know him"

"Of course, I do, I'll take you there myself Max"

"I also need to see the blacksmith"

"Old Billy Morgan, I will introduce you to him, on the way back from the church"

"That's great. One last thing, can you get crystals?"

"Crystals, I can do, but that will cost a fair amount"

“I need a large white piece of crystal, and I don’t care what it costs”

“Oh, I see, you got plenty of money then Max”

“I’m doing alright I suppose”

“So, being a scientific explorer pays well then?”

“Yes, it does”

“And what exactly do you do?”

“I travel around the world with my assistant, and friend Joe, and we find out about other cultures, and other countries, and see how thinks work”

“Well, that sounds like very interesting work, I bet you have some stories”

“I sure do, but I would like to sort out getting married today, so perhaps my stories can wait for another time”

Madeline, and Joe were in the clothing store.

A short lady in a long blue dress, with her brown hair tied up, and under a blue bonnet walked over to them. She had green eyes, and looked about thirty.

“Are you just looking, or do you have money to spend?” She asked sharply.

Madeline pulled out her cash.

“We got five hundred dollars each” she said excitedly.

“Oh well, do have a good look, and please let me know if I can be of assistance” the lady said in friendly tone.

“This dress is so pretty,” said Madeline.

She was looking at a long green dress.

“Get it, get a couple, you can afford it,” said Joe.

Joe was looking at smart suits.

“Joe, can I ask you something please?”

“Of course, Madeline, ask me whatever you like”

“Do you think Max really loves me?”

“Why would you ask that?”

“I just don’t think I deserve a man as nice, and kind as Max, and I wonder if he is just marrying me, because he feels obliged, as he rescued me”

“Madeline, I have never seen Max so happy, and so concerned with his appearance. Also, he was dead set on making sure we didn’t change the past in any way, then he killed seven men to save you, why do you think he did that?”

“Because he loves me?”

“Yes, he loves you, and he wants to marry you more than anything in the world”

“Oh, shucks that makes me wanna cry” said Madeline teary eyed.

“He’s a great guy, and I thank you for making him so happy”

“Oh my, I can’t wait to be married now”

“Well, I don’t think you’ll have to wait long”

“Is that what he is up to today?”
“Look Max really wants to surprise you, so just wait, and see please”

“OK, tell me this though, do women in the future shave their armpits, and keep their downstairs area trimmed?”

“Well, most do, some don’t usually German’s, or feminists”

“What’s a feminist?”

“Someone who believes in women’s rights, and usually hates men I think”

After they had been to the church Frank took Max to the blacksmith.

They stood at the entrance to Billy's barn.

"Hi Billy, this is my friend Max" said Frank peering into the barn.

"Well, howdy Max nice to meet you" said Billy as he emerged from the barn.

Billy was a tall muscular man, with huge shoulders. He looked around forty. He had short blonde hair, and was clean shaven. He had big brown eyes, and a big head. He wore a huge leather apron, and leather gloves.

"Nice to meet you too Billy," said Max.

"Well, I have some errands to run," said Frank.

"Cheers Frank," said Max.

Frank left.

"Can I do something for you Max, need some horseshoes, or some new belt loops for your saddle?" Asked Billy.

"Actually, I was wondering if I could use your equipment for a few hours please," said Max.

"And why the hell would I let you anywhere near my equipment?" Said Billy angrily.

"Because I'll pay you two hundred dollars"

"Well come on in then friend"

Max walked into the barn. There was a roaring fire burning on top of a metal shelf, with a hand pumped set of bellows by it. There was a huge anvil, and various tools hung on the wall. There were several iron desks around the barn. It was very hot, and smokey in the barn.

"So, what you are doing?" Asked Billy.

Max pulled out the gold chain, and held it up.

"I want to melt this down, and turn it into six gold rings," said Max.

"Is that real gold?" Billy asked with wide eyes.

"It sure is"

"I'll get the smelting pot"

Joe, and Madeline left the clothing store with a few boxes each.

"So, shall we drop these boxes off in our rooms?" Asked Joe.

"Yes, then we can take one outfit to the bathhouse, and we'll take a bath, then put our new clothes on," said Madeline.

"Do you mean take a bath together?" Asked Joe worried.

“No silly, you go on the boy’s side, and I go on the girls side. Take a bath together, who ever heard of anything so ridiculous”

They started walking towards the Alamo saloon.

“Oh, I see. I’m sure Max wouldn’t mind having a bath with you,” said Joe.

“There aint enough room in a bath for two people” said Madeline bemused.

“Wait to you see baths in the future Madeline”

“Speaking about the future, do all men shave their balls with a razor in the future?”

“It varies some do, some don’t. I’m well aware Max does”

“Have you seen Max naked?”

“Unfortunately, yes”

“Why?”

“Well, he used to sit in the middle of the living room meditating naked, and then there is the baths he takes. He likes to take really hot baths, and he comes out sweating. He strolls out naked, puts a towel on the sofa, and sits down. He refuses to get dressed until he has stopped sweating”

“I hope he doesn’t use the bathhouse then; he would be arrested if he walked around town naked”

“Well, we better make sure we keep enough money to bail him out then”

At the blacksmiths barn.
Max was using the mould that the blacksmith used to make loops for buckles on saddles to shape the molten gold.
He then hammered the rings into the right size. He used a round pieces of wood which he measured up, to check the internal diameter was correct.

Eventually he had six gold rings.

“Do you have tools for intricate work?” He asked Billy.

“What do you mean by intricate?” Asked Billy.

“Small stuff, like engraving”

“Oh yeah, I’ll get you my engraving kit”

Billy walked over to a desk, and grabbed a leather strap with pointed tools in it.

He walked back, and handed the leather strap to Max.

“Perfect, thank you,” said Max.

Billy watched in amazement as Max started to chip away at a soft piece of hot gold. He carved it into a weird shape like an upside spider. Then he pulled his glove off, and reached into his pocket. He pulled out two shiny diamonds, and placed them down on the desk. He placed a diamond in the middle of the upside-down spider, and gently closed the legs around it. He repeated the process. Then he picked up two of the rings. He heated them one at a time, and attached the upside down gold spider with diamond onto it.

“What have you created sir?” Asked Billy in amazement.

“They’re called diamond rings,” said Max.

“That is so pretty, does that weird upside spider thing that holds the diamond have a name?”

“It’s called a bezel”

“You are one fancy fellow, what do you need all that fancy stuff for?”

“I’m getting married tomorrow, and in England where I’m from we use gold rings, and diamond rings in our wedding ceremonies”

“Oh my, I would love to see an English wedding”

“Well, you’re welcome to come to my wedding, it’s at three tomorrow”

“That’s mighty kind Max, I’ll be there”

“And be in the saloon later, you won’t want to miss what I’m gonna do”

“Max with the two hundred dollars you’ve given me, I am gonna take the rest of day off, buy some new clothes, get a bath, and then I’ll be in the saloon for the rest of the day. Two hundred dollars is more than I get in a month”

“You just reminded me, I need some new clothes, and I could do with a bath”

“You do need a bath Max, you spent so long over the furnace, you look like a Negro”

Max burst into the Alamo saloon fresh, and clean in his new brown suit, snakeskin boots, and a new red Stetson hat. His beard was neatly trimmed, and his hair was brushed, and hanging down. He looked rather dashing.

“Howdy Max” called Billy the blacksmith holding up a glass of beer smiling drunkenly.

The saloon was three quarters full. He spotted Madeline, and Joe sat at a table.

He strolled over to the table feeling a tiny bit nervous, but totally determined.

He reached the table, and stood by Madeline.

“Hi Max, sit down,” said Madeline.

“Madeline, just be quiet, and enjoy what is about to happen,” said Joe.

Max got down on one knee. The whole saloon went silent as people watched in wonder at what was going on.

"Madeline, I love you, now, and forever, will you marry me?"

"Of course, I'll marry you, I love you too"

Max stood up, and Madeline stood up as well. Max pulled the diamond ring out of his pocket. He took Madeline's left hand, and slipped the ring on.

"Oh my God, what is that?" Shrieked Madeline, shocked at seeing the diamond ring.

"It's called an engagement ring my darling, it's what we give to women when we want to marry them," said Max.

"It's the most beautiful thing I have ever seen" said Madeline teary eyed.

"And you are the most beautiful thing I have ever seen"

"Aw Max"

She threw her arms around Max, and they kissed.

When they finished Max looked around, and noticed everyone was staring at him with confused expressions.

"This woman has just agreed to be my wife. We are getting married tomorrow, and you are all invited, it's at three o'clock"

Everyone in the saloon started applauding, and cheering. When the noise had died down.

“I am so happy, I would like to buy everyone a drink, barman serve everyone, and I will pay when you have finished”

There was an even bigger cheer, and everyone rushed to the bar. A couple of saloon girls, and a man in a suit, got behind the bar to assist with the rush.

Max sat down, and so did Madeline.

“Are we getting married tomorrow, Max?” Asked Madeline.

“Yes, we are at three,” said Max.

“Oh my God, that’s why you told me to buy new clothes”

“Are you surprised?”

“Surprised, happy, overjoyed, I could fuck you right now Max Walsh”

“Once I’ve paid for the drinks, we can pop upstairs”

“No, we need to have a drink first, and celebrate”

“Yes, we do. Now you are aware you can’t drink when you’re pregnant?”

“What I never heard that”

“It’s bad for the baby, no smoking tobacco either”

“Oh, you just expect me to watch you drink, and smoke when I can’t?”

“No Madeline, when you are pregnant, I will not drink, or smoke any tobacco, to support you”

“Oh Max, you are too sweet, I don’t know what to say”

“We can still smoke that Jamaican tobacco though”

Mayor Joe McCoy walked over, and placed a bottle of champagne down on the table, and three glasses.

“Well done you two, here is some champagne for you all to celebrate, I will be at your wedding tomorrow” he said.

“Thank you, Mayor, that’s very kind” said Max.

“Thank you, Max, you paid for the bottle, I just brought it to you, I hope you have a lot of money on you sir” said Joe McCoy.

After the rush was over, the barman came over to their table. “Sir, I’m afraid everyone went a bit mad; you owe me four hundred, and eighty-two dollars” he said.

Max pulled out some cash, and counted it out.

“Here you go sir, there’s five hundred, get yourself a drink on me” he said passing the cash over.

“Golly sir, you are welcome here as much as you like” said the barman smiling.

The barman walked away.

“Joe, I got something for you mate,” said Max.

“Yeah what?”

“Hold your hand out”

Joe held his hand out, and Max dropped a diamond ring, and two gold wedding rings into his hand.

“For when you find your future wife mate,” said Max.

“You made these?” Asked Joe surprised.

“Yes, I did”

“How do you know my future wife’s finger size?”

“Intuition mate, intuition”

“You are a fucking genius mate, they look great. Thank you so much”

Max, and Madeline stood at the front of the small wooden church together in front of the preacher.

Madeline was wearing her new green dress, it was long, and flowing, and felt very soft. She had a new pair of red leather boots on. Max wore his new brown suit, with a blue shirt, snakeskin boots, and a red cravat. He also wore his new red Stetson.

The preacher was a short fat man, with a bald head, and narrow grey eyes. He had a large grey beard. He looked around sixty, and was wearing black robes.

The church was packed. Some people were standing. Hundreds of people had excepted Max's offer. In the front row Joe sat in his new suit with Billy the blacksmith, Frank Mitchell, Mayor McCoy, and Wild Bill. They were all smartly dressed.

The preached stood behind by a small high wooden desk with some paper on it.

"Now what are your names?" He asked in a croaky voice.

"I'm Max Walsh, and this is Madeline Hanson," said Max.

"OK we can begin. Do you both agree to be married?"

"Yes" they said together nodding.

"Madeline Hanson, do you take Max Walsh to be your husband in accordance with God's law?"

"I do"

“Max Walsh do you take Madeline Hanson to be your wife in accordance with God’s law”

“I do”

“OK just sign the certificate, and you will be officially married”

“Where I come from, we give each other gold rings,” said Max.

“Well, if you can find a gold ring, be my guest,” said the preacher.

Max pulled out two gold rings. He gently grabbed Madeline’s hand, and slipped her ring on.

“Now slip this on my finger” he said handing her the ring, and holding up his ring finger.

Madeline slipped the ring on.

“We’re married now” she said excitedly.

“Once you sign the certificate” said the preacher turning the paper round.

He handed a quill to Max.

“Ladies first” said Max handing the quill to Madeline.

“Actually, it’s the man who signs first,” said the preacher.

“Who is paying for this wedding?” Said Max firmly.

“Fine ladies first,” said the preacher.

“Max, I don’t know how to write, I’m sorry” said Madeline sheepishly.

“Here, I’ll help you,” said Max.

Max gently took Madeline’s hand, and guided her to put the quill in the ink, and the write an M, followed by a squiggle. He then took the quill, and did the same signature.

“Now you are married,” said the preacher.

“And where I’m from we usually kiss the bride, when we’re officially married,” said Max.

“Don’t you dare start kissing in a church young man, I don’t want God striking my place down with lightning” said the preacher shocked.

“I guess we’ll save that bit for later then,” said Max.

Max, and Madeline turned, and walked down the aisle hand in hand to thunderous applause.

Outside the church Max grabbed Madeline, and kissed her. Which got a few gasps from people nearby.

“Max, you don’t want us to be arrested for indecency” she said worried.

“Sorry, but I had to kiss my bride, I love you Mrs Walsh” he said.

“I’m Mrs Madeline Walsh, I am so happy”

“I’m sorry you can’t read, and write”

“I’m sorry Max, no one ever showed me how, I’m not smart like you”

“I’ll teach you how to read, and write”

“Seriously, you would do that for me?”

“I would do anything for you, you’re my wife”

“Oh goody, when can we start?”

“After our honeymoon”

“What is a honeymoon?”

“It’s a trip people take after they get married”

Chapter 9
Frank Mitchell

Max, and Madeline had taken a train to Chicago for their honeymoon. Max had left Joe some money, and asked him to get a barn for them in town.

Joe went to Frank's office, and walked in.

Frank was sat behind his desk reading a newspaper.

"Howdy Joe, come in, and sit" he said putting down his paper.

"Thank you" said Joe sitting down.

"How are you, Joe?"

"Good thanks, how are you, Frank?"

"Just swell. How can I help you buddy?"

"Max needs a barn in town, he asked me to buy one"

"OK, well there are no barns for sale in town, but I could arrange for a crew to build you one at the end of town"

"Yes, that would be perfect"

"It would cost a fair bit though"

"Max left me some money"

“Where is Max?”

“He has taken Madeline to Chicago for a few days”

“Gosh, he sure knows how to treat a lady”

“Yes, it seems so”

“So why do you need a barn?”

“For Max to do some of his scientific experiments in private”

“Oh see, what sort of experiments?”

“No idea, I’m just the assistant, he is the scientist”

“That reminds me, I had a telegram yesterday, a piece of white crystal is being sent from California by Wells Fargo, should be here in a couple of days, Max asked for it”

“Yes, he’s got a thing about crystals”

“Now is there anything else I can help you with Joe, I am the chief fixer in town, so I can get you anything”

Joe laughed.

“Couldn’t find me a wife could you, I feel a bit left out now Max is married” said Joe half joking.

“Well Joe, I don’t trade people, but I do know a girl who you might like, she is a negro woman, and see works at the bank. Would you like me to introduce you?” Asked Frank.

“OK, I suppose it would worth meeting her” replied Joe curiously.

“It certainly would. I’ll take you over now, but first let me get you’re barn building arranged” “SAMUEL” he yelled.

A young boy who looked around fourteen or fifteen walked out of a back room. He was quite tall, and skinny. He had short blonde hair, and a short fluffy beard. He had blue eyes. He was dressed in leather boots, brown chaps, a blue shirt, and wore an oversized Stetson.

“Yes boss” he said.

“Samuel, I need you to ride over to Dawson’s ranch, and tell Mr Dawson I have a job for him,” said Frank.

“Sure, thing boss,” said Samuel.

Samuel left the office.

“I found him wondering around in the plains a few years ago. His daddy died in the civil war, and his mother shot herself in the head. He was skinny, and close to death. I took him in, fed him, gave him a place to stay, and gave him a job. He is now my trusted assistant,” said Frank.

“That’s very kind of you,” said Joe.

“I have a heart Joe, and I couldn’t just leave that little blighter to die, and to tell you the truth, he is a hard working young man, and a cheeky boy too, reminds me of myself when I was young. Anyway, enough emotional stuff, let’s go to the bank”

Frank got up, and walked over to the door. Joe stood up. Frank opened the door, and the two men left the office.

They walked across the street, and along a bit until they reached the First Bank of Abilene. They waked inside.

Joe was surprised by the lack of security. No screens up in front of the cashier, no armed guards. The bank was a wooden building, with a stone-built section where the vault was. The vault was guarded by a huge black iron door. There was one cashier sat at a desk. The manager sat behind a desk at the back of the bank.

Joe noticed a desk in the corner with a black lady sat at it. She looked gorgeous. She was petite with long brown frizzy hair. She had big brown eyes, and a pretty face. She wore a long blue gown, and a blue bonnet. She was sat writing on paper. Sat on her desk there was a funny wooden box with buttons on it, and a wire coming out of it, and stretching up to the ceiling.

Frank led Joe over to her desk.

“Howdy Ethel May” he said.

“Well good day mister Frank, how is you today?” She said in a southern accent.

"I'm very well thank you my dear, how are you?"

"I'm just swell mister Frank. Can I help you with anything?"

"I just wanted to introduce you to my new Friend Joe"

"Hello Ethel May," said Joe.

"Hello Joe, nice to meet you, you have a funny accent where you from?" Asked Ethel May.

"I am from England"

"Oh, how exotic"

"Not really, it rains a lot there"

"Well, I would love to travel myself"

"Ethel May sorry if I'm being a bit forward but that is the British way, can I buy you a drink later please?"

"Mister Joe, nobody ever asked to buy me a drink before"

"I find that hard to believe, you look lovely"

"Oh, mister Joe, you is a charmer sir, I suppose you could come back at six o'clock when I finish work, and then maybe I would be quite thirsty"

"OK I'll be back at six. By the way what is that?" Asked Joe pointing to the box on her desk.

“That is the telegram box. You can send, and receive messages with it, it is a fine device, it’s like magic to me”

“Wow that is cool”

“Yes it is, it never really gets hot, what does wow mean?”

“Oh, it’s an English expression, we say it when something impresses us. When I first saw you, I thought wow”

“Mister Joe, you really is a charmer. Wow to you as well”

Shit, have I just introduced a new word to this time by accident, thought Joe?

That evening Frank was upstairs in his bedroom. His bedroom was a plain wooden room with an oak framed bed, and a cedar wood chest of draws.

He sat on his bed, and sighed. He missed his family. He made a good life for himself in the old west, but his missed home every now, and then.

He opened the top draw, and took out a photograph. He looked at the colour photograph of his Mum, and Dad, and his little brother Terrance as they stood in front of the house together. His Dad’s Buick was parked in the driveway. He was sixteen years old when the photo was taken by their neighbour. He popped the photo back in the draw. He looked in the draw, where he had a walkie-talkie radio, a 9mm Colt Commander pistol, and a pair of Ray Ban sunglasses. He closes the draw.

He got up, and left his room, he walked downstairs, and through his office. He left the office, and headed to the Alamo saloon.

In the Alamo saloon Joe, and Ethel May were sat at a table.

“This drink is delicious,” said Ethel May.

“It’s champagne with a dash of orange juice, my friend Max’s wife really likes it,” said Joe.

“I take it Max is a Negro too”

“No, he is a white man”

“I aint never heard of a white man being friends with a Negro before. I met some white folk who was nice to me, but they would never be my friends”

“Max is from England like me, we’ve been friends for years, he doesn’t judge people by the colour of skin”

“Well, he sounds like the nicest white man in the world”

“Yeah, he is nice”

“Well, my last master was quite nice, he taught me how to read, and write. That’s how I got a job at the bank. I do the administration stuff, that means I have to write all the records down on paper, and keep them in a book, and I send, and receive telegrams”

“Wow you’re really smart”

“Well don’t be so surprised boy, just cos I’m a woman, and a Negro don’t mean I can’t be smart”

“I’m not surprised, I meant it as a compliment. I admire you, I like smart women”

“Well, that is OK Joe, you are quite the gentleman you know, are all England people like you?”

“No, there are some nasty English people as well. But London where I’m from is nowhere near as bad as the south is here”

“The south is not as bad, now they got to pay Negroes for work, and all. It’s just they don’t wanna give us jobs now that they got to pay us”

“It’s terrible, they are just narrow-minded hicks”

Ethel May laughed.

“I like the way you talk Joe” she said.

Just then a drunken Texas cowboy stumbled over to their table. He was young, and foolish.

“I can’t believe they let niggers in here, what is this place” he said wobbling in front of them

Joe stood up, and took his jacket off exposing his muscular arms through his shirt, and the handle of his Browning 9mm sticking out of his shoulder holster.

"You wanna take a swing at me nigger, with them God damn short monkey hands?" Said the cowboy.

Joe walked over, and slammed his fist into the cowboy's face. The cowboy flew backwards, and landed on a table breaking it.

Wild Bill strolled over.

"What's going on here boy?" He said to Joe.

"This hick insulted my lady," said Joe.

"OK, well you had every right to hit him them," said Wild Bill.

Wild Bill turned, and walked back to his table.

The barman rushed over to Joe.

"Who's gonna pay for the damn table?" He said angrily.

Joe pulled out some cash, and handing the barman a ten dollar bill.

"That's fine, thank you sir," said the barman.

The barman walked back to the bar.

Joe sat down.

“I aint never had anyone defend my honour for me before, you is a special man Joe” said Ethel May.

“I would always defend your honour Ethel May,” said Joe.

A large cowboy came over to Joe, and pulled a Derringer out of his jacket.

You punched my damn brother nigger” he said raising the Derringer.

He suddenly fell on the floor as Frank slammed the butt of his gun into the back of the cowboy’s neck.

Four cowboys approached.

Frank raised his two revolvers, and aimed them at the cowboy’s.

“Pick up your trash, and get the hell out of here” he said menacingly.

“You heard the man boys” said Wild Bill who was stood up, and aiming his revolver.

Two cowboys grabbed their boss who Frank had knocked out.

One cowboy went to the bar to retrieve their guns.

“Leave the guns boy, you can get them in the morning when you are sober,” said Wild Bill.

The cowboy's left, and everyone in the saloon cheered.

Frank sat down with Joe, and Ethel May.

"Thanks Frank," said Joe.

"Yes, thank you mister Frank," said Ethel May.

"My pleasure," said Frank.

The barman came over, and put some drinks down.

"On your tab sir" he said to Frank.

"Thank you, Richie," said Frank.

"Cheers Frank" said Joe downing his old beer.

"Joe, when I saw you, you didn't look scared at all," said Frank.

"You mean when he pointed that tiny gun at me?" Said Joe.

"It can still fire a bullet"

"Yeah, but my gun is bigger" said Joe patting his shoulder.

"Can I see that gun Joe; it looks different to a normal revolver?"

"No sorry Frank, I only get it out if I really have to, I am not a fan of guns, I carry it purely for self-defence"

"Fair enough Joe, we've all got our principles, it's just looks like no gun I've seen before"

"Yeah, it's one of Max's inventions, I can show you it private sometime, I suppose"

"Is Max an inventor?" Asked Ethel May.

"No, he is a scientist, but he does build things every now, and then," said Joe.

"I would like meet Max; he sounds like an interesting fellow," said Ethel May.

"And what do you think of Joe, Ethel May?" Asked Frank.

"I think he is a gentleman, and I like him" she replied.

"And Joe, what do you think of Ethel May?"

"I think she is lovely, and I would like to take her out again sometime" he replied.

Max, and Madeline got off the train at Abilene after their seven-hour ride back from Chicago.

Madeline was wearing a red silk gown, and had a red hat with a red floral design on it. She was carrying a black leather bag in one hand, and carrying a small potted plant in the other hand. Max was wearing a brown checked suit, and a black bowler hat. He had a gold pocket watch in his suit's breast pocket, and attached to his collar with a gold chain. He was carrying two large leather suitcases.

They walked through town together happily.

Frank spotted them, and walked over to them.

“Howdy Max, and Madeline, did you have a nice time in Chicago?” He spoke.

“Oh yes, it was wonderful. They have flushing toilets in Chicago, and on the train, they are the most wonderful thinks I have ever seen” said Madeline excitedly.

“Well, I’m surprised you came back then,” said Frank.

“Of course, we came back, I would never abandon my friend Joe,” said Max.

“Well, I’ll show you to your new place if you like,” said Frank.

“Oh great, Joe managed to buy a barn, did he?” Said Max.

“Not exactly, I got a crew to build one for him,” said Frank.

“Oh, that’s fantastic, thank you Frank,” said Max.

“My pleasure, that’s what I do, fix things for people,” said Frank.

“I can’t wait to see it,” said Madeline.

“Here let me carry that plant for you Madeline,” said Frank.

“Why thank you Frank” said Madeline handing over the plant to him.

“What is this anyway?” Asked Frank.

“It’s parsley, you chew it, and it freshens up your breath,” said Max.

“How marvellous, there’s a few people in town who could do with this,” said Frank.

Frank led them to the end of town where the new barn was.

Frank knocked on the door.

“It’s got a lock on the door, came off of an old money chest” he said.

The door opened, and Joe came out.

“Max, Madeline your back, good to see you, come in” he said excitedly.

“Well, I’ve got some errands to run, but I hope I’ll see you later in the Alamo,” said Frank.

“You sure will, thanks Frank,” said Max.

Frank handing the plant to Joe, and walked away.

Max, and Madeline walked into the barn.

Inside the van was parked on one side covered with a large piece of canvas. There were two desks on the other side, and four wooden chairs, and three rooms at the rear of the barn. The floor was lined with timber.

“This is wonderful,” said Madeline.

“Yes, well done Joe,” said Max.

Joe locked the front door, and Max put his cases down.

“Yes, I had three rooms made at the back, two bedrooms, and there is an empty room I thought we could turn into a bathroom,” said Joe.

“With a flushing lavatory” said Madeline excitedly.

“Yes, I’m sure Frank can get us a toilet bowl, and cistern from Chicago,” said Max.

“What is this plant?” Asked Joe.

“Parsley” said Max.

“Oh cool, to clean our teeth,” said Joe.

“Oh Joe, I need to tell you about our trip, and about the flushing toilets, they are marvellous,” said Madeline.

"Yeah Joe, can you believe it, they have flushing lavatories in Chicago," said Max smiling.

Joe laughed.

"Well, I am not from the future, so it is all new to me," said Madeline.

"Listen guys, would you mind waiting until tonight to tell me all about the trip, I have a girlfriend now, and I'm due to see her tonight," said Joe.

"Joe that is wonderful news, have you asked her to marry you yet?" Said Madeline.

"Not yet, we've only been out twice," said Joe.

"Well hurry up, before someone else asks her," said Madeline.

"I'm sure Joe knows what he is doing, he is a smooth operator," said Max smiling.

"Yes, that's right, I am," said Joe.

"What is her name?" Asked Madeline.

"Ethel May" said Joe.

"That is a lovely name," said Madeline.

Max laughed.

“Ethel May, that’s the sort of name a granny would have” he said sniggering.

“Yes Max, but remember we are in the 19th century,” said Joe.

“Of course we are, sorry Joe,” said Max.

“Right, see that desk over there” said Joe pointing “wrapped up in that cloth is your crystal”

Max rushed over to the desk, and unwrapped the crystal. Inside the cloth was a rough jagged piece of white crystal.

“Perfect, I just need a hammer, a chisel, and some sandpaper, and I’ll cut this into shape,” said Max.

“And come, and see your bedroom guys,” said Joe.

They followed Joe to the rear of the barn, and he opened the door on the left.

Inside their bedroom was a large oak bed frame with a bed spread on it. There was also a cedar wood chest of draws in the corner. There was no window in the room, so it was quite dark. The sun pocked through small openings in the wooden planks. There were three white candles in a candelabra on the chest of draws.

“We need some lighting,” said Max.

“Yeah, I’ve been using an oil lamp at night, and as you can see there are candles in the bedrooms,” said Joe.

“I’ll sort something out,” said Max.

“The mattress isn’t sprung, or memory foam I’m afraid, its basically a big cloth bag filled with cotton,” said Joe.

Madeline walked over, and lay on the bed.

“I think it’s very comfortable” she said.

“Excuse me Mrs Walsh, no shoes on the bed please,” said Max.

Madeline slipped off the bed.

“Well excuse me Mr Walsh, but when you brought me these shoes, you ask me to wear them, and keep my stockings on in bed when we had sex” she said annoyed.

“Max, you kinky boy” said Joe smiling.

“Yes, but the shoes were brand new then, they hadn’t been worn outside,” said Max.

“Well, your future sex stuff was quite strange,” said Madeline.

“Future sex, what did he do?” Asked Joe.

“I would rather not discuss it, but I did enjoy it,” said Madeline.

“Doing stuff, you’ve seen on the internet eh Max?” Said Joe.

“Yeah, I was mate,” said Max smiling.

"What is the internet, some sort of fishing device?" Asked Madeline.

"It's how we get information in the future, using computers," said Max.

"What the hell is a computer?" Said Madeline confused.

"Where is my laptop, Joe?" Asked Max.

"Top draw" said Joe pointing to the chest of draws.

Max rushed over to the chest of draws, and pulled his laptop out. He opened it up, and switched it on.

He moved over to Madeline, and held the laptop up to show her.

"This is a computer" he said as the operation system loaded up.

"Now that is magic surely" said Madeline shocked.

"These are common in the future," said Max.

"But that is a colour picture, that is such a clear picture, how do you make such clear pictures appear on a box?" Said Madeline amazed.

"It is made up of loads of dots of liquid crystal that project different colours onto the screen," said Max.

"Well, that sounds like magic to me," said Madeline.

"Now I hate to ask Max, but did you get me a present when you were away?" Asked Joe.

"Follow me mate," said Max.

Max walked over to where he left his cases. He laid one case down, and unzipped it, he opened it up.

"Is that toilet paper?" Said Joe.

"Yep, fifty rolls," said Max.

"And is that my present?"

Max laughed.

"Of course, not mate, that's for all of us, I not using fucking corn to wipe my arse ever again," said Max.

Max reached inside his jacket, and pulled out a gold pocket watch with a gold chain, and clip.

"Here you go mate, I set the time, you just have to wind it up every morning, it doesn't have a battery" said Max handing the pocket watch to Joe.

"Wow thanks Max that's really cool" said Joe happily "so I guess batteries haven't been invented yet"

"Actually, Joe batteries were used thousands of years ago in ancient Babylon. They got a clay jar, put an iron rod into it, then filled it with lemon juice. The citric acid in the lemon juice reacted with the iron to produce electrons," said Max.

"He is so clever isn't he" said Madeline as she walked over to them.

"How did they figure that out?" Asked Joe.

"Aliens called the Anunnaki showed them how to do it," said Max.

"You, and your aliens Max," said Joe.

"There not my aliens," said Max.

"Do you like my bag?" Asked Madeline holding up her leather bag.

"Yes, that is very nice," said Joe.

"Max got it for me, and other things which I will tell you about later when we meet your girlfriend," said Madeline.

"Surprised you didn't get a fancy Chanel handbag Max," said Joe.

"I would have liked to, but it appears they haven't been invented yet," said Max.

"When were handbags invented?" Said Joe.

“This may surprise you Joe, but I don’t actually know, the history of handbags is not something I have ever studied” said Max sarcastically.

“Bet you wish you did now though,” said Joe.

“Yes, actually I do,” said Max.

Later on in the Alamo saloon Max, and Madeline were sat at a table. Max had a glass of beer, and Madeline had a champagne with a dash of orange juice. There was another glass of beer, and champagne with a dash of orange juice on the table.

Joe walked over to them with Ethel May.

Max, and Madeline stood up.

“Ethel May I would like to introduce you to my good friends Max, and his wife Madeline,” said Joe.

“Hi Ethel May” said Madeline shaking hands with her.

“Hello Madeline,” said Ethel May.

“Hello Ethel May” said Max shaking her hand.

“Hello Max” she replied.

They all sat down.

“Got you some drinks,” said Max.

“Cheers mate,” said Joe.

“Thank you, mister Max, this is very kind of you,” said Ethel May.

“Now can I tell you about our trip?” Asked Madeline excitedly.

“Yes, please do Madeline,” said Joe.

“OK so we went on a train, and I was amazed by how fast, and smooth it was, and they had flushing toilets. I thought it was all magic, but Max explained to me that there are these boxes on the roof called water tanks, and the water come down because of, because of, what is it Max?”

“Gravity”

“That’s right gravity, the water comes down, and fills the toilet thingies with water so you can flush them”

“The toilet thingies are called cisterns”

“Right thanks Max, and I asked Max how the train moves cos it was like magic to me, but I can’t remember, you tell them Max”

“OK there is a big coal fire at the front of the train, and the fire heats up a big tank of water until it gets so hot it turns to steam, that why there called steam engines. The steam is released, and it drives these metal things called pistons up, and down. The pistons turn a big cylinder-shaped piece of metal called a crank shaft, and the shaft drives the wheels, and makes them turn”

“He is so clever, isn’t he?”

“Yes, he is, that was so interesting, I never knew how trains run,” said Ethel May.

“And Chicago was amazing. It was so big, and so busy. People, and carriages everywhere. We stayed in this fancy hotel, what was it called Max?”

“The Palmer House Hilton”

“Wow I didn’t know Hilton was that old,” said Joe.

“Well, this hotel was brand new, and in our room, we had a sweet bathroom,” said Madeline.

“It’s called an ensuite bathroom darling”

“Oh, sorry Max, an ensuite bathroom. It had a bath, and a shower, and a flushing toilet, and some thingy for washing your hands”

“A basin”

“Yes, a basin, and there were these things you turned to make water come out”

“Taps”

“Yes Taps, and there was a hot tap, you turned it, and hot water came out, it was magic. But of course, Max was able to explain how it all worked. They have these big pipes underground called water mains, and they use steam engines to drive a thingy which makes the water flow”

“A pump”

“That’s it a pump, a pump makes the water flow round these pipes, and when it gets to the hotel it goes up to the roof, and fills up big boxes called water tanks, and then that gravity thing makes the water fall down into our ensuite bathroom, so when we turn a tap, it come out, and the hot water is made by a big coal boiler which heats up the metal pipe things”

“A coil”

“Yes, that’s it a coil, and the coil is inside this thingy”

“A cylinder”

“Yes, the coil is inside a cylinder, and the cylinder is full of water, and the hot coil thingy heats the water up”

“Max how do you know so much?” Asked Ethel May.

“I am a scientific explorer, so it is my job to learn about how everything works,” said Max.

“That is amazing, do you travel with Joe?” Said Ethel May.

“Yes, I do, I’m his assistant,” said Joe.

“Wow you must have seen some amazing stuff,” said Ethel May.

"We sure have," said Joe.

"So, you've seen these flushing toilet things before then?" Said Ethel May.

"Yes, we have, haven't we Max?" Said Joe.

"Yes, we have, London has had running water since 1805. The first flushing toilet was invented by Sir John Harrington in the late 16th Century, he worked for Queen Elizabeth the 1st. Alex Cummings came up with U bend equations in the late 18th Century, and the U bend was perfected by Thomas Crapper in 1880," said Max.

"1880, that year hasn't come yet," said Ethel May.

"Sorry I meant 1870, it was very recent. I get mixed up sometimes, too much knowledge in my head," said Max.

"Any way I haven't told the rest of what we did, we went to look at the harbour, which is where you park your ship, and we went to this fancy restaurant, and Max ate snails"

"It was a French restaurant," said Max.

"I had a steak, and we went shopping, this dress I'm wearing is new, it's made of silk, and it cost forty dollars"

"Forty dollars why would anyone spend that much on a dress" said Ethel May shocked.

“I know, that’s what I thought, but it is so soft, and Max brought me this fancy under garments called knickers, they are silk too, three dollars a pair, but they are so comfy”

“I bet Max didn’t mind buying you knickers,” said Joe.

“He certainly didn’t mind taking them off, but that is private,” said Madeline.

“Max what have you become, the king of romance,” said Joe.

“The king of wishful thinking more like,” said Max.

Max, and Joe laughed.

“So, Ethel, how did you, and Joe meet?” Asked Madeline.

“Mister Frank introduced us in the bank where I work. How did you, and Max meet?” Said Ethel May.

“Well, I was working as a whore in a small town called Sherman in Texas, and I was being held against my will. Max rescued me,” said Madeline.

“I was a slave for most of my life, so I know how you feel,” said Ethel May.

“Did you have to sleep with fifteen men a day as well?”

“No, I just had to sleep with the master when he got drunk, he even had sex with me when I was bleeding”

“No way, that is the only time I got off when I was bleeding, I didn’t think a man would sleep with you when you were bleeding”

“I’d sleep with you when you were bleeding,” said Max.

“That is disgusting, you would get blood on your penis” said Madeline shocked.

“Yes, I know but it is your blood, and I love you, therefore I also love your blood,” said Max.

“Oh, well when you put it like that then it’s kinda sweet,” said Madeline.

“Why do women have to bleed Max?” Asked Ethel May.

“He won’t know that he is clever, but he doesn’t know about women’s bodies” said Madeline.

“You might be surprised about how much Max knows about male, and female bodies, tell them why they bleed Max,” said Joe.

“Why don’t you tell them Joseph?” Said Max.

“I am not a great scientist like you, I couldn’t explain it so well,” said Joe.

“Fine. OK, once a month the female body releases an egg from the ovaries, it drops down the fallopian tube into the womb. Now if the egg is not fertilised by a seed, which comes from the man, then the egg will break down, and turn to blood, that blood has to be released," said Max.

"You know what happens inside the body" said Madeline shocked.

"As a scientist I strive to know everything," said Max.

"You must be better than a doctor," said Ethel May.

"Doctors in this town, I would definitely be better, in fact I would probably be better than any doctor on the planet at the moment, at least I would sterilize my equipment properly," said Max.

"He's amazing, bet you're glad to be married to him," said Ethel May.

"I sure am, now when are you two getting married?" Asked Madeline.

"He aint asked me yet," said Ethel May.

"We've only been out three times," said Joe.

"Well, I aint waiting around forever," said Ethel May.

"Can I borrow your ring please Madeline," said Max.

"Which one?"

"Anyone"

“Here you go” said Madeline passing her wedding ring.

Max passed the ring to Joe.

“Let me see you hand please?” He asked Ethel May.

Ethel May held up her hand, and Joe tried to slip the ring on. It was too small for Ethel May.

Joe handed the ring back to Max.

“Slightly too small” he said.

“I’ll fix them tomorrow morning,” said Max.

“OK Ethel May, I will have a surprise for you tomorrow,” said Joe.

“A surprise? Will I like it?” Ethel May asked.

“Yes, you will” said Madeline smiling.

Joe was walking back from dropping Ethel May off at her shack.

He wandered through town, and saw a drunken Wild Bill stumbling along.

Wild Bill saw him.

“Them cowboy’s that harassed you left this morning, so you is safe now boy” he slurred.

“Thanks, Wild Bill,” said Joe.

Wild Bill laughed, and wobbled away.

“Joe” said Frank appearing beside him, and making him jump.

“Oh Frank, you scared me,” said Joe.

“Can I have a quick word with you please Joe?”

Chapter 10
What Year Are You From?

Max, and Madeline were back at the barn. Max had lit the oil lamp so they could see what they were doing. Madeline was looking in the suitcase at her new clothes.

"Oh, there so lovely" she said admiring her new dresses.

She noticed the books they'd brought in Chicago at the bottom of the case.

"Oh Max, we forgot to tell Joe, and Ethel May that we brought some books in Chicago" she said.

"That's OK, we can tell them tomorrow, and also tell them we brought a map, and compass" said Max who sat at the desk with the oil lamp on it rolling a joint.

Max finished rolling the joint, and put it down, he started rolling another one for Joe.

"Come, and sit-down Mrs Walsh, and smoke some Jamaican tobacco with me" he said as he finished rolling Joe's joint.

Madeline came over, and sat next to him. Max lit their joint up.

"Are you gonna teach me to read tomorrow, Max?" She asked.

"Yes, we can start your lessons, it will take a while, but it will be worth it" he said passing the joint to her.

She took a big drag, and blew the smoke in Max's face.

"That's very sexy" he said.

"What does that mean?"

"What sexy?"

"Yeah"

"It means something that makes you feel like having sex, you are sexy to me"

"Aw you sweet man, you are sexy to me then" she said passing the joint back.

Frank was sat behind his desk, and Joe was sat in front. Frank lit his oil lamp.

"Thanks for sparing some of your time Joe," said Frank.

"Well, if I wait long enough, hopefully Max, and Madeline will have finished having sex, they're bloody noisy," said Joe.

Frank laughed.

"You English sure are forward" he said.

"Sorry didn't mean to be rude, we have to get used to different countries all the time, there are places in Africa where tribal people walk around naked. Max loved taking part in their culture"

"Sound like Max is a bit wild at heart"

"I suppose he is"

"Can I see your gun please, I am fascinated by weapons, and I'd like to see what Max has made"

"I suppose so, but you need to keep it a secret, Max likes to keep some of his experiments private"

"No problem, buddy, your secret is safe with me"

Joe pulled out his Browning 9mm, and handed it over to Frank.

Frank took the gun, and looked at it under the oil lamp.

"This looks like a 9mm pistol" he said.

"How the hell would you know that?" Asked Joe shocked.

"I told you, I've been around"

"Max has taught me about logic, and there is only one logical explanation as to how you would know that, you must be from the future"

"Max sounds like a clever man, and I guess it's rubbed off on you a bit Joe. I am from 1974, what year are you from?"

“Max, and I are from 2016”

“Jesus, are you part of a government program?”

“No, one of Max’s experiments went a bit wrong, and accidentally sent us back in time. What happened to you?”

“I was part of the US governments crononaut program. I was sent back to monitor the civil war. When I went back to my position to check in, I was told by my handler that the time link had been Severeed. I arranged to meet him the next day, but he didn’t show up, I never managed to find him again. So, I found myself stuck in 1864”

“Jesus so you’ve been here for six years?”

“Yep, and I’ve made quite a life for myself, I studied this period in time for my research, so I know where all the action is gonna be. This town for instance is gonna cease being a popular cow town in two years, and the action will move to Dodge City, which hasn’t been built yet”

“My goodness. So, do you know how time travel works? Max needs help with his research”

“Sorry Joe, I can’t help you there. I am no scientist. I was just one of the people chosen to go back in time. The scientist would open a window in the lab, and I just had to step through”

“How an earth did they have that technology in the 70s?”

“The government did deals with the grey aliens back in the 40s. The greys shared technology; it was so complex that it took several decades for Earth scientists to get their heads round it”

“So, you mean aliens are real?”

“Oh yes, I have met a few greys, they talk to you telepathically, freaky creatures they are”

“My God, now please don’t tell big corporation run the government, and they are in cahoots with aliens”

“I’m afraid that is all true Joe”

“Oh God, please don’t let Max know that, he has been telling me about this stuff for years, and I thought he was mad”

“The government has brain washed people to think aliens don’t exist. Some people can see through the lies. Max is very smart; he is probably unable to be brain washed. Does he smoke dope?”

“Yeah, he loves the stuff”

“That’s it then, people who get stoned regularly cannot be brain washed, that’s why the government made it illegal”

“They’re starting to legalize it in various states of America now”

“That means their plans are coming to end”

“What is their plan”

“No idea, I was just a lowly worker, I didn’t find out any juicy stuff”

“OK, so if Max can find a way to get us back to 2016, would you wanna come with us?”

“No, not to 2016. If he could send me back to 1974, I would go, but not 2016”

“Well, he doesn’t even know if he can get us to 2016, so I’m not sure if could get you to 74, I can ask him though”

“Actually, would you do me a big favour please Joe. Don’t tell anyone I’m from the future, not even Max. Not yet anyway. I need to think about this, I never expected to bump into other time travellers”

“I don’t feel comfortable lying to Max”

“I know, I’m just asking you not to tell him yet, not until I’m ready”

“OK I can do that Frank”

The following morning. Max, and Madeline were lying in their bed.

“Max, when are we gonna get a flushing toilet?” She asked.

“I’m gonna ask Frank today about getting some stuff, I’ll fit you a flushing toilet as soon as possible”

“Well sort something out soon please. I don’t want to keep going round the back of the barn every time I need to pee, and lords knows where I can go if I need a shit”

“OK, I’ll get on it today, I’ll do that first thing,” said Max.

Max climbed out of bed. Madeline climbed out of bed as well.

Max went to grab his dressing gown.

“Before you put that on, can I have a naked hug please?” She spoke.

Max stopped reaching for his dressing gown, and walked over to Madeline. He threw his arms around her, and they embraced tightly.

“You can always have a naked hug Mrs Walsh”

“Why thank you Mr Walsh”

Joe came out his bedroom in his dressing gown.

Max was sat at a desk fiddling with something. Max was wearing his dressing gown. Madeline was sat beside him in her new silk dressing gown watching him.

“Hi guys” said Joe sleepily.

“Hello sleepy head. The kettle has been set up in the back of the van, so help yourself to coffee, we’ve got no milk, or sugar though,” said Max.

“Thanks mate, what are you up to?” Asked Joe.

“I am just putting my laser rifle together. Just need to fit the last diamond. It has a one carat, two carat, and three carat diamond in it. Each diamond concentrates the laser beam. The one carat is for wounding. The two carat is for killing, and the three carat is for destroying”

Joe walked over to the van, leant in the back, and switched the kettle.

“So, who are you planning on wounding, or killing, or destroying then?” Asked Joe.

“No one, I was gonna use it to dig a hole,” said Max.

“Dig a hole?”

“Yes mate, we need an indoor toilet, and I’m gonna make a temporary one. Right, it’s ready. I’d better test it first”

Max stood up with a white rifle shaped piece of plastic. It looked like a toy ray gun.

“Where are you gonna test it?” Asked Joe.

“I’ll shoot a hole in the back wall of the bathroom; we’ll need a hole for pipe work anyway,” said Max.

Max walked over, and opened the bathroom door. The bathroom was a bare room with a timber floor.

Joe, and Madeline came over, and stood behind him.

“Stand back a bit please, I’ve no idea how powerful this is gonna be” he said turning his head to look at them.

Joe, and Madeline stepped back a bit.

Max aimed the rifle at the right-hand corner of the bathroom, low down.

He pulled the trigger, and nothing happened.

“Shit, forgot to charge the crystal cells” he said.

He rushed over to the van, and used some wiring off the power supply to send a charge into the crystals on the rifle.

He rushed back to the bathroom door, and took aim again.

“It should work this time” he said.

Max took aim, and pulled the trigger.

There was huge cracking sound like lightning. A huge ball of orange light flew out the rifle, and put a large hole in the wall. The hole was big enough to fit a head through.

“Was that the destroy setting?” Asked Joe.

"No that was wound, I think it needs a small adjustment," said Max.

Joe, and Madeline looked at the size of the hole.

"Just don't ever use the destroy mode indoors Max," said Joe.

"Ah, I've just remembered" said Max rushing over to the desk. "Look at this Joe" Max grabbed the map, and passed it to Joe.

"Wow, cool map" said Joe looking at it.

"Yes, it's got all 37 states on it," said Max

Joe walked into Frank's office.

"Hi Frank, how you doing?" Said Joe.

"Good thanks, take a seat Joe, how are you?"

Joe sat down.

"I'm well mate, I'm gonna ask Ethel May to marry me tonight in the Alamo, like Max did. I'm going to the church after this to book the wedding"

"That is fantastic news, well done, glad I introduced you two"

"Yeah, thanks Frank. Max has sent me over to ask you to get some stuff. He is busy blasting holes in the floor at the moment"

“With dynamite?”

“No with his new laser rifle, he put it together this morning, it’s bloody lethal”

“Oh, I see, sounds like fun. What does Max need?”

“Right, he needs a toilet bowl, and a toilet cistern, says they have them in Chicago, and he needs a small thin sheet of copper, so he can make some wires. He also wants some gallium arsenide, and gallium phosphide, but he said they would probably be impossible to get in this time, so he is gonna try, and create his own semi conductive materials”

“Toilet bowl, toilet cistern, and sheet of copper I can do. The other stuff I don’t even know what the hell it is. What is Max trying to do”

“He wants to make some electric lighting”

“Can’t he just make a bulb with an electric filament; he can do that right?”

“Yeah probably, but that is too old fashion for Max”

“Too old fashion. But the light bulb hasn’t even been invented yet”

“I know, don’t get me started”

Joe walked back into the barn. Madeline was sat on a chair by one of the desks.

“Hi Madeline,” said Joe.

“Hello Joe,” said Madeline.

Max walked out the bathroom.

“Hi Joe. I’ve finished now, I got a few bits from the hardware store, the lumber yard, and the railway depot, while you were out. I have made a temporary toilet with a wooden seat. I made a twenty-foot hole in the ground below the toilet. I got some cotton, and a few cloth bags, and made a nice comfy seat on the toilet, I fixed the hole in the wall with some planks of timer, and I hammered a railroad spike into a plank of wood on the wall to create a toilet roll holder. I also got a big bag of saw dust from the lumber yard, and a metal cup from the hardware store. After you have a shit on the toilet pour two cups of sawdust down the toilet to reduce the smell,” said Max.

“Wow you have been busy,” said Joe.

“Yes, Madeline really wanted an indoor toilet, so I’ve done it, did you order my bits?” Asked Max.

“Aw thank you Max, no more peeing behind the barn now,” said Madeline.

“I ordered the toilet stuff, and copper sheet, Frank said it will take three days,” said Joe.

“Three days, that’s not bad, OK when you have a shit on the toilet pour four cups of sawdust down afterwards then,” said Max.

“OK I need to go to the church, and book my wedding,” said Joe.

“Of course, give me your rings Joe, and I’ll make them a bit bigger,” said Max.

Joe pulled the rings out of his jacket pocket, and handed them to Max.

“Right Madeline would you mind going with Joe, so you’re not on your own, the blacksmith’s is a hot sooty place, so I wouldn’t want to take you there,” said Max.

“OK I’ll go with Joe; it will be nice to have a walk,” said Madeline.

“Good, Joe has a gun so he can protect you if anything happens,” said Max.

“Can I have a gun please; I can put it in my bag?” Asked Madeline.

“Yes, you can, but not until I’ve taught you how to use it,” said Max.

“You just have to pull the trigger,” said Madeline.

“Yes, and no, bit more to it than that, the Browning HP which I will give you is a powerful gun, HP stands for high power, it is a forty-five calibre hand gun, and to put that into context, if you fire at a stagecoach, it would go through the stagecoach, through two people, and out the other side of the coach” said Max.

“Wow I didn’t know it was that powerful,” said Joe.

“Yes, and they have quite a kickback on them, so you have to be shown how to hold them, remember I showed you once Joe, never keep your arm straight, always have a slight bend to absorb the kickback or you may break your arm,” said Max.

“OK then, I will wait till you have shown me how to use it,” said Madeline.

“Thank you, Madeline, I’ll show you tonight,” said Max.

Joe, and Madeline reached the small wooden church on the outskirts of town.

They walked inside. The preacher was stood lighting some candles by the pulpit.

“Hello sir,” said Joe.

The preacher looked up from his candles.

“Hello, can I help you?” He asked.

Joe, and Madeline walked over to him.

“I would like to book a wedding please,” said Joe.

The preacher looked at Madeline.

“You married someone the other day, didn’t you?” He asked.

“Oh, I’m not marrying this man, I’m married to his best friend,” said Madeline.

“Oh, I see, no offence, but I couldn’t marry a Negro to a white woman, wouldn’t go down very well, is you a bride a Negro?” Said the preacher.

“Yes, she is,” said Joe.

“That’s good. If it was up to me, I wouldn’t mind who got married, God does not judge people on the colour of their skin, but there would be an outcry in the town if a Negro married a white woman,” said the preacher.

“It’s OK, I understand, not everyone is as tolerant as you are preacher,” said Joe.

“So went do you want to get married sir?”

“Tomorrow please”

“Three o’clock, OK?”

“Yes, that would be fine thank you”

"No problem, I'll need five dollars off you please for the service"

"No problem"

Joe pulled some cash out of his pocket, and handed a five dollar bill to the preacher.

"Excellent, well just bring your bride here at three tomorrow, and I'll get you married"

That evening Joe walked into the Alamo saloon with Ethel May. They walked over to where Max, and Madeline were sat.

On the table was a bottle of champagne, and four glasses.

"At last, your here," said Max.

"I told you Maxwell, Ethel May doesn't finish work till six," said Joe.

Joe pulled out a chair for Ethel May.

"Why thank you sir" said Ethel May taking her seat.

Joe stood next to her.

"Are you gonna sit down Joe?" Asked Ethel May.

"I just need to ask you something first," said Joe.

"OK well ask away then," said Ethel May.

Joe got down on one knee by Ethel May.

"What are you doing Joe?" She said confused.

"Ethel May, will you make me the happiest man in the world by agreeing to marry me please?" Said Joe.

"Oh Joe, I was hoping that would be the surprise, I suppose you look good, and you're a real gentleman, so yes I will marry you Joe Brown" she said smiling.

"Give me your hand please," said Joe.

Ethel May held up her right hand.

"Other hand please," said Joe.

Ethel May raised her left hand, and Joe slipped the diamond ring on her finger.

"My goodness what a pretty ring, just like?
said Ethel May.

"Yes, my dear, it's called an engagement ring, it's what gentlemen in England give to their ladies when they agree to marry them," said Joe.

"Wow, I love your England ways" said Ethel May smiling.

"THIS WOMEN JUSTIN? AGREED TO MARRY ME, WE'RE GETTING MARRIED TOMORROW AT THREE" yelled Joe.

There was thunderous applause from the people in the saloon. Wild Bill hurried over to them.

“Well done you two, I will be at your wedding, are you gonna buy everyone a drink?” He asked.

Max stood up.

“Take a seat Wild Bill, I’ll get some bottles, and deliver one to each table” he said.
:
“OK, whiskey please sir,” said Wild Bill.

Wild Bill went back to his table.

Max looked around, and counted. There were eight tables occupied in the saloon, excluding their own.

“Pour the champas Joe, I’ll be back in a minute,” said Max.

Max walked over to the bar.

“Hi buddy, I’m glad you didn’t cause a stampede again,” said the barman.

“Yes, I thought I’d get a bottle of whiskey for each table please,” said Max.

“Sure, thing buddy,” said the batman.

The barman placed eight bottles of whiskey on the bar, then he helped Max to give a bottle to each table.

"How long you staying in town buddy?" Asked Wild Bill when Max dropped a bottle off on his table.
I
"Don't know a while," said Max.

"Well, you are welcome to stay as long as you like, I really like you Max," said Wild Bill.

"Thanks, Will Bill," said Max.

Max walked back over to the bar after the whiskey had been handed out.

"That's sixteen dollars please," said the barman.

Max handing him a twenty-dollar bill.

"Here buddy, keep the change, get yourself a drink" he said.

"Well thank you kindly sir," said the barman.

Max walked back to the table.

He sat down, and sipped his glass of champagne.
"Bit sour, but I'm thirsty" he said.

"Thanks for sorting the drinks out, Max," said Joe.

“No problem, mate, and congratulations to you both,” said Max.

“Thank you, Max, and thank you for making this ring, Joe told me. You are a very clever man,” said Ethel May.

“He is clever, he’s been teaching to read today, I’ve been learning about the alpha something,” said Madeline.

“The alphabet dear,” said Max.

That night Max took Madeline round the back of the barn. There were a couple of rocks on the ground. He handed Madeline the Browning HP 9mm.

“Now pull the hammer back with you other hand. That’s it, careful let it click into place” he said.

Madeline held the gun up.

“It’s quite heavy” she said.

“OK now bend your arm slightly, and close one eye, now line up the little point at the end of the gun with one of those rocks”

“OK done that”

“Pull the trigger”

BANG

The rock shattered, and Madeline fell backwards, Max caught her.

“Oh my, that was powerful, and loud” she said.

“Yes, one more shot dear, then we better go home, before someone comes to investigate. Now put you right foot forward a bit, and bring you left foot back slightly, now you will be better balanced. Now shoot the other rock” he said.

Madeline aimed the gun, and pulled the trigger.

BANG

The other rock shattered, and this time Madeline stayed upright.

“This is fun” she said.

“Yes great, now let’s go home” he said.

“Is this my gun now?”

“Yes, it is”

“Oh goodie”

The next day Joe, and Ethel May got married. They had a quick ceremony like Max, and Madeline.

The saloon crowd was in the congregation, along with Joe McCoy, and Frank.

That evening after having celebratory drinks in the Alamo saloon, they made their way back to the barn.

Max opened the door, and held it open while Madeline, Joe, and Ethel May Brown entered the barn.

Max walked over to the oil lamp, and lit it. Joe locked the front door.

“This is where you live?” Said Ethel May.

“Yes, my dear, my bedroom is at the back next to Max, and Madeline’s bedroom,” said Joe.

“Is this where you do some work as well?”

“Yes, Max does his scientific experiments here”

“Wow I would love to see a scientific experiment”

“What do you think about travelling back in time Ethel May?” Asked Max.

“Now that sounds like magic,” said Ethel May.

“Max, no science talk tonight please, I just wanted to enjoy my wedding night, and tomorrow we’ll tell Ethel May about our science stuff,” said Joe.

“OK Joe, no problem, mate,” said Max.

“Where is your outhouse, I need to pee before bed?” Said Ethel May.

“Our outhouse is indoors, I’ll show you, and light the candle in there,” said Joe.

Joe led Ethel May to the bathroom.

“Aw isn’t it great that Joe is married now” said Madeline excitedly.

“Yes, it is, I’m very happy,” said Max.

Soon they were all in their beds. Ethel May was very impressed by using an indoor outhouse, and even more impressed by toilet paper.

Max, and Madeline lay in bed together.

“Max”

“Yes Madeline”

“What does wow mean?”

“It’s something you say when you’re impressed by something. Is it a term you’re not familiar with?”

“No, but I’ve heard you say it before, and Ethel May said it tonight. Is it an English phrase?”

Yes, it is, possibly a future word, that's why you've never heard it before"

"Aw Max, can you hear them fucking next door?"

"Yep, sure can"

"Aw, how romantic"

"If you say so"

"Yes, I do, would you like to fuck me, Max?"

"Hmm let me think about that"

Chapter 11
Tommy the Texas Ranger

The next morning Joe walked out of his bedroom in his boxer shorts, and Ethel May followed in Joe’s dressing gown.

Max was sat at one of the desks fiddling with a metal box. Madeline was sat near him drinking a mug of coffee.

“Howdy you two, how was your wedding night?” Said Madeline.

“It was fantastic” said Ethel May smiling.

“I’ll make you some coffee, take a seat,” said Joe.

Ethel May got a chair from the side, and sat near to Madeline. Joe walked over to the van, and snook under the canvas, and into the back of the van.

“I take it the trouser snake came out to play,” said Max smirking.

“Don’t be so rude Maxwell,” said Joe.

Madeline, and Ethel May started laughing.

“Trouser snake, that is a funny expression” said Madeline giggling.

“Yes, it must be one of their England expressions” said Ethel May also giggling.

Joe came back with two mugs of coffee.

“Wow that was fast” said Ethel May taking a mug off Joe.

“Yes, we have a fast way of making coffee, one of Max’s inventions,” said Joe.

“Wow he is very clever,” said Ethel May.

“Yes, I am,” said Max smiling.

“What are you up to Max?” Asked Joe.

“I’m making a new electromagnetic crystal power supply, when I was at Billy’s two days ago, I got an iron box made, and yesterday I chiselled the crystal into shape, and now I’m putting everything together,” said Max.

“So, I guess it’s time to tell Ethel May about us?” Said Joe.

“Would you like me to explain it mate?” Asked Max.

“No, it’s my job,” said Joe.

“Tell me what, what is it with you guys?” Asked Ethel May.

“You know when Max said yesterday about going back in time?”

“Yeah, and I said that would be like magic”

“That’s right, well imagine if it was possible, image if you could travel back in time one hundred years”

“I can’t imagine something that is not possible”

“You said Max was clever, didn’t you?”

“Yes, I think he is clever”

“Well imagine if he was clever enough to travel back in time”

“What are you trying to tell me Joe, speak in a way I can understand”

“Joe, and Max are time travellers from the future,” said Madeline.

“WHAT!” Yelled Ethel May shocked.

“We come from the year 2016,” said Joe.

“Don’t you go making fun of me Joe Brown, I though you was a gentleman” said Ethel May angrily.

“Max some help please,” said Joe.

“OK mate,” said Max.

Max got up, and rushed over to his bedroom. He came back a minute later, and showed Ethel May his laptop. She looked at the screen in shock.

“Is this witchcraft?” She said nervously.

“No Ethel May, this technology from the future,” said Max.

“So, you Max, and you Joe come from the future?” Asked Ethel May.

“Yes, that’s right Ethel May, but I’m still the same gentleman you fell in love with, I just come from a different time,” said Joe.

“And you knew about this Madeline?” Said Ethel May.

“Yes, and I was shocked at first, but Max, and Joe are lovely people, and I’m so glad I met Max, I love him dearly, and Joe loves you, that’s why he told you about where he’s from, this is something they have to keep secret, but he wanted to tell you because he loves you,” said Madeline.

“Well in that case, thank you Joe for telling me your secret, it may take me sometime to understand what I have just heard though,” said Ethel May.

“You take as long as you need darling. To be honest with you I don’t understand it, Max is the one who brought us back in time,” said Joe.

“By accident Joseph, and I now have the tools to take us back to the future, ha, back to the future, I’ve always wanted to say that,” said Max.

“What do you mean, you have the tools to take us back to the future?” Asked Joe.

“I have built the other crystal power unit, so I can now begin the experiment,” said Max.

“Right now?” Said Joe.

“Why not, it will take six hours for the power supplies to overload,” said Max.

“What about the stuff you ordered?”

“Joe, I think we can find toilets, and copper much easier in 2016”

“Hang on, are you saying we’re going to 2016?” Asked Madeline excitedly.

“That is the plan, although I can’t guarantee it, time travel is a bit tricky,” said Max.

“I can’t believe what I am hearing,” said Ethel May.

“OK I know this has been thrown at you suddenly, but in the future Ethel May black people have a much better time, we can take any job we want, you could be a scientist, or a member of the government,” said Joe.

“Seriously, there is no discrimination against black people in the future?”

“Well, there is some, Max help please”

“Ethel May, there will always be people that discriminate against people due to the colour of their skin, the difference is, that in the future there are laws against it,” said Max.

“Laws that give black people equal rights to white people?” Said Ethel May.

“Yes” said Joe.

“Well then, I’m in,” said Ethel May.

“I’ll start the process then,” said Max.

Joe walked into Frank’s office. Frank was sat behind his desk.

“Hi Frank. I need to talk to you urgently” said Joe really fast.

“Slow down buddy, take a seat, and talk to me,” said Frank.

Joe sat down.

“What’s up Joe?” Asked Frank.

“Right Frank, Max is trying to get us back to 2016, he has an experiment set up now, and in just over five, and half hours we might be able to get back to 2016,” said Joe.

“Well, that’s great news, I hope it goes well”

“I’m here to invite you to come with us”

“That’s really kind Joe, but I told you 2016 is not for me”

“Yeah, I know, but when we’re back in 2016 Max can try, and find a way to send you back to the 70s”

“Do you think he would do that?”

“Yes, I do, he is a really nice guy”

“Look Joe, the reason I told you not to tell Max that I’m a time traveller is because I don’t trust scientists, I’m stuck here because of scientists”

“Max isn’t like a normal scientist, he had been shunned by main-stream science, mainly because he burnt down the National Physics lab in England, but also he hates the government”

“I still don’t know”

“Give him a chance I’ve known him for many years, and he is a lovely guy, he would always help someone out in need, he risked messing up the timeline to save Madeline, and he did it again to save a couple who were gonna be killed, and also he did it to save some Comanche Indians”

“Seriously?”

“Yes seriously”

“OK, I’ll give him a chance them. SAMUEL”

Samuel came into the office from the back.

“Yes sir” he said.

Frank opened a draw in his desk, and grabbed an envelope.

“Samuel, I have to go away for a while, not sure when I’ll be back, could be a really long time, now take this letter to Mr Dawson, you’ll be staying at his ranch, and working there while I’m gone. You know Mr Dawson, he is a nice guy, and he will look after you, and treat you well,” said Frank.

“OK Frank, I’ll miss you” said Samuel taking the letter.

Frank stood up, and walked over to Samuel. He embraced the boy.

“I’m gonna miss you too boy” he said teary eyed.

“Thank you so much Frank for all you done for me, I so glad you found me” said Samuel also teary eyed.

“I’m glad I found you too Sammy, get going now please boy,” said Frank.

Frank let go of Samuel, and he walked out the back to get his horse.

Frank sobbed.

"I'm gonna miss that little fellow" he said.

"He could have come with us," said Joe.

"No, this is his time, and I don't want to take him away from it. Dawson is a friend of mine, and we discussed what would happen if I had to leave, I know he will look after the boy well"

Max, Madeline, and Ethel May were sat together in the barn sharing a joint.

"You're right, this Jamaican tobacco is really sweet, and it's making me feel lightheaded," said Ethel May.

The front door opened, and Frank walked in, followed by Joe.

"Hiya Frank," said Max smiling.

Frank sniffed the air.

"Is that marijuana you're smoking" he said.

"Yeah man, want some" said Max holding the joint out.

Frank walked over to Max, and took the joint off of him.

"I never knew you knew about marijuana Frank," said Max.

"There is a lot you don't know about me Max," said Frank.

“Yeah, well there is a lot you don’t know about me Frank,” said Max.

“Like you come from 2016,” said Frank.

Max started chocking.

“Joe, for fucks sake. What don’t you understand about keeping a secret?” Said Max shocked.

“It’s not Joe’s fault, I worked out he was from the future because I am from 1974”

“Oh, I see. 1974, where you part of the US governments secret crononaut program?”

“Yes, I was, I got stuck here when the time portal shut down”

“I knew it, didn’t I tell you Joe, I said the US government had cracked time travel, using alien technology I bet”

“OK Max, no need to be so smug, I’m sorry I took the piss out of you for believing in aliens, and the fact that big corporations ran the government,” said Joe.

“I accept your apology, Joe. Now Frank, I’m guessing you want to come to 2016 with us, then you would like me to find a way to send you to 1974?” Said Max.

“Yeah, Joe said you could probably do that,” said Frank.

"Probably is an apt term. No certainty though, I don't even know if this experiment is gonna work, but I can try my best, and I suppose if anyone can do it then I can, but it would help me greatly if I could get my hands on alien technology though"

"Well, I can't help you with that I'm afraid, I was just a lowly worker, and it took the scientists over twenty years to work out how to use the alien time travel window"

"Window? Interesting. So, they opened up a time window in the lab, and you just had to step through?"

"Yes, that's right, you are exceptional clever Max"

"Please don't say that to him Frank, his head is big enough as it is," said Joe.

"Well, I think he is very clever, and wonderful," said Madeline.

"I don't know what to think, I'm so confused," said Ethel May.

"Well five hours to go, and we'll see if this works," said Max.

"Fingers crossed," said Joe.

"I cannot believe we've bumped into another time traveller. The chance of that happening must be a million to one," said Max

"I'm pretty damn surprised myself," said Frank.

"Oh, I get it now. That's why Lusanna told me to go to Abilene," said Max

"Who's Lusanna?" Asked Frank

"My spirit animal"

"Spirit animal?"

"It's a long story"

Just over five hours later there was a huge cracking sound like lighting.

Max rushed over to the front door, and opened it. He looked outside. He came back in, and shut the door.

"FUCK" he yelled making everyone jump.

"Didn't work then?" Said Joe.

"I'm not in the mood Joe" said Max moodily.

Madeline jumped up, and rushed over to Max. She threw her arms around him, and embraced him tightly.

"Oh Max, I'm sorry" she said.

"It's not your fault Madeline," said Max.

"I'm gonna take you to the bedroom, and cheer you up my darling husband," said Madeline.

"OK that would be nice," said Max.

Madeline took Max's hand, and led him to the bedroom.

"Sorry guys, look like I have to go back to the drawing board, Joe go get a train, and take your wife to Chicago" he said as he walked to the bedroom.

Max, and Madeline walked into the bedroom, and shut the door.

"Sorry about that Frank," said Joe.

"Don't worry, I suppose time travel is quite hard," said Frank.

"Is Max going to draw a picture?" Asked Ethel May.

"No get back to the drawing board is a future express for start again," said Joe.

"Oh, I see," said Ethel May.

"Come on Ethel May, I'm gonna take you to Chicago, and we better get a move on before those two get noisy," said Joe.

Two days later.

Joe, and Ethel were in Chicago. Max had kept himself busy fitting the toilet bowl, and cistern. He had fitted a shower using the pipe with the holy bottle cap on it. The shower was over where the temporary toilet had been. Max put a wire mess over the hole. Max had made a drainage tunnel on the other side of the bathroom, where he had fitted the toilet, using his laser rifle to make the tunnel. He had used his laser rifle to dig a well behind the barn. He had fitted the pump, and boxed it over with wood to hide it. He had laid the pipe work, and water treatment unit under the floor in Mr, and Mrs Brown's bedroom. Why not he though, they were not here to object to him pulling up their floorboards. He put them all back neatly afterwards. The water heater was in the corner of the bathroom near the door.

He had used a Stanley knife from his tool kit to cut strips of copper off the sheet he got. He had used the strips of copper to make wiring for lightbulbs. He made a small switch with wood. When the switch was turned a certain way, it lined up the wires, and when you turned it, it moved the wires, and broke the connection. He was unable to make LEDs as some of the materials he needed had not been discovered yet. He took light bulbs out the back of the van, and put one bulb in the bathroom, and each bedroom, and two bulbs in the main area.

He had been checking the data on his laptop to figure out what went wrong. Both power units had discharged a forty-gigawatt surge of electromagnetic energy at the same time. He came to the conclusion that the waves must have somehow cancelled each other out. Possible, maybe? He still didn't have a clue how time travel worked.

It was late afternoon, and Max, and Madeline were having some dried beef to eat, with a cup of coffee.

There was a knock on the door.

“I’ll get it” said Max putting his plate down on the desk.

He got up, and walked over to the door. He opened the door, and Frank burst in.

“Shut the door Max” he said in a panic.

Max quickly shut the door, and locked it.

“What’s up Frank?” He asked.

“There are six Texas Rangers in town, they have a wanted poster with your picture, and Joe’s picture on it,” said Frank.

“Oh no, that must be big John’s brother,” said Madeline.

“It gets worst though; they are offering a hundred bucks to anyone who tells them where you are,” said Frank.

“Shit, but no one knows we live here, do they?” Said Max.

“No, just me, and Dawson’s crew, Dawson is my friend, and I know he wouldn’t give you up, he aint a big fan of Texans anyway, Texas fever killed half his cattle”

“OK so we just stay hidden for now until they pass through”

"I don't know Max, these guys seem pretty determined, maybe you should get out of town"

"Slight problem with that Frank, Joe, and Ethel May are in Chicago, and I have no way of getting word to them, so we have to stay put"

"Do you know where they are staying in Chicago?"

"No idea, they went off two days ago, they might not even be in Chicago"

"We don't need to worry; six Texas Rangers are no match for your future weapons," said Madeline.

"I can't use my future weapons in this town. We need to keep a low profile, and assault rifles, or laser rifles are not very discreet. What if I challenged then to a gun fight?" Said Max.

"Max, this aint a Hollywood Movie, gun fights were actually very rare in the old west," said Frank.

"OK rare, but not unheard of?"

"Max, if you are wanted by the Texas Rangers, and you kill the Texas Rangers you will still be wanted, but if you kill a law man, they will put a huge bounty on your heads, and every bounty hunter in the US will be after you"

"I've got it, I'll shave my beard off, cut my hair, and speak like an American"

“That might actually work”

“Of course, it will work I am a fucking genius”

“There is a slight problem Max, I have met big Franks brother on several occasions,” said Madeline.

“Fuck, fuck, fucky fuck fuck” said Max annoyed.

“I can go, and see if I can find out any more information,” said Frank.

“Ooh I know, speak to Wild Bill, he likes me, he can run them out of town”

“Wild Bill is an alcoholic, he couldn’t run one Texas Ranger out of town, let alone six”

“That makes sense, I’ve never seen him without a drink in his hand, shit, and I spent all day fitting the bathroom, and electric lighting”

“I’ll go, and see what I can find out,” said Frank.

Frank walked into the Alamo saloon, and walked over to the table where the six Texas Rangers were sat.

“Hi fellow, my name is Frank Mitchell”

“Howdy Frank, I’m Ranger Tommy Bridgewater, and these are my deputies,” said a tall handsome man.

He had long blond hair, and a large moustache. He had piecing blue eyes. He looked around thirty.

All the Texas rangers were dressed in black chaps, black leather boots, white shirts, and brown trench coats. They all wore large black Stetson's, and star shaped silver badges.

"Now I hear you are looking for two limeys', one of them is Negro," said Frank.

"That's right sir, one of them killed my brother, you know where they're at?" Said Tommy.

"I seen them two days ago boarding a train, they had a woman with them, pretty girl she was," said Frank.

"Well, we had a fellow tell us he saw the white guy, and the lady yesterday"

"Probably just after your money, wanted to buy himself some whiskey I'll bet"

"Actually friend, this guy refused to take our money, he said his brother had been killed, and he sympathised with me"

"I see, well they must have come back then"

"No, he said the Negro had just got married, and taken his wife somewhere on the train, so he is probably out of town, but this white fellow, I think he is somewhere in this town"

"How did you managed to track them down?"

“We’re Texas Rangers, tracking people down is what we do”

“Say fellow, can I buy you a drink?”

“Of course, friend, we’re Texans so we’re good at drinking”

Frank smiled at them, and walked off to the bar.

“Howdy Frank,” said the barman.

“Howdy Richie, have you got anything super strong to drink?” Asked Frank.

“I got this moonshine from Paddy, he said it’s an old Irish recipe, I reckon you could strip paint with it” Richie said holding up a bottle.

“Perfect, I’ll take the bottle then please friend, and can you tell me where the Texas Rangers are staying”

“Sure, my friend, I’ll give you the moonshine for free, and the Rangers have booked three rooms, 2, 5, and 6”

“Thank you, Richie,”

“My pleasure Frank, give them bastards hell, I can’t stand fucking Texans”

Frank took the bottle of moonshine over to the Texas Rangers.

"Now boys, this is Irish whiskey, and I have been told that the Irish are the best drinkers in the world, and only they can handle this stuff," said Frank.

"Give me that" said Tommy grabbing the bottle.

"Be careful it's strong," said Frank.

"Yeah boss, I heard them Irish are good drinkers" said one of the Texas Rangers.

"Damn you Jake, Texans are the best drinkers in the world" said Tommy pouring the moonshine.

"Now drink damn it"

The Texas Rangers all picked up there glassed, and downed the moonshine.

"Good lord that is strong" said one of the Texas Rangers.

"Damn you Wyatt, we are Texans we can outdrink anyone," said Tommy.

He filled the glasses again.

Max, and Madeline were sat in the barn fretting. Max was holding his M16 assault rifle, locked, and loaded.

There was a knock at the door.

Max jumped up, and walked over to the door. He held his rifle in one hand.

“Who goes there?” He said in an American accent.

“It’s Frank”

Max opened the door. Frank came in, and Max shut the door, and locked it.

“OK, so I’ve found out where there the Texas Rangers are staying, and they will be so drunk tonight, they’ll probably be unconscious,” said Frank.

“What did you do, spike their drinks?” Asked Max.

“No, I goaded them into drinking Irish moonshine” said Frank smiling.

Max laughed.

“Nice one Frank, that might be enough to kill them” he said.

“Well, I was kinda hoping you might have some future poison, or something?” Said Frank.

“No but I have a spare plastic bottle”

“And how does that help us?”

“Simple, we catch a couple of rattlesnakes, and we get them to bite the bottle, and the bottle will catch their venom. Then I fill a couple of syringes up with venom, and inject the Texas Rangers twice on their bodies, so it looks like they have been bitten by a rattlesnake"

"You are a fucking genius Max, but I'm not comfortable handling poisonous snakes"

"Actually, rattlesnakes are venomous, and the key to handling a venomous snake is to hold its head, so it can't bite you"

Frank, and Max had gone away from town into the wilderness. Max was busy picking up rocks, and looking under bushes, while Frank held the plastic bottle.
Madeline was waiting back in the barn holding Max's M16, she had been told if anyone tried to break in, to point the rifle, and pull the trigger.

Max found a rattlesnake under a bush. He pulled some of the bush away. The rattlesnake started shaking its tail, making a rattling noise.

"Yeah, like that scares me, I'm a fucking scientist" said Max looking at the rattlesnake.

He shot his hand out quickly, and grabbed the snakes head. The snake started thrashing its body around. Max lifted the snake up by its head, and grabbed the thrashing body with his other hand.

"Stop struggling snakey or I will eat you for dinner tonight" he said.

He walked over to Frank. Frank put the bottle down, and stepped back.

“I can’t believe you’re holding that thing, look at the size of it,” said Frank.

“This is a western diamond back, but it’s only a snake Frank, big animals are more scary to me” said Max calmly.

Max put the snakes head against the bottle. The snake’s fangs shot out, and punctured the bottle. Max watched as the thick yellow venom oozed into the bottle.

Once the snake had finished, Max put it on the ground. It looked at Max, hissed at him, and slivered away sideways.

Max pulled a syringe out of his pocket, and filled it with the rattlesnake venom.

“Is that enough now?” Asked Frank.

“No one more should do”

“Why didn’t you wait until you had all the venom before you filled the syringe?”

“Because I believe if the venom is left exposed to oxygen it will degrade”

“I see, so you need another snake then?”

“Yes Frank, would you like to catch it?”

"No way"

Max laughed.

The next day Frank, Max, and Madeline turned up at the Alamo saloon, and walked inside.

Joe McCoy, Wild Bill, and old Doc Valley were chatting at the bar.

The doctor left them, and walked out the bar.

"What's going on?" Asked Frank.

"Howdy Frank, five Texas Rangers died last night. The doc checked them; it looks like they were all bitten by a snake" said Wild Bill.

"Oh, now that's strange, I thought I saw six Texas Rangers in here yesterday," said Frank.

"Well, we only found five of them, so maybe one of them went home," said Wild Bill.

"OK cheers Bill," said Frank.

He turned to Max, and whispered to him.

"We did three each, didn't we?"

“I did two in room 2, and you did two in room 6, then we did one each in room 5” whispered Max.

“Is it possible to be immune to rattlesnake poison?”

“Yes, it is possible, usually if you’ve been bitten, and injected with a small dose of poison like from a baby rattler, then you could build up a resistance to the venom”

“Shit what are you gonna do Max?”

“I’m gonna wait for Joe, and Ethel May to get back, then I’m gonna get out of town”

Joe, and Ethel May were on the train home from Chicago, sat in the rear carriage. They had, had a lovely time. Ethel May was wearing a silver necklace with an emerald pendant on it. She adored it. They sat looking out the window at the dusty landscape going past. They were back in the west now, it looked completely different from the east.

The train began to slow down, and came to a stop. Joe looked around wondering what was going on. The carriage they were in was half full, other passengers looked confused, this was an unscheduled stop.

A few minutes later two tall guys burst into the carriage with their revolvers drawn. They wore grey trench coats, black Stetson’s, and had bandanna's up over their faces, so just their eyes were visible.

“Now listen to us good people, and do as you’re told, and I guarantee nobody will be harmed, if you don’t do as we say, I can’t guarantee your safety” said one of the outlaws.

The other outlaw opened up a black leather bag.

“Now as we approach you, you must drop your cash, and any jewellery in this here bag, OK” he said.

They began making their way down the carriage collecting cash, and jewellery.

“Joe, I don’t wanna lose my lovely necklace that you got me” whispered Ethel May.

“Don’t worry darling, I will handle this” Joe whispered back.

Joe pulled out his Browning slowly, and quietly. He eased the hammer back. He watched the two outlaws as they made their way down the carriage.

As they got close Joe jumped up with his gun raised.

“Sit down bo”

BANG

BANG

The outlaw never had a chance to finish his sentence. Joe shot them both in the head.

The other passengers in the carriage stood up, and started applauding.

“Well done boy”

“Good for you young man”

“You showed them bastards”

The other passengers were very grateful to Joe.

Joe opened the window, and leaned his head out. He threw up. That was the first time he had ever killed someone.

Chapter 12
On the Run Again

Madeline watched in amazement as Max, and Frank were busy converting the Transit van into a camper van.

They built a frame out of wood, and put two bunks beds on the left front side of the back of the van. On the right front side they built a wooden shoe rack. They used tree sap to glue the shoe rack, and the bunk beds to the sides of the van. Max cut a hole in the wooden partition at the front of the back of the van that separated the back of the van from the front seats. He used tree sap to glue a piece of canvas over the hole, as a curtain. He hammered a nail into the top of the wooden partition, and bent it upwards with the hammer. He pocked a hole in the bottom of the canvas, then lifted it up, and hooked it on the nail. This way the curtain could be opened, and closed. The hole in the partition allowed light from the front of van into the back.

At the rear of the van, they built two small wooden cubicles. Max fitted the toilet in one, and a shower in the other one. The shower was just a pipe hanging down from the ceiling. He put a cork in the pipe to stop to water coming out, and when the cork was removed the water flowed out the pipe. He used canvas to make curtains cover the openings of the cubicles for privacy. He cut two holes in the chassis of the van to use as drainage from the shower, and the toilet.

The space in between the cubicles at the back of the van, and the bunk beds at the front had two wooden boxes which were glued to the floor with tree sap. The built a shelf to put the power supply, water heater, and kettle on. The shelf had wooden panels on either side of it, and on each side of the wooden panels Max fitted two small pieces of wood to act as a sliding mechanism like a draw. He slid a wooden panel on top of the shelf into the pieces of wood. This was to cover the power supply, water heater, and kettle so they didn't fall off the shelf when the van was moving.

Max wired up light bulbs into the toilet, and shower. He had to stick pieces of timber along the path of the wires, so the bare wires weren't touching the vans metal shell.

They fitted two wooden chairs in the back one on each side glued to the boxes. The chairs were covered with cushions which Frank made out of cloth, and cotton wool.

Billy the blacksmith had made them a large iron box with an opening lid, they glued wood to the roof of the van, and strapped the box down with seatbelts which they cut out the front of the van. The box was to be used a water tank, which had to be manually filled. Max cut two holes in the iron box, and with great difficulty he cut two holes in the roof of the armoured van, it took over two hours to hammer, and chisel through the armoured shell, and he went through five chisels as they kept getting warn out. He connected two pipes from the iron box, one to the toilet cistern, and the other to the water heater. The water heater then connected to the shower pipe. Max set the water heater to forty degrees centigrade, an ideal temperature for bacterial growth, however the water heater didn't store water, it heated water as it passed through.

Finally, they used the pump to fill water bottles, which they used to fill the iron water tank. It took twenty, five litre bottles to fill, meaning the water tank had a one thousand litre capacity.

The van was now a camper. It had no kitchen, there simply wasn't enough space. On the road they would need to cook by campfire.

They filled the two boxes up in the back of van. One of them had two suitcases, a big back of weed, the bag of guns, and the medical bag. The other one had Max's bag of scientific equipment, a bag of towels, and a bag of tin plates, tin cups, cutlery, and the map, and compass.

They took the bedding off the Walsh's bed, and the Brown's bed, and put them on the bunk beds.

They were now ready to escape.

Joe, and Ethel May stepped off the train at Abilene station. Joe was wearing a new black suit, a black bowler hat, and carrying a leather suitcase. Ethel May was wearing a new blue silk gown, and a blue bonnet. She was carrying a small leather bag.

They left the station, and strolled through town hand in hand.

"Hold it right there Negro" said Tommy the Texas Ranger jumping out in front of them, brandishing two colt revolvers.

"What have we done?" Asked Joe.

“You are wanted dead or alive Negro, just give me an excuse to take you in dead,” said Tommy.

“I think you are mistaken” said Joe calmly.

“No way I seen the poster, I aint got it now. Your buddy Max let a rattlesnake into our room, and killed all my deputies, and then stole the wanted poster, but I know you are the Negro who helped him escape after he killed my brother”

“I don’t know anyone called Max”

“I tell you what Negro, you tell me where Max is, and I’ll let you live?”

“I’m over here” called Max from behind Tommy.

Tommy spun round, and saw Max holding a strange type of rifle.

“You killed my brother” he said angrily.

“And now you can join him,” said Max.

Max raised his M16, and shot Tommy in the head.

Tommy fell to the ground with blood pouring from his head.

Women in the town started screaming.

“Can’t believe you said you didn’t know me” said Max smiling at Joe.

“What the hell’s going on?” Said Joe.

“Time to get out of here, come on,” said Max.

They walked round the corner where Madeline was waiting, holding her Browning pistol with two hands.

“Thank you for watching my back darling,” said Max.

“My pleasure,” said Madeline.

“Joe, draw your gun, and take point, I’ll watch the rear, and ladies in the middle please,” said Max.

The posse moved quickly through town to their barn.

Max unlocked the door, and they all rushed inside.

“Joe, give Madeline your case, and she’ll put it in the back,” said Max.

Joe handed his case to Madeline.

“Come with me Ethel May, and I’ll show you were the ladies sit,” said Madeline.

Frank rushed over holding the AK47.

“Howdy Joe, is it time to go Max?” He spoke.

“Yes, jump in,” said Max.

Joe, and Frank climbed into the front of the van. Joe looked through the hole in the partition in the back of the van where Madeline, and Ethel May were sat.

“What’s happened to the van?” He asked.

“Me, and Max spent all day turning it into a camper van, you, and Ethel May have your own bed, so do Max, and Madeline, and I sleep in the front,” said Frank.

Max lit the oil lamp, and threw it into the Brown’s old bedroom. The lamp smashed on the floor, and set fire to the wood.

Max went to the front of the barn. The large barn doors had been sealed shut, they just used the small front door. Joe had nailed a big block of wood onto the doors to seal them shut.

Max raised his M16, and fired a shot at the wooden block. The block cracked in the middle, and just about held in place.

“That’ll do,” said Max.

Max climbed into the driver’s seat, and handed his M16 to Joe.

“I don’t know how to use this,” said Joe.

“Just put it on the floor, I can’t carry it, and drive at the same time” said Max as he shut his door.

Max fired up the engine. He put the van in first gear, and slowly crawled forward. The van bumped the barn doors. The cracked block of wood fell apart, and the barn doors crept open.

Max drove out slowly.

Billy the blacksmith looked in amazement from the doorway of his workshop. A few people in the town stared in shock at the strange white moving box.

Once the van was out the barn, and onto the dusty road, Max floored the accelerator, and the front wheels span, and kicked up dust.

The towns people fled in fear, and Billy moved into his workshop, and shut the door.

Soon the van was bumping along the dusty road, and moving out of town.

There were a few houses dotted about on the outskirts of town.

They were soon out of town, and bumping along a dusty trail westwards.

"What the hell is going on?" Said Joe.

"Six Texas Rangers came to town looking for us, we tried to kill them all with snake venom, but it would seem the leader was immune, he wasn't immune to a bullet through the head though," said Max smirking.

"Snake venom," said Joe.

“You should have seen it Joe, Max just walks up, and grabs rattlesnakes by their heads, I’ve never seen anything like it” said Frank.

“We extracted rattlesnake venom, then we injected it into the Texas Rangers while they were asleep,” said Max.

“You never cease to amaze me Max,” said Joe.

“Yeah, I know Joe, I’m pretty amazing aren’t I,” said Max.

Madeline, and Ethel May were in the back of the van talking.

“So how was your trip to Chicago Ethel May?”

“Oh, it was great, just like you said, the flushing toilets are amazing, and it was so busy, and so many big buildings. We stayed in the Palmer House Hilton, which was lovely, and we ate at a few nice restaurants, and see this necklace?”

Ethel May pointed to her chest. She was wearing a silver chain, with a silver crucifix on it.

“Oh, that’s lovely,” said Madeline.

“Joe got it for me from a jewellers”

“Wow so you had a great time then?”

“Yes, it was lovely, I’m so happy to be married to Joe”

“Ah that’s great, I know how you feel, I’m so happy being married to Max”

“And on the way back these two bandits tried to rob our train, and Joe shot them both so they couldn’t take my necklace”

“Oh, wow that’s amazing”

In the front of the van.

“Is that right Joe, you killed two bandits?” Asked Max.

“Yes, I had to, they would have taken the necklace I brought Ethel May” replied Joe.

“Well good for you Joe, I’m very proud of you,” said Max smiling.

“Yeah, well done Joe,” said Frank.

“Thanks guys,” said Joe.

“So Frank, do you know any government secrets?” Asked Max.

Frank reached into a bag he’d brought with him, and pulled out the photo. He held it up.

“This photo was taken in 1960, it’s my family. My Dad was a section commander for a CIA black ops unit, that how I got into the crononaut program,” said Frank.

“Wow, so what secrets did you find out?” Said Max.

“Loads, what would you like to know?”

“Who shot JFK?”

“Well, it wasn’t Lee Harvey Oswald, he was set up to be the patsy. Lyndon B Johnson hired three top assassins from a CIA team known as Operation 40. They were the tramps in Dealey Plaza who were photographed being led away by police, only they weren’t dressed very tramp like, they had shiny shoes on for one thing. I’m not sure which one of them fire the fatal shot, but the three men were E Howard Hunt, David Morerales, and Jim Sturgess”

“Wow that is brilliant, I’m so glad I know the truth. Now have you met any aliens?”

“I’ve met a few grey aliens”

“And is the government in league with them”

“I think so, the grey aliens gave us the time travel window”

“I knew it, I told Joe, didn’t I” said Max defiantly.

“Yes, I’m sorry Max, sorry I doubted you, you were right all along” said Joe sheepishly.

In the back of the van.

“So, if your master had sex with you all the time, did you ever get pregnant?” Asked Madeline.

“Yes, I had five babies”

“Five babies, what happened to them?”

“They were taken off me, and sold”

“Oh, that’s terrible”

“I know, but back then black people were just property, I got sold when I was a baby, I never knew my Mumma, and Poppa”

“Oh, I’m so sorry that happened to you, I’m a Texas girl, but I never agreed with the slave trade”

“Thank you, Madeline. If you were a whore for seven years, did you ever have a baby?”

“I got pregnant three times, but I went to the doctor, and he got rid of them”

In the front of the van.

“Where are we actually going now?” Asked Joe.

“No idea, I just wanted to get out of town,” said Max.

“Well, we have a serious problem now boys. Now a lawman has been killed, there will be a large bounty on Max’s head. Every bounty hunter in the US will be looking for you, but worse than that, when word gets to the East, they will send Pinkerton agents to look for you,” said Frank.

"Pinkerton agents, not exactly a scary name, what are they fairies in pink two-twos?" Said Max smirking.

"The Pinkerton detective agency was started by Allan Pinkerton in 1850, they are the most determined detectives in the US at the moment, they were a forerunner of modern detectives, and if the Pinkerton's are after you, they will not quit," said Frank.

"So, I guess we head for Mexico then?" Said Max.

"Max, the Mexican border isn't the same as in your time, US lawmen, and bounty hunters regularly cross the border to track down suspects"

"Canada then?"

"Same problem my friend, borders don't matter to law enforcement in this time"

"So, the only logic thing we can do, is hide, and not stay in the same place for more than a day"

"That may buy us some time"

They set up camp that night in a valley where they had encountered some Buffalo's. Frank had managed to shoot one. The rest of the herd had charged away.

Tonight, they feasted on Buffalo steaks. They sat by a roaring campfire eating, and drinking water.

"Buffalo meats well tasty," said Joe.

"Enjoy it while you can Joe, the Buffalo will soon be hunted to near extinction in a campaign by the government to eradicate the plains Indians," said Frank.

"That's not fair," said Max.

"I know Max, these aren't fair times I'm afraid, especially for the Indians," said Frank.

"You are aware that they are actually called Native Americans, they don't exactly come from Indian do they," said Max.

"I know Max, but that's what us white Americans call them, I'm afraid," said Frank.

"So did you bring anything modern with you when you came back in time Frank?" Asked Joe changing the subject.

"Yeah, that photo I showed you, a pair of Ray Ban sunglasses, a transistor radio, and my guns are supposed to be of the time, but they are Colt Peacemaker 1973 models. I also brought a Colt Commander 9mm," said Frank.

"Why bring a transistor radio, they aren't any radio communications in this time?" Asked Max.

"We got sent messages on the radio sometimes, after the window shut down, I left the radio on every day for four months until the battery ran out, hoping to get a message," said Frank.

“We’ve got a working radio in the van” said Joe.

“Yes, we have, what did you broadcast on FM or AM?” Said Max.

“We used the frequency one thousand AM,” said Frank.

Max got up, and walked over to the van. He opened the passenger door, and climbed in. He switched the radio on. Bryan Adams started playing as that was the last CD they were listening to. He switched the system over to radio. He tuned it in to one thousand AM. Static came through the speakers. Max left the radio, and jumped out the van. He shut the passenger door, and walked back to the camp fire.

“Right, I’ve tuned the radio, and we’ll leave it on all night just in case” he said.

“But that will flatten the battery,” said Joe.

“Yes, but the crystal batteries in the hybrid system can start the engine if the battery gets flattened, and then where the engine is running the alternator will charge the battery,” said Max.

“Oh, I see,” said Joe.

“You know, sometimes when you guys speak it is like you are talking a foreign language,” said Madeline.

“A radio is a device for broadcasting sound, like you have telegraph lines to send messages, a radio sends sounds, like talking, and music, and crystal batteries provide the power for our electric devices. An electric device is anything that requires an electrical current to power it. Electricity is a force of power that is developed by spinning a copper coil inside a magnetic outer core. A magnet is a piece of metal that attracts other pieces of metal. An alternator is a power generator that supplies electrical current. Have I missed anything," said Max.

"I think you need to talk me through it slowly please Max," said Madeline.

"Yeah, I'm even more confused now, if a radio is like a telegram system, then where are the telegraph lines?" Asked Ethel May.

"A radio is a wireless communication device invented by my beloved hero Nikola Tesla in about 1898. It was first used by Guglielmo Marconi in 1903, he stole the design off Tesla when he worked for him, and is widely credit as the inventor of the radio, bloody charlatan," said Max.

"How can you send a message without any wires?" Said Ethel May.

"Now you're getting technical, I will try, and explain this as simply as I can. You use an electrical device which is called a broadcast unit. The broadcast unit converts sound into invisible waves of energy which are call radio waves, which are sent through the air, the radio waves are picked up by a radio receiver, and converted back into sound," said Max.

"That has got to be magic," said Ethel May.

"It's just science. When the first trains were invented, I bet a lot of people thought they were magic," said Max.

"I don't think I will ever be as smart as you Max," said Madeline.

"Well, I brought a book out with me to read us all a bedtime story, this was one of my favourite books when I was a child, it is what inspired me to become a scientist. It is called the Curious Case of Dr Jekyll, and Mr Hyde, by Robert Louis Stevenson," said Max.

"That's what inspired you to become a scientist, that explains so much," said Joe.

"Yes, it was actually based on the true story of Deacon Brodie the engineer who invented the drop gallows. He was a respectable engineer by day, and a thief by night. He was actually hanged using his own invention, now that's proper irony. Anyway, I shall begin," said Max.

It was early in the morning the next day.

"MAX, WAKE UP" yelled Frank from the front of the van.

Max opened his eyes, and yawned. He was lying in bed naked with Madeline on the top bunk.

"MAX" yelled Frank.

"What" said Max sleepily.

“There was a message on the radio last night,” said Frank.

“What” said Max still half asleep.

“There was a message on the radio last night” repeated Frank.

Max quickly climbed out of bed, and grabbed his boxer shorts from the floor. He put them on, and moved over to the hole in the partition.

“What message?” He asked.

“Right, it said to go to a house five miles Northwest of Fort Worth, Texas, on the banks of the Trinity River,” said Frank.

“Oh great, it would be in Texas,” said Max.

“What’s going on” said Joe sleepily.

“Looks like we’re going back to Texas,” said Max.

“Did you say Texas?” Said Madeline sleepily.

“Yes, I did,” said Max.

“Wont that be dangerous?” Asked Joe.

“Life is dangerous Joe,” said Max.

“It sure will be dangerous, the Texas Rangers are after us, and the Governor of Texas is also after us,” said Madeline.

“Well, I guess we better try, and avoid them then,” said Max.

“We’re going to have to travel south. I suggest we take the Chisholm trail,” said Frank.

“What’s the Chisholm trail?” Asked Max.

“It’s a trail set up for cattle drives. It runs from Abilene to central Texas,” said Frank.

“So, we need to go back to Abilene?” Said Max.

“Well south of Abilene,” said Frank.

“This plan just gets better, and better,” said Max.

“I guess Texas is the last place they’d think of looking for us,” said Joe

Once everyone was up, they started a campfire, and cooked some Buffalo meat for breakfast, with water to drink.

They sat by the campfire eating.

“We’ll have to travel at night obviously if we’re gonna use a public trail,” said Max.

“Yes, although we are still likely to come across some cowboy camps at night,” said Frank.

“Well hopefully if they see a Transit van pass by, they will assume they were dreaming,” said Max.

“Is OK if I have a shower, I smell a bit,” said Madeline.

“Sorry Madeline, I don’t know when we’ll next be able to fill the water tank, so we are all going to have to smell for a bit, and only flush the toilet when you shit, not when you piss, we need to conserve water for drinking,” said Max.

“OK, as long as you don’t mind sleeping next to me when I stink,” said Madeline.

“Madeline I wouldn’t never mind sleeping next to you, you are my beautiful wife, and I love you,” said Max.

“Aw thank you Max. I love you too, even when you stink,” said Madeline.

“Do you still love me if I stink Joe?” Asked Ethel May.

“No, I don’t like stinky people,” said Joe.

“What” shrieked Ethel May shocked.

“Sorry darling, I was joking, I will always love you,” said Joe.

“Good, I should hope so too” said Ethel May firmly.

“We’re not far from the Arkansas river if everyone wants to wash, and you could fill the water tank up Max,” said Frank.

“Washing in the river is fine, although we have run out of shower gel, and shampoo, but I can’t fill the water tank with river water too much bacteria in it,” said Max.

“OK fair enough,” said Frank.

“We do have loads of soap, I got a load from Chicago,” said Joe.

“Oh yeah, Chicago, did you get me a present?” Asked Max.

“Yeah, the soap,” said Joe.

“Very funny Joe”

“I wasn’t joking Max”

“OK, well given the circumstances I suppose soap is quite handy”

Joe started laughing. He got up, and wandered over to the van. He opened the side door, and climbed inside.

Joe came back a couple of minutes later carrying some bits.

“Here Max” he said passing him a revolver.

“Wow thanks Joe, an antique gun,” said Max smiling.

“It’s a smith, and Wesson model no. 3,” said Joe.

“Cool” said Max admiring the gun.

“Here Madeline” he said passing her a gold bracelet.

“Wow thanks Joe” she said.

“Ethel May picked that for you,” said Joe.

“Aw thank you Ethel May, it’s lovely” she said putting the bracelet on.

“Here Frank” said Joe passing him a gold pocket watch with a gold chain.

“Wow thanks Joe, that’s very kind” Frank said smiling.

“You can be like Max, and me now” said Joe holding up his own pocket watch.

Max held up his pocket watch.

“Nice one thanks Joe,” said Frank.

“We can be the pocket watch gang,” said Max.

Everyone laughed.

It was slow progress to Texas, travelling only at night-time. Crossing a few rivers. Luckily the Chisholm trail took them to the fords, and low points of the river, so they could drive across.

They gave two groups of cowboys the fright of their lives when they drove passed. One group shot at the van. The bullets bounced off the armoured shell of the van which scared the cowboys even more.

It took three nights to reach Texas. On the fourth night they found the house by the Trinity River.

The house was a small wooden shack with nothing extraordinary about it from the outside.

Chapter 13
Confrontation

Max parked the van at the side of the shack. There was nothing around to use to hide the van.

They all got out of the van, and had good stretch. They walked over to the front door of the shack. Frank knocked on the door.

They waited for a minute, there was no answer. Frank knocked again. Still no answer. The door had no lock or handle on it.

"How do you open this door?" Asked Max.

"I'm guessing you need a security card to open it," said Frank.

"I'll grab an axe," said Joe.

Joe walked off to the van. He came back a minute later with an axe.

Joe raised the axe, and slammed it hard against the door. The axe bounced back, and sent vibration through Joe, making him drop the axe.

"Ow, fuck. That aint wood, it's fucking solid," said Joe.

Max banged on the door.

"Hmm, I think it's got some sort of metal reinforcement" he said.

“So how are we gonna get in?” Asked Joe.

“My laser, photon cannon,” said Max.

“Laser, photo cannon,” said Frank.

“Yes, it has three settings, setting one is a powerful laser beam which cuts through most materials, setting two is a burst of photon energy which will kill someone, and setting three is a large burst of photon energy which will destroy a large house,” said Max.

“I take it you built that,” said Frank.

“Yes, I did, back in a minute,” said Max.

Max rushed off to the van. He came back a minute later carrying his laser rifle.

“That’s looks like a kids toy” said Frank.

“Observe” said Max.

Max held the laser rifle close to the door, and fired a short burst on setting one. The laser beam punched a small hole in the side of the door halfway down it. Max kicked the door, and it swung open.

Max walked inside with his laser rifle raised, ready to use.

It was dark inside the shack. Max found a light switch on the wall by the door. He pressed it, and a florescent strip light in the middle of the ceiling slowly clicked into life.

Inside the shack they could see the walls were lined with steel to reinforce the wooden structure. There was a desk with some radio equipment, there was a chest freezer, and some cupboards. There was a large cabinet on the back wall. There was a kitchen sink near the cabinet with one tap. There was a large microwave, kettle, and a toaster on a worktop next to the sink.

There was a large wooden table with six chairs around it in the middle of the shack. There was also an electric heater.

There were two rooms at the right side of the shack. Joe had a look inside them.

“There is a toilet, and shower in these rooms” he said.

“I wonder where the power is coming from,” said Max.

Frank looked in the freezer.

“There’s some microwave meals in here” he said.

“What’s that?” Asked Madeline pointing to the microwave.

“It’s called a microwave, it is used to heat food up, using concentrated waves of electricity,” said Max.

“So is the stuff in this room from the future?” Asked Ethel May.

“To you it is, to Joe, and me it all looks like old stuff from the 70s,” said Max.

Max examined the radio equipment.

“Right, the broadcast unit is here, it must be set up to send a broadcast automatically,” said Max.

“Shouldn’t there be someone based here?” Asked Joe.

“I would assume so, but I have no idea to be honest,” said Frank.

“Well, I suggest we have dinner then,” said Max.

Frank turned the electric heater on.

“I suggest we have a shower here as well, they have some shampoo, and condition in the shower room,” said Joe.

Max turned the tap on the sink, and cold water flowed out of it. It was orange at first, before turning clear.

“The water hasn’t been run for a while, they must have a bore hole, and an electric pump,” said Max.

Frank checked inside the large cabinet.

“Wow” he said looking inside.

“What have you found?” Asked Max.

“There are three AK47’s, five 9mm pistols, and a load of ammo,” said Frank.

“Excellent” said Max.

Joe looked through the cupboards.

“Fantastic” he said.

“What have you found?” Asked Frank.

“There’s loads of tinned food in here, and there are some jars of coffee, and bags of sugar, ooh, and there’s a big bag of salt,” said Joe.

“Any plates, and cutlery?” Said Max.

“Yep, six plates, six bowls, six mugs, and six sets of cutlery,” said Joe.

“Let’s get cooking then,” said Max.

“All the microwave meals are TV dinners, there’s either roast beef, or roast chicken,” said Frank.

“How can we eat a TV dinner if there is no TV?” Said Max.

“Quite easily I reckon, I’m blood hungry,” said Joe.

Madeline, and Ethel May were stunned by how quick the microwave cooked the food.

They all sat round the table eating their TV dinners, and drinking black coffee with sugar.

“Wow, we’re like one big happy family sitting down together having dinner,” said Max.

“Yeah, this is nice,” said Joe.

“I’m a bit bothered as to why this place was abandoned,” said Frank.

“This food is delicious,” said Madeline.

“Is this what food is like in the future?” Asked Ethel May.

“Some of it, we have a massive variety in the future,” said Joe.

“Yeah, we’ve got McDonald’s in the future,” said Max.

“Oh, I do miss McDonald’s,” said Frank.

After dinner Frank washed the plates. Joe went, and got towels from the van, and Max started fiddling with the radio equipment.

He tried transmitting on different frequencies.

“Hello, can anyone here me, this is station fifteen” Max said into the microphone.

“How do you know it is station fifteen?” Asked Frank.

“There is a label on the microphone that says station fifteen,” said Max.

“Ah I see,” said Frank.

Joe came back with towels for everyone.

Madeline went into the shower.

Max suddenly jumped up from the desk where the radio equipment was, and sprinted to the shower.

He burst in.

“Max, you scared me, I was just about to take my clothes off,” said Madeline.

“I just need to do something with the shower first, so you don’t catch anything,” said Max.

Max opened the shower curtain. The shower was an old electric type. He switched on the shower, quickly jumped back, and shut the curtain.

“Once you are undressed, the shower will be OK to use” he said.

“OK, thank you Max,” said Madeline.

Max left the shower room, and went back to the radio desk.

“What was that about?” Asked Joe.

“I didn’t want Madeline to catch Legionaries disease,” said Max.

“What the hell is Legionaries disease?” Asked Frank.

“Legionella is a bacterium that grows in water, it can be found in high numbers in water systems that haven’t been used for over a week. If the bacteria is inhaled it can cause a type of Severe pneumonia” said Max.

“Well, I’ve never heard of that,” said Frank.

“It was first discovered in 1976,” said Max.

“Ah I see, so in my time it wasn’t know about,” said Frank.

“Well, the Romans knew about it a couple of thousand years ago, they used to line their aqueducts with silver, and silver kills bacteria,” said Max.

“How an earth did they know that back then?” Asked Frank confused.

“My guess would be they acquired the knowledge from the Atlanteans”

“Yeah, that’s make sense”

“Are you telling me Atlantis was real?” Said Joe.

“Yes, it was” said Max, and Frank together.

“Have you looked in the draw on the desk Max?” Said Frank.

Max opened up the draw, inside was a piece of paper. Max pulled it out.

“Emergency frequency” he said reading the paper.

“What’s the frequency Max?” Said Frank.

“You’re supposed to say what the frequency Kenneth” said Max.

Max, and Joe both laughed.

“What does that mean?” Said Frank confused.

“It’s a song by REM,” said Joe.

“Came out in the 80’s or 90s after your time Frank, the frequency is 1307 medium wave,” said Max.

Max tuned the radio.

“Hello, can anyone hear me, this is station fifteen” Max said into the microphone.

“Station fifteen please state name, and authorization code, over” came the crackly reply.

Frank grabbed the microphone.

“This is Frank Mitchell, code is monkey fox seven four, over” he said.

“Who is that with you Frank, over?” Came the reply.

“I am with some other time travellers from 2016, over”

“Are they from a new project in 2016”, over?”

“No, they accidentally went back in time, over”

“OK, I’ve heard weirder stories than that. I’m Colonel Steven Baines US Airforce, I’m at station one, over”

“Where is station one, over?”

“It’s two miles south of Fort Laramie, Wyoming, it’s a large compound made of adobe walls, over”

“OK, it will take us about five days to reach you sir, over”

“No problem, see you when you get here, over, and out”

Frank put the microphone down.

“What are abode walls?” Asked Max.

“It’s clay mixed with straw, it’s what they used to build strong walls in the old west” said Frank.

“Oh, right good, even I can learn something new,” said Max.

That evening they all had a shower. They brought there bedding into the shack, and slept in there for the night.

The next morning, they all sat round the table, drinking coffee. Max, Joe, and Frank had filled the water tank on top of the van up by filling up plastic bottles from the kitchen sink in the shack. They had put all the tins of food, a can opener, the bedding, and the towels back in the van.

"COME OUT WITH YOUR HANDS RAISED, YOU ARE SURROUNDED" yelled a loud booming voice.

Frank got up, and peeked out the door. There was a large group of Texas Rangers stood outside. Their leader was a huge man with a fluffy white beard. He was wearing a black suit, and a large black Stetson. He had a Sharps rifle in his hand.

Frank shut the door. Max was on his feet brandishing his laser rifle.

"We got a problem," said Frank.

"I can get rid of any sized force in a minute or two with this" Max said holding up his laser rifle.

"There leader is the famous captain William Wallace, nicknamed Bigfoot Wallace, we can't kill him, as that would have serious consequences on the timeline," said Frank.

"OK then, we can use the AK47's in the cabinet to scare them away then," said Max.

"OK, but don't hit Bigfoot if you can help it," said Frank.

"Which one is Bigfoot?" Asked Max.

"He is the giant," said Frank.

Max, and Frank grabbed an AK47 each from the cabinet.

"Come on Joe," said Max.

"I've never fired an assault rifle before," said Joe.

"Can I fire one please?" Asked Madeline.

"No darling, this is a serious fix we're in, and there is no time for inexperienced gun users," said Max.

"Exactly so that rules me out then," said Joe.

"Fine, two AK47's should be enough to scare this lot off, get ready to run to the van when I say," said Max.

Max, and Frank walked over to the door.

"Max, you open the door when I give the word, and I will empty my clip," said Frank.

Frank cocked the rifle, and raised it ready.

"Now" he said.

Max flung the door open, and Frank leant out the door firing the AK47. The sound of automatic gunfire echoed around the shack. The noise was ear splitting.

Frank swung the rifle side to side keeping it low. Hitting Texas Rangers in the legs.

The Texas Rangers started firing back. Max quickly shut the door when Frank ran out of bullets. The bullets from the Texas Rangers weapons pinged against the door, and the walls of the shack.

Frank took Max's place by the door.

"Joe, Madeline, and Ethel May can you grab all the weapons, and ammo from the cabinet please, and get ready to run" said Max.

Frank ejected his clip, and loaded a new clip into his AK47.

"Now" said Max.

Frank flung the door open.

Max fired his AK47. He swung the rifle from side to side as the loud sound of automatic gunfire echoed through the shack. He held his gun slightly higher inflicting more damage on the Texas Rangers. He made sure to avoid the giant.
Frank slammed the door shut as soon Max ran out of bullets.

“WE ARE BRINGING BIGGER GUNS OUT NEXT, SO ANYONE WHO WANTS TO LIVE SHOULD RUN AWAY NOW” yelled Max.

Bullets started pinging off the shack again.

Max handed his AK47 to Frank. He walked over to the table, and grabbed his laser rifle. He put the power on setting two. Then he walked back over to door.

“I promise I won’t kill the giant,” said Max.

“You better not,” said Frank.

“Now” said Max.

Frank flung the door open, and Max stepped outside the door. He fired the laser rifle to his left side. A burst of photonic energy shot out of the rifle and exploded against a couple of Texas Rangers vaporising their bodies. He aimed his rifle at Bigfoot.

“Back off Bigfoot, or we will kill you, and all your men” he said menacingly.

“You won’t get away with this” boomed Bigfoot raising his rifle.

Max quickly fired another burst of energy to his right side vaporising two more Texas Rangers. He swung the rifle back, and aimed at Bigfoot.

“Drop the gun Bigfoot” he said.

“Fuck you outlaw,” said Bigfoot.

Bigfoot fired his Sharps rifle into Max’s chest. The bullet slammed against his kevlar vest. It felt like he’d been punched in the chest by Lennox Lewis.

“You fucker” chocked Max.

Max fire his rifle at the ground in front of Bigfoot, and kicked up a huge pile of earthy dust into his face.

Max turned to the door of the shack.

“Now get to the van” he said.

Frank rushed out holding his AK47, and holding another AK47 on his shoulder. Madeline rushed out with two pistols from the cabinet, and a few clips in her bag. Ethel May rushed out with three pistols in her bag, and a few clips. Finally Joe rushed out with an AK47 on his shoulder, and holding six clips of AK47 bullets.

They quickly climbed into the van. Madeline, and Ethel May jumped into the back. Frank, and Joe jumped into the front, and Max climbed into the driver’s seat. Max fired up the engine, and slammed the van into first gear.

The front wheels spun, and kicked up dust as Max floored the accelerator. The van surged forward through the dust.

Bullets began pinging against the van, as the remaining Texas Rangers, including Bigfoot started firing at them.

Max skidded the van past them, just missing hitting Bigfoot. They hurtled away at speed.

“That Bigfoot is a nutcase, totally fearless,” said Max.

“That’s what history says about him, he once faced down forty Comanches single handed,” said Frank.

“Trust us to get the nuttiest Texas Ranger after us,” said Max.

“How did he know we were there?” Asked Joe.

“The van being parked outside was probably a bit of a giveaway,” said Max.

“Right Fort Laramie is Northwest of us, but I don’t fancy driving there during the day in a modern vehicle,” said Frank.

“Well, I don’t fancy staying in Texas to get hunted down,” said Max.

“How much fuel have we got?” Said Joe.

“Half a tank,” said Max.

“What happens when we run out?” Asked Frank.

“We need to learn how to make peanut oil, rapeseed oil, or just find some oil,” said Max.

"Oh fuck," said Joe.

"What's up mate?" Asked Max.

"We forgot the coffee" Joe said solemnly.

"Joe, I've got the sugar, and the salt in my bag, and Madeline has the coffee in her bag" called Ethel May.

"You're the best ladies, thanks" said Joe smiling.

After 48 hours of travelling the men were exhausted as they'd been taking it in turns to drive. Madeline, and Ethel had been using their beds, although they hadn't sleep well with all the bumping.
They were travelling through the plains in the early morning sun.

"We need to stop, and stretch our legs, and I wouldn't mind some hot food, I'm a bit fed up of cold beans, and cold soup" said Joe.

Frank was driving.

"Where are we Frank?" Asked Max.

"We're still in Texas, near the salt plains, we've got a way to go until the Kansas border," said Frank.

They were driving through a valley with hills on either side of them.

“We’re still in Texas, it would not be safe for us to stop,” said Max.

“I’m gonna pass out soon,” said Joe.

“Climb in the back, and have a sleep,” said Max.

“Oh fuck,” said Frank.

Max, and Joe looked up, and saw what Frank was worried about.

In front of them about five hundred yards away was a line of Union Calvary soldiers. They had two hand operated Gatling guns, but more worryingly they had two Howitzer cannons.

“Stop the van now” said Max urgently.

“You worried about the Howitzers?” Said Frank stopping the van.

“Is that what the cannons are called?” Asked Max.

“Yep” said Frank.

“This van is bullet proof, but I’m sure if it is cannon proof. I’d rather not test it now, so turn around,” said Max.

“Check the mirror buddy, there are soldiers behind us as well,” said Frank.

“He’s right, we’re surrounded” said Joe checking the side mirror.

The soldiers started marching towards the van. Horses pulled the Howitzers, and the Gatling guns.

“Can you see anyone famous that can’t be killed like General Custer?” Said Max.

“I don’t think so,” said Frank.

Max picked up his laser rifle, and selected setting three.

“That’s good enough for me” he said, as he climbed over Joe, and opened the door.

“Max don’t go outside” said Joe worried.

“I’ll be back,” said Max smiling.

He jumped out the van, and shut the door behind him.

He aimed the laser rifle, and fired a huge burst of photonic energy at one of the Howitzers. A big blue photon ball slammed into the Howitzer, and exploded with such force it vaporised around thirty soldiers.

The soldiers started firing at Max. The Gatling guns where quickly set up, and began firing.

“Ow shit” said Max as a bullet hit him in the leg.

He fired at the second Howitzer with the same results, the cannon plus thirty soldiers were vaporised.

“Arr fuck” he said as a bullet stuck him in the left arm from behind.

He span round, and saw soldiers charging towards them.

He fired the laser rifle, and vaporised around forty soldiers.

He was stuck again in the leg, and then again. Blood started pouring from the holes in his body.

Max raised the rifle again, and suddenly his vision blurred, and felt dizzy. He was losing blood fast. He collapsed on the ground.

Frank jumped out the van with an AK47, and let rip cutting down thirty five soldiers.

The Gatling was aimed towards Frank.

Frank was hit by a hail of bullets from the Gatling gun. He collapsed onto the ground with blood pouring from his stomach.

On the other side of the van.

Max lay on the floor feeling cold, and weak. He raised the laser rifle, and tried to aim it. His vision went all starry, then he blacked out.

Frank reloaded his AK47 as lay on the floor bleeding.

He unloaded another clip as soldiers charged towards him. Twenty soldiers were cut down by the automatic gunfire.

Joe jumped out of the van with an AK47. He stood over Max, and began firing at the soldiers in front of them. He unloaded the rifle, then he ducked down on the ground.

“Max, how do I reload this?” He spoke.

Max was unconscious on the ground.

Joe looked under the van.

“Frank, how do you reload the AK?”

Frank was unconscious on the ground.

Joe pulled out his Browning 9mm. He stood by the open door of the van, and started firing his Browning, taking out one soldier at a time.

The soldiers charged towards him.

The Gatling gun was aimed at him.

We are so fucked though Joe as his Browning ran out of bullets.

He quickly reloaded with the only spare clip he had on him.

Twelve bullets now stood between him, and a hundred soldiers charging towards him.

The soldiers on the Gatling gun aimed at Joe, and cranked the handle.

Chapter 14
Dreams

Frank was in the garden with his parents Chuck, and Marge. His little brother Terrance was also there. He was sat at a round patio table with his Mum, and brother. His Dad was by the barbecue cooking burgers, and sausages. The garden was large with two beech trees, a large lawn, a couple of flowering areas, and the patio that they were sat on. The house was a large detached colonial house. Built in the eightieth century.

Chuck came over with a large plate of burgers, and sausages. He put the plate on the table, and sat down. They all made their own burgers, and hot dogs. Frank put tomato relish on his burger, and mustard on his hot dog.

It was a fine summers day, and everyone was happy enjoying the family time. Frank, and Terrance didn't get to see their dad much as his work with the CIA took him overseas a lot of the time. Whenever Chuck was home, he made a great effort to spend time with his family.

This was back in 1960. As far as Frank knew his dad was an international banker. In 1972 he would find out what his dad really did, and in 1973 he would join the crononaut program. Then in 1974 he would get stuck back in 1864.

Frank sat happily looking at his family. This was a wonderful day. The weather had been perfect, and so had the food.

As Frank sat looking at his family the world started to darken. Suddenly everything was dark. Frank could see a light ahead of him. He walked towards the light. As he got close, he could see someone standing in the light. He moved towards them, and saw it was his Grandmother Mabel. Mabel reached out her hand. Frank took her hand, and moved into the light.

Max was in his flat in Colliers Wood which he had brought with Joe after they made some money selling the formula for secret garden. He was sat on the sofa in the small living room wearing jeans, and a Van Halen t-shirt. The living room had white walls, and a green carpet. There was a three-seater sofa, a glass coffee table, and a cabinet with a TV, DVD player, and Sky box on it.

As Max sat on the sofa two young children rushed into the living room. There was a boy, and a girl. They looked around four years old. The boy was a mini version of Max without a beard. He was dressed in blue trousers, and a Spider Man t-shirt. The girl was a mini version of Madeline wearing a pink princess dress.

“Hello Daddy” they shrieked jumping on Max.

“Hello children” said Max surprised.

Madeline entered the living room, she was wearing black leggings, and a Bryan Adams t-shirt, she had a huge stomach.

“Hi babe” she said.

“Hi darling,” said Max.

"Oh, bloody hell, I need to pee again, the baby keeps kicking my bladder," said Madeline.

Madeline left the room.

"Daddy, can we go to McDonald's?" Asked the little boy.

"Yay Daddy can we, can we?" Said the little girl.

"I suppose so," said Max.

What an earth are the children's names thought Max.

Madeline came back in the room.

"Mummy we're going to McDonald's," said the little girl.

"No, we're not Angelica, we went there yesterday," said Madeline.

"But Daddy said we can go," said the little boy.

"Well Daddy is naughty then for saying that" Madeline said giving Max an evil look.

"Sorry I forgot we went yesterday; I didn't sleep well last night," said Max.

"Can we go to the park then?" Asked the little boy.

"Yes, Joe we can," said Madeline.

“Joe, and Angelica what lovely names,” said Max.

Madeline gave Max a confused look.

“Are you feeling alright Max?”

“Yes darling, I just didn’t sleep well last night, had a bad dream that I was alone, and now I’m really happy to have you all with me” Max said.

“Aw you sweetie Max, you always got us with you” said Madeline in a gooey voice.

“Park, park” said the children together.

“OK let’s go to the park” said Max standing up.

They all went to the hall, and put their shoes, and jackets on. They left the flat, and walked to Max’s car.

Max was shocked to his Seat Ibiza which he had when he was 19. He pulled the keys out of his pocket, and unlocked the doors. The kids climbed in the back, and sat on their booster seats. Madeline climbed into the passenger seat, and Max got in the driver’s seat.

“Madeline when did we get back from the past?” Asked Max.

“I don’t know what you are talking about Max, now get driving please before I need to pee again,” said Madeline.

Max fired up the engine, and set off. He had no idea where the park was!

“Madeline, where did we meet?” Said Max.

“If you don’t remember that, then you are in big trouble” said Madeline angrily.

“As far as I remember it was the Sherman saloon”

“Are you feeling alright Max?”

“No, I had a bad dream last night, and now I don’t feel myself”

“Aw sorry to hear that Max. We met at college, we studied Chemistry together, and made loads of money with secret garden, then we got married after I got pregnant”

“So, you don’t come from 1870 then?”

Madeline laughed.

“No Max, I was born over a hundred years after 1870”

“I am so confused”

“I know you are you should have turned right, you’re going the wrong way”

“Actually, I’m going the right way darling, I’m going to St Georges hospital to get myself sectioned, I have lost my mind”

Max could hear a crackling sound, like a campfire. He could feel the warmth.

"He's waking up," said Madeline.

Chief Rattlesnake, and the Medicine man came over, and looked down at Max.

Max opened his eyes, and looked up at them all.

"Are you OK Max?" Asked Madeline.

"I'm fine Mother, I have just been overdoing things with my science experiments, I must have passed out," said Max.

"I'm not your mother" said Madeline shocked.

"Look Mum, if Rachael wants a pony, I will get her one for her birthday, me, and Joe made a bit of money doing a botanical experiment," said Max.

Joe walked into the Tepee.

"How's he doing?" He asked.

"Who's Rachael?" Said Madeline.

"That's his cousin," said Joe.

Joe walked over, and crouched down by Max.

“Hi Max,” said Joe.

“Mr Freetown, how are you sir, have you come round for a smoke?” Said Max.

“Who’s Mr Freetown?” Said Madeline.

“That was our neighbour when we lived in Colliers Wood, an old Caribbean fellow from Aruba. He used to come round, and smoke with us,” said Joe.

“He seems delirious,” said Chief Rattlesnake.

Max looked at Chief Rattlesnake.

“Ah Professor Woo, what are doing here, I handed my homework in yesterday,” said Max.

“Professor Woo was our chemistry tutor in College,” said Max.

“poo?sa? niwʉnʉrʉ” said the chief to the medicine man.

“taahkatʉ kwasikʉ” replied the medicine man.

“His crazy talk shouldn’t last more than a day,” said the chief.

“Oh Mother, I am sorry, but I feel very tired, I must sleep now,” said Max.

Max let out a huge yawn, and closed his eyes.

“Are you sure he’ll be OK?” Asked Madeline.

"Yes, he will be fine, he was not as badly injured as Frank," said the chief.

Max woke up with a splitting headache, he felt like he'd been hit by a freight train.

"Oh man, what is going on" he said sleepily.

"Oh Max, are you OK?" Said Madeline looking down at him.

"Hi Madeline, where are we?"

"We're in a tepee"

"What" said Max sitting up, and falling back in pain.

He looked around. He was in a tepee with a buffalo skin over him.

"Whose tepee is this?" He asked.

"We're with the Comanches," said Madeline.

"How you doing mate" said Joe from the other side of him.

Max looked round, and saw Joe, and Ethel May looking at him with concerned expressions.

"Joe, how did we get here mate?" Max asked.

“Right OK mate, well we were fighting hundreds of Union soldiers. You, and Frank were down. I fired an AK47 at them, but when it ran out of bullets, I didn’t know to reload it,” said Joe.

“You just press the eject button above the magazine, and then shove a new magazine in, and pull the bolt back,” said Max.

“Yes, I know now Madeline showed me, but I had never used an assault rifle before. So anyway, I got my Browning out, and started shooting, I emptied the clip, and then reloaded with the last clip I had on me. So basically, it was me with twelve bullets against a hundred soldiers. They aimed the Gatling gun at me, and cranked the handle, I thought I was going to die, but the Gatling didn’t fire”

“Yes, that makes sense, the early Gatling guns were notorious for jamming. Madeline how did you know how to reload an AK47?” Asked Max.

“I watched you, and Frank doing it in the shack,” said Madeline.

“Wow I love you Madeline” said Max in a gooey voice.

“Aw Max, I love you too,” said Madeline.

“Well anyway thank God the Gatling gun did jam, but I still had a hundred soldiers shooting at me, then suddenly I heard loads of screaming, and a load of horses being ridden by Comanches came thundering along. The Comanches started firing guns, and arrows, and throwing spears whilst they were riding their horses. They're the best horse riders I've ever seen. They saved us, and took us back to their camp, which is where we are now. The medicine man removed the bullets from your arms, and legs, and put some special ointment on your wounds," said Joe.

"And how is Frank?" Asked Max.

"Frank is dead I'm afraid"

"Oh fuck, I liked Frank"

"Yeah, we all did mate, he got hit eight times in the back with the Gatling gun"

"Shot in the back, those fucking cowards" cried Max angrily.

"Any way you need to rest for a few days, the van is outside"

"And what happens if the Union army attacks us?"

"There are scouts on watch duty"

"And what are they gonna do if they see hundreds of Union soldiers charging towards them"

"They have the AK47's we found in the shack, and Madeline showed them how to use them"

"Madeline, you showed them" said Max looking at Madeline.

"Yes, I sure did," said Madeline.

“You are a genius my darling. I had a dream about us, we had two children, and you were expecting another one”

“Aw Max, that’s lovely. Hopefully that dream will come true soon” said Madeline smiling.

“Anyway Max, do you still think we should go to the house near Fort Laramie?” Asked Joe.

“Well, we’ve got nothing else to do, and there may be a scientist there who can help us. I still haven’t come up with any plans to get us home. If there is someone there who knows the theory of time travel that would be a huge help. I feel like utter crap,” said Max.

“OK we’ll get going when you’re up to it, you need to rest for a few days. You got shot five times Max. It was a miracle you didn’t get any bones broken. The medicine man had to remove a few bone fragments from your shoulder where a bullet chipped it, but you should make a full recovery, just rest now mate,” said Joe.

“And I will be right here to look after you, if there is anything you need just ask,” said Madeline.

“I really need to pee,” said Max.

“I’ll get a plastic bottle from the van, and Madeline can assist you,” said Joe.

A few days later Max was able to walk, slowly. He stood outside the tepee. Chief Rattlesnake came over to him.

“Thank you chief, I owe you my life,” said Max.

“Our debt to you is repaid Max, we owed you our lives,” said the chief.

“I hope you didn’t lose to many men saving us”

“We lost some, including my son”

“Oh chief, I am so sorry”

“It’s OK Max, my son died in battle, that is a noble, and honourable death. His spirit is with the ancestors now watching over us”

“Yes, and so is Frank’s spirit, he also died in battle”

“Well, I know you must be going now Max as your destiny lies elsewhere, I will have your guns brought back to you”

“No chief the guns are yours now, along with four future handguns, if they can help you to survive longer than I’ll be very happy”

“Max, you are truly the nicest white man I ever had the pleasure to meet”

Joe was driving the van, Ethel May was sat next to him, and Max, and Madeline were in the back. Max was laying on the bottom bunk. They had swapped bunks, so Max didn't have to climb to get into bed. Madeline was sat on the chair on the opposite side to the bed.

"What sort of gun do I have Joe?" Asked Ethel May.

"It's a Walter PPK. The same gun James Bond uses," said Joe.

"Who is James Bond?"

"He is a spy in the future"

"A spy, like in the civil war, the North sent spies to the South"

"Yes, that's right"

"So, you have civil wars in the future, do you?"

"Erm, not where we live"

"So, what do spies do in the future then"

"They spy on rival companies, or countries that they're ordered to go to"

"I don't understand"

"Yeah, me neither, spies are very mysterious. I've just had a thought. Madeline, can you ask Max something please"

“You can ask me yourself Joe. It was my arms, and legs that got injured, not my ears” said Max from his bed.

“OK, what happens if we burst a tire?” Asked Joe.

“I made the tires myself one night while you were on a date. They are neoprene with titanium braiding. They are pretty indestructible,” said Max.

“What the hell is neoprene?”

“It’s what they make wetsuits out of”

“So, they won’t burst then?”

“Hopefully not, there is one spare wheel, but the shower, and toilet cubicles are on top of it”

After three nights of driving, and camping out during the day. They reached the mining town of Denver, Colorado. Joe Parked the van up by some trees. They all got out. Joe pulled up a few bushes, and used them to hide the van.

They made their way into town. The town was larger than Abilene. A typical western town with rows of wooden buildings either side of a dusty road. There were horses, and carts parked up all over the dusty road. It seemed like a bustling town. A good place to lay low for a night or two.

They entered the Silver saloon, and hotel. A large wooden building. Through the two swinging stable doors they walked.

The place was very busy. Lots of men dressed in miner's suits, men dressed in suits, and a few cowboys, and of course the saloon girls wearing their bright frilly dresses.

They walked up to the bar. A short plump lady with long brown hair, and big brown eyes came over. She wore a red frilly dress, and looked around forty.

"Howdy folks, what can I get for ya?" She asked.

Max looked at an advert on the bar.

"Does the Colorado Silver Bitter have silver in it?" He asked.

The bar lady laughed.

"All the new folk in town ask that, I'm afraid it doesn't, that is just the name of it" she said.

"OK then, we'll take two glasses of Colorado Silver, and two glasses of champagne with a dash of orange juice please," said Max.

The bar lady got their drinks for them.

"That's a dollar, and a half please" she said.

Max gave her a three-dollar coin. She gave him his change.

"Oh, do you have any rooms available?" Asked Max.

"Yeah, a few. Buck for two hours, or three bucks for the night"

“Two rooms for one night please”

“Six bucks please”

Max handed her a ten-dollar bill.

She handed him two keys, and some change.

“Room nine, and room twelve” she said.

“Thank you” reply Max.

They found a free table at the back of the saloon, and sat down.

After a few drinks. They retired to their rooms for the night.

The next day Max, Madeline, Joe, and Ethel May went out for a walk after their lunch in the saloon.

They wandered along the wooden sidewalk. They walked past the only brick building in town, the First Bank of Colorado, and crossed to the other side of the dusty road. They heard a commotion coming from the bank. Men yelling, and women screaming. They turned back to face the bank, and saw two men with bandanna's pulled up over their faces rushing out of the bank. They had their revolvers in their hands, and one of the men was holding a large cloth bag.

“WE’VE BEEN ROBBED” yelled someone from the bank.

"Quick Joe, shoot them, I can't use my arms properly at the moment," said Max.

"Oh shit, OK" said Joe nervously.

Joe pulled out his gun.

BANG BANG

The two outlaws fell to the ground with blood pouring from their heads. Their hats lay beside them.

Max, and Joe turned, and saw Madeline holding a smoking pistol.

"Got em" she said smiling.

"Put the gun away quick before someone sees it," said Max.

Madeline put the gun back in her bag.

A short slim man with a sheriff's badge on came over to them. He had long brown hair, and blue eyes. He wore black chaps, a white shirt, and a black leather waistcoat. He looked like he was in his twenties, and wore a brown Stetson.

"Howdy folks, I'm deputy Smallholdings, which one of you shot the Jonas brothers?" He spoke.

"I did," said Madeline.

"Really, you did?" The deputy said surprised.

“Yes, she did, she is a crack shot,” said Max.

“Well then, you folks need to come with me to the marshal,” said the deputy.

They all followed the deputy to the marshal’s office. The townsfolk applauded them as they walked along.

The walked into the marshal’s office.

The marshal walked over to them. He was a tall slim man. He had short grey hair, and a grey trimmed beard. He had green eyes, and looked around fifty. He was wearing a black suit, and a large black Stetson.

“Who are these fine looking people deputy?” He asked.

The deputy pointed at Madeline.

“Sheriff this young lady just shot dead the Jonas brothers” he said.

“Really, well I am impressed, I’m marshal William Daniels, who are you fine people?”

“I’m Max Walsh, this is my wife Madeline, and this is my friend Joe Brown, and his wife Ethel May”

“Pleasure to meet you folks. Willie, go, and fetch the mayor, he’ll want to meet these people” said marshal Daniels.

The deputy rushed away.

The marshal took a key out of his breast pocket, and used it to unlock a draw in his desk. He pulled out a bundle of cash.

“This is for you mam” he said handing the cash to Madeline.

“What, really, why is that?” She said surprised taking the cash.

“There is a one-thousand-dollar reward for capturing the Jonas brothers dead or alive, and as you killed you, that means you get the reward” said marshal Daniels.

The deputy came back with a short plump man. He had patchy grey hair, and a handlebar moustache. He looked around sixty. He had blue eyes, and wore a black pinstriped suit, and a black bowler hat.

“Hello, I’m Mayor Baxter Stiles, please to meet the folk that took out the Jonas brothers. They have been causing havoc all other Colorado for over a year now”

That night there was a big celebration in the Silver saloon in honour of Madeline.

Everyone in the place was buying drinks for her.

The mayor, and the marshal were there consuming mass amounts of alcohol themselves. The whole place was buzzing with a happy vibe. People were overjoyed that the Jonas brothers no longer plagued them.

The next morning Madeline woke up with a splitting headache. Someone was knocking on the door.

Madeline got up, and threw on her dress. She walked over, and opened the door.

Joe, and Ethel May were at the door.

“Oh, come in” Madeline said sleepily.

“How are you, Madeline?” Asked Ethel May.

“Not great, I think I drunk too much, how are you two?” Madeline replied.

“We’re pretty tired after Max woke us up at two in the morning,” said Joe.

“What, why did Max wake you up?” Asked Madeline.

“He needed the van key, said he wasn’t feeling well,” said Joe.

Madeline rushed over to Max. She noticed he was sweating; she felt his forehead.

“My God, he’s burning up” she said worried.

Joe rushed over.

“Max, can you hear me” he said.

“Yes, said Max shivering.

“Are you OK?” Asked Joe.

“Well, I’ve ruled out lead poisoning, I think I may have sepsis,” said Max.

“What did you do last night?” Said Joe.

“I had to use the toilet in the van, I’d rather not go into detail, then I had a shower, and then I injected myself with antibiotics,” said Max.

“So, you will be alright then?” Said Madeline.

“I’m sure I’ll be fine,” said Max.

“How did you get sepsis?” Said Joe.

“I would guess being shot five times, then being operated in unsterilised conditions,” said Max.

“Oh shit, but the antibiotics will help?”

“They should do Joe, we’ve only got two doses left though, I hope that is enough”

“What happens if it’s not enough”

“You’ll have to buy me a coffin”

Chapter 15
The House Near Fort Laramie

Joe came back to the van with a bottle of whiskey for Max. He opened the side door, and handed the bottle to Madeline. Max was lying in bed. He'd had another shot of antibiotics earlier, but he was still feeling very sick.

Joe climbed into the driver's seat, and shut the door behind him. Ethel May was sat on the passenger seat next to the driver's seat. The map, and compass lay on the seat next to Ethel May. Joe had studied the map, and knew roughly which direction to go.

He fired up the van, and gently set off.

"Are you alright Joe?" Asked Ethel May.

"Yeah, I'm fine darling, just a bit worried about Max" replied Joe.

Max sat up in bed, and gulped down some whiskey.

"Orr fuck that's strong stuff" he said as the whiskey burnt his throat.

"Go easy on it" said Madeline holding the bottle.

"I need to drink loads to kill the bacteria that has overwhelmed my system" said Max grabbing the bottle.

He gulped down some more.

“Oh, I feel better now, fancy a fuck babe” he said drunkenly.

“Max don’t be so rude, anyway you’re not well enough” said Madeline blushing.

“Joe I just thought of a way to get us back to the future,” said Max.

“Really?” Said Joe.

“Yes mate. I can build a flux capacitor,” said Max.

“Are you drunk?” Asked Joe.

“I should bloody hope so mate”

“And what are you going to power the flux capacitor with? A lightning bolt?”

“That’s it, well done Joe, a lightning bolt, if we get a lightning bolt to strike the power supply then that will reverse the process”

“Would a lightning bolt be powerful enough?”

“Not really, we can jump a few decades at a time”

“What, and just keep using lightning bolts?”

“Yeah”

“How can we predict where, and when lightning will strike?”

“We’re from the future, we can look at old weather reports”

“Max, did you bring a bunch of old weather reports with you?”

“No but lightning will strike the clock at Hill Valley in 1955”

“Max, are you just using the plot of Back to the Future as your theory?”

“Well, it worked for Marty, didn’t it?”

“And was Back to the Future a real-life documentary”

“I think so, I like it”

“Aren’t you one who kept telling me the power generated by a lightning bolt would be nowhere near enough to break the time barrier”

“Yes, a lightning bolt generates one point twenty-one gigawatts of power, my power supply unit can generate forty gigawatts of power”

“So how does a lightning bolt help us then?”

“Screw you man, I’ll fight you after I’d had a nap”

Max passed out.

“What was Max talking about?” Asked Madeline.

"He was talking about a film from the future. He's too drunk to make any sense at the moment," said Joe.

"How long will it take us to get to Fort Laramie?" Asked Ethel May.

"I've got no idea, a guy in town said to head north, and it would take about four days by horse, so I guess we may be a bit faster. The horses in this van don't need to stop for a rest," said Joe.

"Where are the horses?" Said Ethel May.

"It's a future expression, the engine in the van is equivalent to about one hundred, and fifty horses"

"Wow, and it fits in the front of us?"

"Yep, this is 2016 technology"

On the third night they arrived at the House. It was surrounded by orange-coloured high walls.

Max had finished off the antibiotics, and the whiskeys. He was feeling better, but still felt terribly weak.

Joe drove around the walls until he found a door. A large wooden door embedded into the walls.

Joe climbed out the van, and approached the door.

He banged on the door, and waited.

He heard a clicking sound, like locks being unlocked.

The door creaked open slightly, and a large man stuck his head round the door. He was tall, and wide. He had short blonde hair, blue eyes, and was clean shaven. He was wearing a black suit, and a black Stetson.

“Can I help you pilgrim?” He said with a deep voice.

“Hi, I’m Joe. We were with Frank Mitchell”

“So where is Frank?”

“He got killed in a fight with some Union soldiers”

“Damn it boy, what the hell were you doing fighting Union soldiers?”

“It couldn’t be helped they ambushed us”

“OK, I suppose shit happens. Where are the rest of your people?”

“In the van”

“You got a fucking van” the man said shocked.

“Yes”

“And you’re driving it through the old west?”

“Yes, but only at night”

“Jesus Christ boy, do you care about causality, or the integrity of the timeline?”

“Sorry, but you need to talk to my friend Max, he is a scientist”

“OK boy, bring your van inside, and park behind the house”

“OK thank you sir”

Joe walked over to the van, and climbed in. He drove towards the door. The Colonel opened the door all the way. Joe drove inside. Inside the walls there was a small log cabin. Joe drove round the back, and parked the van. He switched the engine off.

“Right, we’re here now,” said Joe.

“Is the man friendly?” Asked Ethel May.

“I’ll let you judge that for yourself,” said Joe.

They all got out the van. Madeline helped Max who was still very weak. They walked around to the front of the cabin. The colonel was waiting for them.

“Howdy folks, I’m colonel Steven Baines,” said the colonel.

“Hi, I’m Max Walsh” Max said croakily “this my wife Madeline, and my friend Joe, who you’ve already met, and his wife Ethel May”

"Well pleasure to meet you all, come inside," said the colonel.

They followed the colonel into the cabin. Inside the cabin there were plain wooden walls, and a wooden floor. There was a large timber table, and some timber chairs in the middle of the room. On the table there was an oil lamp providing light for the room. There were two doors on the left side of the room, which led to other rooms, the kitchen, and the bedroom.

"I expected it to be more modern," said Max.

Max started coughing.

"Are you sick Max?" Asked the colonel.

"Yes colonel, I have sepsis, and we've run out of antibiotics, have you got any?"

"Yes, I have a medical kit downstairs"

"Downstairs?"

The colonel walked over to the table, and pushed it back. He crouched down, and lifted a trapdoor in the wooden floorboards. Under the trapdoor was a steel hatch with a wheel lock on it. He turned the wheel, and lifted the hatch. Electric light shone up from the hole in the ground. There was a fixed ladder leading down to the basement.

"After you folks" said the colonel pointing to the hole.

They all made there was down the ladder. The colonel came down last, shutting the hatch after him, making sure the wooden hatch came down over the steel hatch.

They found themselves in a large stone basement area. There was a florescent strip light on the ceiling. There was a small kitchen area on one side, with a sink, and a microwave, and kettle on a worktop next to the sink. There were cupboards below the sink, and worktop. There was a large chest freezer next to the worktop. On the other side of the room there were two doors, one was labelled WC, and the other was labelled SHOWER. At the back of the basement there was a desk with two chairs. On the desk was radio equipment, and a large computer monitor. Next to the desk was a huge cabinet that almost reached the ceiling. The cabinet was two feet wide, and four feet deep. Inside was a computer server from the 70s.

The colonel open one of the cupboards, and pull out a small jar with pills in it.

“Here” he said passing the jar to Max.

“What are these?” Asked Max taking the jar.

“Penicillin” said the colonel.

“Oh, thank you,” said Max.

“What’s this?” Asked Madeline pointing to the computer server.

“That’s a computer,” said the colonel.

Max, and Joe started laughing.

“What” said the colonel looking at them.

“Sorry colonel, we’re just laughing at the size of your antique computer,” said Max.

“It’s got to be big boy; it has a five-hundred-megabyte hard drive” said the colonel.

Max, and Joe laughed even harder.

“Sorry colonel” Max pulled out his phone “this is a telephone with a computer inside it, it has an eight-gigabyte hard drive, that’s eight thousand megabytes. Look at the size of it”

“My goodness, how technology has progressed. Is it 2016 you are all from?” Said the colonel.

“Have you got a chair please colonel, I’m feeling a bit dizzy,” said Max.

“Sure, Joe give me a hand,” said the colonel.

The colonel walked over, and opened a cupboard door next to the computer server. Inside the cupboard were some wooden folding chairs. He took three out, and handed them to Joe. Joe set one up for Max to sit down, and then set the other two up for the ladies. The colonel grabbed the two chairs from the desk, and brought them over for Joe, and himself.

They all sat in a circle facing each other. The colonel got a glass of water of water from the kitchen area, and handed it to Max.

“Thank you, colonel,” said Max taking the glass.

The colonel sat down, and Max took a couple of penicillin pills.

“Anyone else needs a drink then just help yourself, I got one for Max as he looks very ill,” said the colonel.

“I like your fancy chairs that fold up,” said Madeline.

“Don’t you have folding chairs in 2016?” Asked the colonel.

“Me, and Ethel May aren’t from 2016, we live in this time,” said Madeline.

“Max, is it correct you are a scientist?” Said the colonel.

“Yes colonel, I am a highly skilled physicist, and a competent chemist,” said Max.

“So, I would assume you know about causality then?”

“Colonel, I am aware of causality, however as far as I’m concerned causality can go fuck itself”

“I don’t know what the hell kind of scientist you are, but do have any idea what happens if we change things back in the past?”

“I would guess that we would create a whole new timeline, and the world in the future would be very different”

“That’s right boy, only there is a good chance the world might not still exist in the future”

“We have only made very minor changes, married two women, and killed a few people”

“What do you mean by a few?”

“Less than a thousand, I reckon”

The colonel went bright red, and started panting.

“Do you want a glass of water colonel?” Asked Joe.

“Fucking hell boy you’ve doomed us all. You’ve fucked the timeline so hard, the timeline is dead, we’re all dead, there is no future” said the colonel panting.

“You’re being very over dramatic colonel, where did you get the idea from that killing a few people in the past would destroy the future?” Said Max calmly.

“That’s what the greys told us” said the colonel still panting.

“Well, I’m an expert physicist, and I know all about M theory, and I can assure you, the world will be fine. Don’t worry about the evil greys, I have a weapon that can shoot down their crafts,” said Max.

“We shot down one of their crafts in 1947 at Roswell with a missile,” said the colonel.

“Is that how you first met them?”

“That’s classified”

“I’m guessing the crononaut program is also classified?”

“Yes, it is, well it was, it has been shut down now”

“Shut down, so you’re stuck here?”

“Yes, I am”

“Can you tell me anything about the technology you used to time travel, like how did it work?”

“Well, that is classified, and to be honest with you, I didn’t really understand it. There was this large screen like a big flat TV screen, and it would create a window to the past, and you just had to pass through the screen, and you ended up in the past, I’ve no idea how it actually worked”

“It sounds like the device connected a point in the past to the current point in time via some sort of quantum time tunnel”

“Do you know how to make a quantum time tunnel Max?” Asked Joe.

“No idea, that is some mega complicated science,” said Max.

"He's right, it took a team a scientists twenty years to work out how the technology worked, and another five years to actually use it. How did you travel back in time?" Said the colonel.

"I accidentally bent the timeline with a forty-gigawatt shock wave," said Max.

"Forty gigawatts. We needed two thousand gigawatts of power to run the time window. We had to use ten nuclear reactors"

"Wow, how far could you go back?"

"Well put it this way, one of our crononauts was eaten by a T-Rex"

"Fascinating, and how far could you go into the future?"

"We weren't allowed to go into the future, something about messing with destiny, and causing irreversible damage to the time space continuum"

"This is very useful information, I think"

The colonel looked at Joe.

"Is he really a great scientist?" He asked.

"Well yes, he is an amazing physicist, but a bit a dodgy when it comes to chemistry," said Joe.

"A bit dodgy at chemistry, how can you say that?" Said Max annoyed.

"Do you remember that LSD you made?" Asked Joe.

"Oh that. Well, it may have been a bit too strong"

"A bit, we were in hospital for two weeks"

"He made LSD that put you in hospital for two weeks?" Said the colonel.

"Yes, he did. We were found dancing in the street in our pants, and we were taken to hospital. We spent a week tripping out, and a week recovering," said Joe.

"It was fun though, most of the time, well some of the time," said Max.

"Yeah, great fun, I kept being attacked by a fury purple monster," said Joe.

"Oh, that was just Medusa"

"Medusa?"

"Yeah, one of the nurses, she had purple hair, every time I saw her it looked like she had big purple snakes coming out of her head. She turned me to stone a couple of times as well"

"Now you're making the future sound quite scary, purple snakes coming out of people's heads," said Ethel May.

"No, it wasn't real, we were just seeing things. There aren't really ladies with snakes for hair," said Joe.

“Yeah, the future is fun, you don’t have to drive for days to get antibiotics, unless you live in the middle of nowhere,” said Max.

“Any way you crazy kids must be hungry, help yourselves to food from the freezer, I’m popping out for a couple of hours on urgent business,” said the colonel.

After they had finished eating their microwave meals, Ethel May, and Joe were washing the plates, and cutlery. Max, and Madeline were sat down.

“Are you OK Max?” Asked Madeline.

“I’m just thinking,” said Max.

“About what?”

“I’ve got an uneasy feeling. Joe, can you do me a favour please?”

“Yeah, what do want mate?” Said Joe.

“Can you climb the ladder, and check if the hatch will open, please?” Said Max.

“Whys that mate?”

“I’ve got an uneasy feeling. The colonel doesn’t know us that well, and he has left us alone in his basement. Maybe I’m being paranoid, but the colonel was not pleased about us messing with the timeline. Now think about it Joe, he is a military man, and if he sees us as a threat, what do you think he would do to us”

“OK, I’ll check the hatch”

Joe dried his hands on a towel hanging off one of the cupboards. He walked over to the ladder, and began climbing. Soon he reached the top. He tried to turn the wheel to unlock the hatch. He put all his strength into it, but it wouldn’t budge. He descended the ladder, and walked over to Max.

“The hatch appears to be locked” he said.

“Just as I suspected. Now Joe, in fact all of you, can you look around, and see if there is an emergency exit, please” said Max.

Madeline stood up.

“So, what are we looking for?” She asked.

“A secret door-way,” said Max.

Joe, Ethel May, and Madeline began looking around. Madeline checked the toilet. Ethel May checked the shower, and Joe checked the cupboard by the computer server.

“Can’t find any secret doorways,” said Joe.

“It wouldn’t be obvious. Check behind the computer server,” said Max.

Joe grabbed the computer server, and tried to pull it away from the wall.

“Fuck this thing is heavy” he said.

Madeline, and Ethel May rushed over, and helped Joe.

They managed to slide the large cabinet away from the wall slightly. Joe had a look behind it.

“There is a small hatch here” he said.

“That must be it,” said Max.

Joe pulled the hatch open, and used the torch on his phone to look inside.

“There’s a long tunnel” he said.

“OK I think we need to get out of here” said Max standing up.

Suddenly they heard a clicking sound coming from the main hatch.

“Shit, I think he’s back,” said Joe.

“Everyone draw your weapons, and get them ready to fire” said Max urgently.

Joe pulled out his Browning, and pulled back the hammer. Madeline, and Ethel May pulled their guns out of their bags, and pulled back the hammers. Max drew one of his Berettas, and struggled pulling back the hammer. He could just about hold it with two hands.

They stood ready aiming their guns towards the hatch.

The colonel came down the ladder alone. He reached the bottom, and turned around.

“Woe, what’s going on” he said seeing the guns pointing at him.

“Who’s with you colonel?” Asked Max.

“No one’s with me,” said the colonel.

“Where did you go?” Said Max.

“That’s classified,” said the colonel.

“Joe shoot him in the head please,” said Max.

“Hold on a damn minute. Now I have shown you great hospitality, and now you wanna kill me”

“Where have you been?”

“I had to talk to one of my men”

“Soldier, or scientist?”

“A soldier”

“And how many soldiers are coming to kill us?”

“Are you crazy?”

“Max come on, maybe there is nothing sinister going on,” said Joe.

“Something is not right here,” said Max.

“Do you really think I wanna do you harm?” Asked the colonel.

“I don’t” said Joe putting his gun away.

The sound of clicking could be heard again as the main hatch opened.

Max fired his Beretta hitting the colonel in the chest. The colonel fell to the ground clutching his wound. Blood oozed out of his chest, and pooled on the floor.

“Damn, I was aiming for his head, but I can’t hold the gun up, I’m too weak,” said Max.

“Allow me darling,” said Madeline.

BANG

Madeline put a bullet through the colonel’s head.

“COLONEL WHAT’S GOING ON” a man yelled from the top of the ladder.

Chapter 16
Ziggy

The man stood at the bottom of the ladder facing them. He was dressed like a cowboy. He had short brown hair, and was clean shaven. He had blue eyes, was tall, and slim, and looked like he was in his early thirties. He had two six shooters in his side holsters.

"What the hell is going on" he said.

"We're defending ourselves from your attack" said Max struggling to hold his Beretta up.

"What attack?" Said the man.

"Who are you?"

"I'm lieutenant Micky Hayes, are you Max?"

"Yes, I'm Max, and I know you came to kill us, how many more men are upstairs?"

"Max, buddy, you've got this all wrong. The colonel asked me to bring a wagon here to take you to our laboratory, so you could meet one of our scientists to help you guys"

"Are you serious?" Said Joe.

"Yes, I swear on my daughter's life" said lieutenant Hayes.

“I’m so sorry lieutenant, Max has got mental health problems, he suffers with paranoia,” said Joe.

“That’s OK, I understand, it’s a pretty weird situation, perhaps you could lower your weapons”

“What so you can shoot us?” Said Max.

“Max please calm down, lower your gun mate,” said Joe.

“OK fine, I will take the one weapon I have on me, and put it away,” said Max.

Max holstered his Beretta. Joe holstered his Browning, and the ladies put their pistols in their bags.

“OK, so who shot the colonel?” Asked lieutenant Hayes.

“Well,” Madeline started saying.

“That was me,” said Max interrupting.

“OK then, well I didn’t particularly like him, so no harm done I suppose” said lieutenant Hayes.

“What seriously?” Said Joe surprised.

“Yep, now come with me. Where are your horses?” Said lieutenant Hayes.

"We tethered them around the back, they have plenty of hay, and plenty of water. They could do with a nice rest after our long journey," said Max.

They all followed lieutenant Hayes up the ladder, and out the front of the cabin. There was a chuck wagon waiting. A simple wooden wagon, with large wooden wheels, and a piece of white canvas arrange like a tubular tent on the back. Two large horses were strapped to the front of the wagon.

"You can ride shotgun big fellow" lieutenant Hayes said to Joe.

"Erm, OK" said Joe sheepishly.

Madeline, and Ethel May climbed into the back, and helped Max climb up.

"Thank you, ladies, I'm starting to feel better now, that penicillin has really helped," said Max.

The wagon set off slowly.

"How far is it?" Asked Joe from his shotgun position.

"It's around six miles, will take about forty minutes, just look out for any hostiles" said lieutenant Hayes.

"But it's dark, I can't see much"

"Just stay sharp partner"

In the back of the wagon.

Madeline learnt over, and whispered to Max.

“Why didn’t you tell him about the van?”

“I don’t trust these people, it’s a good idea to keep your cards close to your chest in these sort of situations” whispered Max.

“And why did you say that you killed the colonel?” Asked Madeline.

“I didn’t want you getting into trouble”

“Aw that’s very sweet, but I don’t want you to get in trouble”

“It’s a bit late for that darling, I feel like we’re being led into the lion’s den”

They all got off the wagon. There were at the foot of a large rocky hill, or possible mountain it looked quite high. Lieutenant Hayes got a torch out of his pocket, and shone it on some bushes. He walked over to the bushes, and moved them apart. He turned to face them.

“This way” he said.

They walked over to where lieutenant Hayes was stood. Hayes took out a black card, like a credit card. He held it up to the rocky surface behind the bushes. There was a clicking sound, and the rock face moved out like a swinging door.

“Inside” Hayes said.

They walked through the rocky doorway. Hayes came behind them, and shut the door.

The followed Hayes, and his torch down a long stone corridor. It looked like it had been tunnelled into the rock. At the end of the corridor was a huge steel blast door. Hayes held his card against a sensor, and the blast door slowly opened.

Inside they found themselves in a huge laboratory. There were desks everywhere. Some had bottles, and test tubes set up doing some sort of experiments. Other had 70s computer monitors on them. There were large jars with human organs in them. It looked like a supervillains evil lair.

There was a huge desk at the rear of the lab with four monitors on it. There were two people sat at the desk.

Lieutenant Hayes walked over to the huge desk. Max, Madeline, Joe, and Ethel May followed him.

The two people who were sat down stood up, and turned around. One of them was a tall, skinny man, with balding brown hair, and a brown moustache. He had blue eyes, and looked around sixty, and wore a large white coat. The other man, was not actually a man. He had a large grey head, and huge black eyes. He was in fact a grey alien!

“Vell hello, Vot do we have here?” Said the man in a German accent.

Lieutenant Hayes turned, and faced Max, Madeline, Joe, and Ethel May. He was holding a six shooter in each hand.

“These are the people from 2016 sir. Now take out you weapons slowly, and put them on the floor”

“Do as he say,” said Max.

They took out their weapons, and placed them on the floor. Max only took out one of his Berettas.

“Now step back please” said lieutenant Hayes.

They took a step back. Hayes holstered his guns, and walked forwards, he bent down, and picked up the guns.

“He still has a gun” they all heard the voice inside their heads.

The grey alien was pointing at Max.

Max pulled out his Beretta quite slowly. The grey alien pointed a small silver pointed object at him.

Max collapsed onto the floor unconscious.

“You killed my husband” said Madeline angrily.

Madeline dropped to the ground, and held Max. Lieutenant Hayes quickly grabbed Max’s other Beretta.

“Oh, my dear, ve haven’t killed your husband, he is just sleeping,” said the German.

“That’s Max on the floor, and his wife Madeline. Do you wanna know the names of the niggers?” Said lieutenant Hayes.

“No, I don’t give a shit what the filthy niggers are called. Madeline that is a lovely name. My name is Herman Brundel of the Third Reich. Where is Colonel Baines?” Said Herman.

“He was killed by hostile Indians on the way back from getting me” said lieutenant Hayes.

“Oh, that’s a shame we keep losing people, we should have picked a safer time period,” said Herman.

“You’re a fucking Nazi” said Joe angrily.

“I’m a proud Nazi, and you don’t have the right to speak to me you filthy nigger” said Herman angrily.

“Don’t you talk to my husband like that” said Ethel May angrily.

“You filthy niggers don’t understand. Ve Aryans are the master race, you are mealy our slaves” said Herman smiling.

“Don’t talk to them like that” said Madeline angrily.

“My dear Madeline. You are a fine Aryan specimen, and you are very welcome here. But you do not understand the truth about niggers. Niggers come from hell, they are on earth to perform evil, to murder, and rape Aryans. I worked alongside the great Josef Mengele. I saw his wonderful work. He understood, the niggers, the Arabs, and the Jews must be dealt with in order to save the world,” said Herman.

“That’s just your bullshit Nazi propaganda,” said Joe.

“No nigger, Dr Mengele managed to prove that Aryan DNA, and nigger DNA is different,” said Herman.

“Of course, it’s different, we look different,” said Joe.

“Yes, Dr Mengele discovered you have an extra sequence of DNA which makes you prone to evil,” said Herman.

“That’s bollocks,” said Joe.

“You do not understand the science. You could never understand it, your brains are not as developed as an Aryan brain”

“You’re just a fascist scumbag”

“My Max understands science better than anyone, he will tell us the truth when he wakes up,” said Madeline.

“Yes, and you Madeline, and your Max can join us once Max tells you the truth,” said Herman.

“You’re out of luck buddy, Max won’t help you, he hates fascists, and he hates Nazis,” said Joe.

“Take these filthy niggers to the cells” said Herman angrily.

Max woke up. He opened his eyes, and came face to face with a grey alien. He was sat on an armchair in a small black room. There was a blue light on the ceiling. The alien sat in an armchair facing him.

“Hello Max” said a voice in his head.

“Can you not talk in my head please, that’s just weird” said Max sleepily.

“OK fine, is that better for your poor head,” said the alien.

“I’m talking to an alien?”

“Yes Max, this is not a dream, call me Ziggy”

“Ziggy, is that your name?”

“No, but you don’t have the right to know my name, so call me Ziggy”

“Oh, I don’t have the right do I Mr high, and mighty grey alien”

“Just Ziggy is fine Max, and remember you are lower being to me. Like a rat is to you”

“How long have you people been practising science?”

“Around two billion years”

“Exactly, if I had been practising science for two billion years, I would be a damn site smarter than you buddy”

Ziggy laughed.

“I like you Max; you are mildly amusing”

“Thank you, Ziggy, I would like to say the feeling is mutual”

“Are you wondering why you are here?”

“Hmm let me guess. You want me to join you, in your mad plan to control the universe?”

“Not quite Max. We have no desire to control the universe, just the Earth”

“Oh, that’s OK, us Earth folk need controlling”

“You do, you are silly children with ideas beyond your experience”

“And what gives you the right to control us?”

“What gives you the right to eat animals. It’s simple you are more advanced than the animals. We are far more advanced that you, and you petulant children need looking after”

“OK Ziggy, if you’re so smart, tell me how do you travel through time?”

“You dare to test me. Fine. I’ll try, and keep this simple. The universe works on vibration, and frequencies. Time tunnels exists within the fabric or space time. These tunnels exist outside of the third dimension so humans can’t see them. We use a dark matter detecting window to locate the tunnels, then we project a strong radio wave frequency through the time tunnel to create a stable link”

"So, you can time travel using radio waves?"

"Yes Max, as long as you have a powerful enough antenna"

"And I'm guessing you could build a time window?"

"Yes Max, I could. But I won't, I have no desire to help you"

"But isn't it better for the integrity of the timeline if we return to our own time?"

"That is of no concern to me. We are changing things here anyway"

"What are you people up to?"

"Come, and talk to Herman he can explain.

Madeline was sat at a small square table in the laboratory. Lieutenant Hayes was stood near watching her. She had a glass of champagne in front of her, which she refused to drink.

Herman came over to the table.

"Please drink the champagne my dear. We mean you no harm" he said.

"Where are my friends?" Asked Madeline.

"The niggers are safe. They are not your friends, they are evil, you aren't able to see that yet, but in time you will"

Max walked over to the table followed by Ziggy.

Max rushed over to Madeline, and crouched down by her.

“Are you OK, darling?” He asked concerned.

“I’m fine, how are you?” She replied.

“Better for seeing you”

Max learnt in, and they kissed passionately.

“STOP THAT” yelled Ziggy.

Max got up, and turned to face Ziggy.

“It’s true then, the power of love can defeat evil” he said smiling.

“Sit down please Max,” said Herman.

Max sat at the table next to Madeline.

Herman sat down.

“Pleasure to meet you Max, I am Herman Brundel” he said.

“Oh great, let me guess, is this the First Reich?” Said Max.

“I suppose you could call it that”

“No, no, and no is my answer”

“Vhat, are you saying no to?”

“I’m not helping you, with some crazy Nazi plan to take over the world, and kill all the Jews”

“Ve don’t Vant to kill anyone. You must understand Max, you are a man of science. Aryans are the master race. We need to rule the world, and keep the unworthy people in check”

“You fascists are the same. What makes you better than a black person Herman?”

“Dr Mengele managed to prove that Aryans are the master race, and niggers are evil”

“Dr Josef Mengele, that crazy butcher, how many people did he kill with his barbaric experiments?”

“Sacrifice is necessary for the greater good”

“Spoken like a true fascist”

“I am a fascist, and a proud Nazi, and when we have finished our work the Third Reich will be unstoppable”

“Oh shit, I’ve just worked out what you’re up to. You are going build advanced weapons, and give them to the Nazi before World War two starts”

“Clever boy” said Herman grinning.

Lieutenant Hayes pushed Madeline into the cell with Joe, and Ethel May. The cell was a small stone walled room with a single bed in it. Joe, and Ethel May were sat on the bed. Ethel May got up, and hugged Madeline.

“Madeline how are you?” Asked Ethel May.

“I’m OK thank you Ethel May, how are you two?” Asked Madeline.

“We’re OK thanks,” said Ethel May.

Ethel May, and Madeline sat down on the bed.

“How’s Max?” Asked Joe.

“He’s OK thanks. I saw him recently. He refused to help them. Then they took me away. Max jumped up from his seat, and tried to stop lieutenant Hayes taking me, the grey creature pointed something at him, and Max froze,” said Madeline.

“I can’t believe that we bumped into an alien, and a Nazi in the old west,” said Joe.

“What is going to happen to us?” Said Ethel May.

“We’ll be OK, Max will think of something I’m sure,” said Joe.

“Yes, Max will save us,” said Madeline.

“I hope so,” said Ethel May.

"Any idea what they want to do?" Said Joe.

"Well, they said something about helping the Nazis to win World War two," said Madeline.

"Oh fuck, that would be a disaster," said Joe.

"Who are the Nazis?" Said Ethel May.

"They're a group of fascists. They hate all non-white people. They killed six million Jews in World War two," said Joe.

"I can't believe that whole world would be at war," said Madeline.

"Yes, the first world war was 1914-1919, and the second world war was 1938-1945. Millions of people lost their lives in each world war," said Joe.

"And what would happen if the Nazi won World War two?" Asked Ethel May.

"It would be bad news for black people, we would all be slaves treated worse than you could imagine," said Joe.

"Oh, I hope Max is OK," said Madeline.

Max was sat at the table in the laboratory. Lieutenant Hayes returned from the cells.

"If you hurt them, I swear it will be the last thing you ever do, I will kill you all slowly, and painfully" said Max defiantly.

Herman, Ziggy, and lieutenant Hayes started laughed.

"Oh Max, you do amuse me, I really like you," said Ziggy.

"What the hell does a grey alien get out of this deal?" Asked Max.

"We would rule the world with the Nazis, and we can carry out our experiments on Earth humans in abundance," said Ziggy.

"What do you actually do with humans?"

"We are interested in your DNA, and we are interested in controlling humans to make you our slaves," said Ziggy.

"You evil soulless fucker"

"Oh, Max that isn't a very nice thing to say. I have a soul, all living creatures do. I just don't possess human emotions like empathy, guilt, and compassion"

"You're all fucking evil, I would never help you, or be like you"

"Lieutenant Hayes, as Max vont cooperate please go, and kill the prisoners," said Herman.

Lieutenant Hayes started walking away.

“WAIT” yelled Max.

Lieutenant Hayes stopped.

“Yes Max,” said Herman.

“OK, here is the deal, if I help you, then you must let us go, and give our guns back so we can protect ourselves in the old west,” said Max.

“You’re in no position to make deals Max,” said Ziggy.

“OK then, kill my friends, and kill me, then you can’t make me help you,” said Max.

“You are very clever Max. You have a deal,” said Herman.

“Shake my hand, and give your word as a gentleman then” said Max standing up.

Herman walked over to him, and held out his hand. Max took his hand, and they shook hands.

“You have my word Max,” said Herman.

“OK what do you want me to do?” Asked Max.

“We need crystals for our energy weapons, you will go out, and get as much as crystal as you can find,” said Ziggy.

“That’s it?” Said Max.

“That is all you have to do, and then you, and your friends can leave with your guns,” said Herman.

“Ziggy can’t you go out in your space craft, and beam up some crystals?” Said Max.

“I do not have a space craft with me,” said Ziggy.

“Can’t you build one?”

“Not with the material you have on Earth”

“OK fine, and where do I get crystals from then?”

“In the deserts of northern Arizona, you will find petrified wood which contains quarts”

“How far away is northern Arizona?”

“It is four hundred miles away, south, southwest”

“And are you going to provide me with transport, and a weapon to defend myself?”

“You can take the wagon outside, and here take this” said lieutenant Hayes passing a rifle to Max.

Max took the rifle, and looked at it.

“Winchester Model 1873. How many bullets are in the magazine?” He asked.

“Fifteen” said lieutenant Hayes.

“And can I take a spare magazine please?” Said Max.

“No that will enough for you. Just use the bullets sparingly,” said Herman.

“And how much crystal do you want?” Said Max.

“Five logs of petrified wood should be enough,” said Ziggy.

“How many miles a day can the horses do pulling a cart?” Asked Max.

“About fifty” said lieutenant Hayes.

“OK, sixteen days travel, and a day collecting wood, I’ll be gone for seventeen days you know,” said Max.

“That’s fine Max, ve vill feed the prisoners, they vill still be alive vhen you get back,” said Herman.

It was daylight when Max left the laboratory, and started riding along. He had no intention of helping Nazis, and grey aliens. With the weapon in the van, he would have no trouble taking them out. He just had to find the cabin again.

Max began riding in the direction he reckoned the cabin was in. The Winchester was in a leather holster on the side of the wagon.

He had been riding for around twenty minutes when a young women came running towards him waving her arms. Max pulled the reins, and stopped the wagon. The women looked like she was in her late teens, early twenties. She wore a long blue dress, and a blue woollen shawl. She had a blue bonnet on. Her hair was long, and blonde. She had green eyes, and a slender figure, and she was very pretty.

“What’s up lady?” Said Max.

“Please help me mister, they took my Daddy away. They accused him of rustling, I think they’re gonna hang him” she said desperately.

Max held out his hand.

“Jump on” he said.

She took his hand, and he pulled her up onto the front of the wagon.

“That way” she said pointing.

Max swung the reins.

“YAH” he yelled.

The horses started moving. Max pulled the reins to the left, and steered them the way the young lady had pointed.

“I’m Max by the way”

“Thank you, Max, I’m Peggy Sue. Are you Australian?”

“No Peggy Sue, I’m English”

“Oh swell, thanks for stopping”

“You’re welcome, how many men took you Daddy away?”

“I think there was six of them”

“Well then, should be OK, as long as Winchesters are accurate, and don’t jam up”

Chapter 17
Rescue

Max stopped the wagon behind some rocks. Max, and Peggy Sue climbed down from the wagon. Max grabbed the Winchester. They both ducked down behind the rocks.

Around five hundred yards away was a group of men, dressed like cowboys. They had thrown a rope over the branch of a tree, and tied it to the saddle of a horse. Two of the cowboy's dragged a short skinny man over. He was dressed in brown cloth trousers, and a brown smock. They were in open country. The tree was a bare dead one in a patch of grassy ground, surrounded by desert.

"I'm just a simple farmer, I aint rustled no cows," said the man.

"That's my Daddy" whispered Peggy Sue.

Another cowboy put a lariat around the man's neck, and pulled it tight.

Another cowboy pulled the horse forward. Peggy Sue's Daddy started lifting off the ground.

"Oh my" said Peggy Sue sobbing.

"He not dead yet" said Max aiming the rifle.

BANG

He hit the side of the rope, and frayed it a bit.

“Fires slightly to the left” he said.

He aimed the rifle again, and shot the rope. The rope snapped, and Peggy Sue’s Daddy fell to the ground.

The cowboy’s hit the deck, and began looking around, and pointing their six shooters.

“Who the hell is there” said one of the cowboys.

“It’s marshal Wyatt Earp” said Max in an American accent.

“Who the hell are you?” Said another cowboy.

“Don’t they recognise the name Wyatt Earp” Max whispered to Peggy Sue.

“I aint never heard of Wyatt Earp” she whispered back.

“Oh, fuck it,” said Max.

He aimed the rifle, and shot one of the cowboy’s in the head.

The cowboy’s realised where the shot had come from, and started firing at the rocks that Max, and Peggy Sue were hiding behind.

Bullets pinged against the rocks making rock dust fall to the ground.

“Stay down,” said Max.

Once the firing had stopped, Max quickly aimed the rifle again. He took out three more cowboys' as they were reloading there six shooters.

The two remaining cowboys started firing again.

Dust, and tiny bits of rock fell down onto Max, and Peggy Sue.

The firing stopped, and Max quickly took aim, and shot another cowboy. The last cowboy had taken cover behind the tree. Peggy Sue's Daddy was laying on the ground.

Max fired a shot at the tree. The bullet was not powerful enough to go through the tree.

"Damn, if I had a Skorpion sub-machine gun I could cut that tree down," said Max.

"I aint never heard of a Skorpion sub-machine gun," said Peggy Sue.

"There from Czechoslovakia," said Max.

In about ninety years he thought to himself.

"I'll have to go, and get him" said Max standing up.

"Be careful Max" said Peggy Sue worried.

"I'll be fine, just stay there"

Max walked towards the tree over the soggy blood-soaked ground. His feet squelched as he moved.

The cowboy appeared from the behind the tree. He unloaded his six shooter as fast as he could hitting Max in the chest five times. Max aimed the rifle, and put a hole through the cowboy's head.

Peggy Sue's Daddy stood up.

"Thank you, mister, how come you aint hurt, he emptied his gun into your chest?" He spoke.

"I've got a tough chest, I'm English," said Max.

Peggy Sue ran over to her Daddy, squelching through the pools of blood.

"Daddy" she shrieked throwing her arms around him.

"Oh Peggy Sue" he said hugging her tight.

After she had hugged her Daddy, Peggy Sue jumped on Max, and embraced him tightly.

"Thank you so much Max" she said.

"Yes, thank you mister, if there is anything we can do for you just say the word," said Daddy.

"Yeah, get yourself a rifle so you can defend yourself, I won't always be around," said Max.

“I’m just a simple farmer, I aint got no money to buy rifles”

“Here take this one, it has six bullets in it, and I’m sure bullets don’t cost too much” said Max holding out the Winchester.

“Gee thank you mister, you are too kind” Daddy said taking the rifle.

“I know, come on I’ll give you a ride home in my speedy wagon”

Max finally arrived at the cabin, as the sun was setting. He stopped the wagon by the front door in the adobe walls. He got off the wagon, and tried the door. It was locked.

“Shit this is when I could do with a gun” he said to himself.

He kicked the walls. They were pretty solid.

Bet Joe could punch these walls down with his muscular arms he thought to himself.

Max began to think. The walls were around twelve feet high. Max was six feet high. If he stretched his arms up his height would increase to around seven, and half feet. The top of the wooden box on the back of the chuck wagon was around three feet off the ground. So, if Max stood on top of the chuck box with his arms stretched up he would be around ten, and a half feet high. So, then he would just have to jump a foot, and a half to reach the top of the wall.

Max pulled the horses closer to the wall, and manoeuvred them into position so the wagon was beside the wall. He climbed up on to the chuck box, and stood up on it. He stretched his arms up.

Here we go he thought to himself.

He bent his legs, and springed back up as hard as he could. He jumped up, and grabbed the top of the wall. He struggled to hold himself up, he was still not back to full health. He tried to pull himself up, but he had no strength in his arms. He kicked his legs against the wall trying to grip. The rough surface of the wall had good grip. Max pushed his feet against the wall, and used his arms, and legs to struggle up, and over the wall.

Once he was on the other side, he hung on the wall deciding how to land, when suddenly his arms gave up. He fell, and landed on his back sending up a huge cloud of dust.

Max coughed, and covered his eyes as the dust descended.

Once the dust had descended Max opened his eyes, and stared up into the night sky. He looked at twinkling stars above him. Some of the stars were thousands of light years away. Max wondered where the grey aliens came from, had they travelled thousands of light years to reach Earth?

Max slowly pulled himself up. He walked around the back of the cabin, and found the van. He tried the driver's door, and it opened. You beauty Joe, you forgot to lock it he thought. Max climbed into the driver's seat. He checked the ignition barrel, there were no keys there. Joe still had them. Max was unable to start the van as the key had a microchip in it which was needed to disable the immobilizer.

Max decided to have something to eat, he was starving. He got his laser rifle from the back of the van, and walked to the front of the cabin. A quick blast with the laser rifle on setting one, and the lock was destroyed. Max opened the front door. He walked into the cabin, and made his way down to the basement.

Joe, Ethel May, and Madeline sat on the bed in their cell. There were eating bread rolls, and drinking water. They had been given two bread rolls, and a cup of water each for dinner.

“At least they’re feeding us” said Madeline chewing her bread.

“Yeah bread, and water I really feel like a prisoner now,” said Joe.

“I wonder how Max is?” Said Madeline thinking out loud.

“He’s obviously cooperated with them,” said Joe.

“How do you know that?” Asked Ethel May.

“Because they are feeding us. The only way Max would cooperate with them if they threaten to kill us. So, Max has agreed to do something for them in exchange for our lives,” said Joe.

“Poor Max having to do something he doesn’t want to do, I know how that feels, it’s not nice at all,” said Madeline.

“No, it isn’t nice,” said Ethel May.

“I wouldn’t know,” said Joe.

The cell door suddenly opened, and lieutenant Hayes placed a tin plate with some dried meat on it down on the floor.

“You’re only getting this because there is an Aryan in the cell” he said.

“How’s Max?” Asked Madeline.

“He’s on his way to Arizona to pick up something up for us” said lieutenant Hayes.

Lieutenant Hayes slammed the door shut.

“Where’s Arizona?” Said Madeline.

“Me, and Max ended up there once, we were in Vegas, and we tried some mentally strong cocaine. I can’t remember what happened the rest of the night, but we woke up on a bench in a town called Peach Springs, in Arizona,” said Joe.

“So where is Arizona?” Asked Madeline.

It’s south, it’s near Mexico, so it must be south of us,” said Joe.

“How far?” Said Madeline.

“No idea,” said Joe.

“It’s approximately four hundred miles south, southwest,” said Ethel May.

“How do you know that?” Asked Joe looking at her in surprised.

“I used to study maps in my spare time when I was a slave. My master had a fine collection of maps,” said Ethel May.

“So, if it’s four hundred miles away then I guess Max will get the van,” said Madeline.

“He can’t I have the keys,” said Joe.

“Then he’ll have to go on horseback, that will take ages,” said Madeline.

“Max won’t be going to Arizona, I bet right now he is planning how to rescue us,” said Joe.

Max cuddled up in bed in the back of the van. He’d had a roast chicken TV dinner, and a can of Pepsi. Then he used the toilet in the basement, and had a nice hot shower afterwards. He was now ready to have a nice rest. He’d carried out one rescue today, so the next rescue could wait till tomorrow.

Max was restless in the night. He could hear noises that sounded like aircraft. He climbed out of bed, and noticed the daylight was streaming through the hole in the partition. What was that noise?

He pulled on his boxer shorts. He opened the side door of the van, and blinked, and squinted as the daylight hit him.

Soon he was able to see. To his surprise he was stood in a large green field. He could hear waves crashing against the shore. He looked out to the horizon, and could see the sea. He heard a roar above him. He looked up to the sky, and saw a formation of around fifty Spitfires flying above him.

He looked to the horizon again, and saw what look like an F117 Stealth Bomber approaching the Spitfires. Suddenly a huge blue flash came out the front of the Stealth Bomber, and a massive shockwave erupted towards the Spitfires. The Spitfires disintegrated as the wave of energy tore them apart.

Max woke up sweating. That was a powerful dream he'd had. Showing him what would happen if Herman was allowed to carry out his plan.

The cell door opened, and lieutenant Hayes walked in.

"Madeline, can you come with me please?" He spoke.

"Why?" Asked Madeline.

"Just do as your told please," said Hayes firmly.

Madeline got up, and walked over to Hayes. He motioned for her to leave the cell. Hayes followed her, and slammed the door shut.

Madeline followed Hayes down the stone walled corridor, and into the laboratory. He led her over to a door which had a picture of a shower on it.

Hayes opened the door. Inside the shower room there was bench, and a shower with a plastic screen around it. There was a red silk dress hanging over the bench, and some silk knickers on the bench.

"Just leave your clothes on the floor, and wear the new clothes when you finish your shower. I'll leave you to it," said Hayes.

"What?" Said Madeline confused.

Hayes left, and shut the door.

Oh well, I could do with a shower she thought to herself.

Max was sat in the basement drinking coffee. He finished the coffee, and put his cup down by the sink. The basement was starting to smell bad as the colonel's body lay on the floor by the ladder decomposing.

Max walked over to the ladder.

"You fucking stink" he said to the colonel's body.

Max climbed the ladder. He shut the hatch behind him. He walked out the front door of the cabin. He walked around the back of the cabin to the van. He opened the driver's door of the van, and learned over to release the handbrake. He pushed the van back so the back of the van was against the wall. He leaned over, and pulled up the handbrake. He grabbed his laser rifle from the passenger seats, moved backwards out of the van, and shut the driver's door.

Max climbed onto the bonnet of the van, and from the bonnet he climbed onto the roof. He climbed on top of the iron water tank. He walked to the rear of the van. He reached up, and placed his laser rifle on top of the wall. He then reached up, and grabbed the wall. He was feeling must better now. He pulled himself up, and sat on the top of the wall. He flipped himself around, and hung off the wall, he reached up with his right hand, and grabbed the laser rifle. Once he had the rifle he let go with his left hand, and fell to the ground. He landed hard, and rolled on the ground sending up dust.

Max got up off the ground, and brushed the dust off himself. He walked around to the front of the walled compound, and found the horses grazing on a patch of grass near the front. Max climbed up onto the wagon, he put his laser rifle in the leather holster on the side of the wagon. He swung the rains.

"YAH" he yelled.

The horses started moving.

Madeline was sat at the square table in the laboratory looking amazing in her new red silk dress. It was low cut showing off her impressive cleavage, and was down to her knees. Quite short for old west standards.

Madeline, Ziggy, Herman, and lieutenant Hayes sat together having lunch. They were having roast beef, roast potatoes, and vegetables, with gravy. They had white wine to drink.

“Are you enjoying the food my dear?” Said Herman.

“Yes, thank you, its lovely,” said Madeline.

“I told Max ve vould look after you, and your friends vhile he is away, lieutenant Hayes gave some roast beef, and a bottle of wine to your friends in the cells to enjoy,” said Herman.

“Thank you, that’s very kind of you,” said Madeline.

“Not at all my dear, ve not bad people you see,” said Herman.

“Madeline, I sense you are not from 2016,” said Ziggy.

“No, I’m from this time, and so is Ethel May,” said Madeline.

“I see, so Max, and Joe married women from the past, they clearly don’t mind changing the timeline then,” said Ziggy.

“And where are you from Ziggy?” Asked Madeline.

“The zeta reticuli star system on the other side of the Milky Way galaxy,” said Ziggy.

“Where is that?” Said Madeline confused.

"Thirty-nine light years away," said Ziggy.

"So, are you from the future?" Said Madeline.

"Not really, I'm over twenty thousand years old," said Ziggy.

"Wow I didn't know anyone could live that long"

"You Earth humans have a genetic age limit of one hundred years, humans on other planets live up to one thousand years. The beings that designed you added the age limit, and gave you an aggression gene as well, that why Earth humans are so violent"

"I thought God made us"

"What you call God, we call the creation. The creation is a powerful force that governs the universe. The beings that made you were made by the creation, they are known on Earth as the Anunnaki. You are a descendant of the Martian humans that occupied Atlantis. That's why white people are the master race. Oriental people are hybrids of grey aliens, and Africans that why they are so smart. Africans where the inhabitants of Earth who were engineered by the Anunnaki to be slaves, so you see black people are destined to be slaves"

"You see my dear, Ziggy is very wise, so it is true what he says, white people are the master race, oriental people are our equals, and black people are our slaves, and the Hebrews are just evil people that need to be dealt with," said Herman.

“I can’t believe that Joe, and Ethel May are my friends, and they shouldn’t be slaves” said Madeline horrified after hearing Nazi ideology.

“Oh, my dear, I tell you vhat if you join us then Joe, and Ethel May vill be yours to look after, and you can treat them however you vish,” said Herman.

“Well don’t be surprised if Max comes back, and rescues us, and kills all of you”

Herman, Ziggy, and lieutenant Hayes started laughing.

“That would be amusing, one man trying to kill us all with one Winchester rifle,” said Ziggy.

“Where the fuck is this place” muttered Max.

Max was lost. Wandering around in the desert.

Why didn’t I bring water with me he thought as the sweat dripped down off his nose? It was scorching.

How hard can it be to find a fucking mountain thought Max.

He heard heavy footsteps behind him. He looked around, and saw five native Americans on horses galloping towards him.

Max grabbed his laser rifle.

He watched as the native Americans got close. They looked different to the Comanches. They wore buffalo skin coats, and trousers with red, and white lines painted on them. Three of them had rifles in their hands, and the other two had shotguns.

They lined up in front of the wagon.

The native in the middle was tall with broad shoulders. He had long black hair, and big brown eyes, he looked like he was in his thirties. He moved forward slightly ahead of the others.

"Just hand over your wagon white man, and you won't be hurt" he said.

"Sorry I need this wagon to get around," said Max.

"White man, you are outnumbered so give up" said the native.

"You are outgunned my friend," said Max smiling.

"What is that you are holding?"

"A weapon of the Gods"

The native laughed.

"You are no God"

"Observe my good man"

Max aimed the rifle at a large rock. He fired a burst of laser energy, and sliced the rock in half.

The natives all backed up in fear.

Max pointed the rifle at the natives.

“Believe or not I’m on your side. I killed Union soldiers to protect a Comanche tribe” he said.

“We are Sioux. We got our guns from Union soldiers we killed in battle” said the native.

“I’m Max”

“I am Screaming Eagle”

“Nice name, sounds like a good name for a bottle of wine”

“We are sorry we threatened you almighty one”

“That’s OK noble warrior. If you point me in the direction of the nearest mountain, I will forgive you”

Screaming Eagle pointed.

“Around four miles that way” he said.

Madeline tried some of the chocolate sponge cake with cream she had been given for dessert.

“Wow this is delicious” she said excitedly.

“Ve only have the best food to eat,” said Herman.

“I made the sponge cake” said lieutenant Hayes.

“Wow you are a great cook,” said Madeline.

“Yes, he is Madeline, if you join us, you can learn how to make sponge cake,” said Herman.

“That’s a very kind offer Herman, but I expect Max will rescue me soon. He killed seven men to rescue me last time, and there is only three of you,” said Madeline.

“Max would have used a modern pistol which holds more bullets, and fire much quicker than an old six shooter, and I noticed he had a kevlar vest on to protect him from being shot. He no longer has his modern pistol, and his kevlar vest will not help him against my weapons,” said Ziggy.

“Oh dear, I guess Max won’t be able to rescue me then” said Madeline, remembering what Max had told her, keep your cards close to your chest.

“Don’t worry Madeline, ve vill take good care of you while Max is away, and when he comes back if you don’t want to join us you can leave,” said Herman.

Max pulled up in the wagon at the foot of the mountain. He climbed off the wagon. Max checked around the bushes. It all looked like rock to him. Where was the entrance.

He took a step back. He tried to remember when lieutenant Hayes had brought them there. He had pushed two bushes apart.

Max studied the bushes at the foot of the mountain. He spotted two that were slightly bent apart.

“Ah ha” he said.

He walked between the bushes, and rubbed the surface. It felt like rock.

He stepped back, and aimed the laser rifle. He pulled the trigger, and held it, sending out a stream of energy. He moved the laser rifle around cutting a hole in the rock.

I hope they don’t have an intruder alarm he thought.

Max took out his phone, and switched the torch on. He looked through the hole he had just cut. He could see the stone tunnel. He climbed through the hole, and entered the tunnel.

He moved slowly, and quietly down the tunnel. He needed the element of surprise to pull this rescue off without his dear friends getting hurt.

He reached the solid steel blast door. This was where he was likely to lose the element of surprise. No other way to get in though.

He stepped back, and aimed the laser rifle. He pulled the trigger, and held it. The laser beam shot out, and began to cut through the steel. It took a few seconds to punch through the steel, Max had to slowly manoeuvre the rifle around cutting a hole. A big piece of steel fell to the floor with an almighty crash.

Element of surprise gone.

Max climbed through the hole as quick as he could. He ducked down behind a desk as he heard footsteps approaching.

Lieutenant Hayes came over to investigate the sound.

Max jumped up, and put a short laser blast through lieutenant Hayes heart.

Lieutenant Hayes looked at him in shock, he began coughing up blood. He fell to the floor with blood dripping from a partially cauterized hole in his chest, and died.

Max kept low, and moved through the laboratory.

“It was probably something falling over on the other side of the lab, Hayes vill sort it out,” said Herman.

“I have a bad feeling all of a sudden,” said Ziggy.

“There is nothing to worry about, we are perfectly safe here,” said Herman.

“Guess again Nazi boy” said Max jumping up from behind a desk.

"How the hell did you get in?" Said Herman shocked.

"With this" said Max aiming his laser rifle.

A blast of laser energy shot through Herman's head. Herman's head dropped face first onto the table with a neatly cauterized wound.

Max aimed the gun at Ziggy. Ziggy vanished.

Madeline jumped up, and rushed over to Max. She threw her arms around him, and they embraced tightly.

"Thank you, Max, I knew you would come" she said relieved.

"Of course, I would come back for you, my love. You look stunning in that dress. Great cleavage," said Max.

"I have no idea what cleavage is, but this not the time for compliments, we have to get Ethel May, and Joe"

"OK, lead the way"

Madeline, and Max rushed through the laboratory, and down the corridor to the cells.

Max fired a short burst with the laser rifle, and destroyed the lock. He pulled the door open.

"Bout time, we're getting bored" said Joe annoyed.

“Well, you can have fun on the speed wagon soon” said Max walking through the door.

Joe, and Ethel May jumped off the bed. Joe embraced Max, and Ethel May embraced Madeline.

“Wow where did you get the dress from? It’s a bit revealing,” said Ethel May.

“Herman gave it to me,” said Madeline.

“Well. we can’t fault the old Nazi boys fashion sense. Come on lets go,” said Max.

They rushed back to the lab.

“Where are our guns?” Said Max.

“I think it was this desk” said Joe opening a draw in a desk “got them”

Everyone grabbed their guns. Max holstered his two Berettas.

“Have your weapons ready, I took out Hayes, and Herman but Ziggy beamed away before I could get him,” said Max.

Everyone held their weapons up ready to use.

They moved over to the blast door. Max climbed through, and looked down the tunnel. Madeline came through the hole, followed by Ethel May, and then Joe.

“Joe take the girls outside; I have to destroy the lab,” said Max.

Joe, Ethel May, and Madeline made their way outside.

Max held the laser rifle through the hole in the blast door. He set the rifle to setting three. He aimed the rifle up, and fired.

Outside Joe, Ethel May, and Madeline came face to face with Ziggy.

Chapter 18
Fragile

Joe pushed Ethel May, and Madeline to the ground as a bolt of blue lighting shot towards them. The blue bolt stuck Ethel May slicing off her left arm just below the shoulder. Ethel May screamed as blood trickled from the partially cauterized wound.

Joe fired his Browning at Ziggy. Ziggy disappeared.

There was a huge explosion behind them.

Max dived out the hole in the rock as the mountain began to implode.

“Mission accomplished, holy fuck what happen?” Said Max noticing Ethel May.

Joe rushed to Ethel May’s side.

“She’s hurt badly Max, she’s bleeding” said Joe sobbing.

“Joe, pick up Ethel May please, Madeline grab Ethel May’s gun please, and follow me,” said Max.

Max led them over to the wagon. He jumped in the back. Joe lifted an unconscious Ethel May up, and Max gently pulled her into the wagon. Joe climbed into the back, and helped Madeline up.

Max pulled off his jacket, and ripped his left sleeve off his shirt. He wrapped the sleeve around Ethel May's wound.

"Apply pressure here Joe" he said.

Joe held the wound tightly.

"Madeline hold her head, so she doesn't get it bumped on the journey," said Max.

Madeline moved over to Ethel May's head, and gently held it.

Max climbed out the back of the wagon, and climbed up on the front.

He grabbed the rains, and swung them as hard as he could whipping the horses firmly.

"YAH, YAH, YAH" he screamed.

The horses started moving.

Max swung the rains again.

"FASTER" he yelled.

The horses started trotting. They got up to nearly twenty miles per hour as Max kept geeing them along.

Twenty-five minutes later, after pushing the horses as hard as Max could, they arrived back at the walled cabin.

Max burned the doors away with his laser rifle. He moved the wagon through the hole in the walls.

He manoeuvred the wagon around the back of the cabin. Max jumped off the wagon. He rushed over to the van, and opened the side door. He climbed into the van, and found his medical bag. He rushed back to the wagon, and jumped into the back.

"How is she?" He asked.

"I don't know" said Joe crying.

Max leaned over, and checked Ethel May pulse. Then he checked her breathing. Ethel May looked really pale.

"OK she has a weak pulse, and shallow breathing. I think she has lost a lot of blood, and there isn't anything I can do about that," said Max.

"Give her some of my blood then" sobbed Joe.

"Joe, I don't what her blood type is," said Max.

"We're both black, so we should have the same blood" said Joe desperately.

"Well, it doesn't work like that I'm afraid mate, you are of Caribbean descent, and Ethel May is African so there is a slight difference between you. What is your blood type Joe?"

"I'm O positive"

“OK that’s good mate, O goes with any blood type, but if she is rhesus negative, then your blood could kill her”

“And what happens if we do nothing?”

“OK I get your point, it’s worth a try”

Max opened up his medical bag, and reached inside. He pulled out a large syringe.

“OK Joe, I don’t have a transfusion kit, so I’m going to use the largest syringe I have, the five hundred millilitres. I will draw blood from your arm, and inject it into Ethel May. It’s very unorthodox, but it’s all I can do. I will take one litre of blood from you,” said Max.

“Take as much as you need to save her,” said Joe.

“I will not take more than one litre from you Joe, as that would compromise your health”

“I don’t care, just save her”

“I’ll do my best”

Max passed some plasters to Madeline.

“Watch” he said.

Max held up a plaster, and took the back off it. Then he stuck it on the vans floor.

"After I pull the needle out of Joe's arm you need to put a plaster over the wound, do you understand that?" He asked.

"Yes" said Madeline.

"Good, I have to transfer the blood as fast as possible before coagulation sets in," said Max.

"OK, I don't understand that, but I'll put a plaster on Joe's wound as soon as the needle comes out," said Madeline.

Max reached into his medical bag, and took out a tourniquet. He placed the tourniquet around Ethel May's right arm, near the shoulder, and tightened it.

"OK, here we go, Joe clench your left hand into a fist, and then release, keep doing that please to get the veins up" said Max.

Joe started clenching, and unclenching his fist.

"OK stop now please," said Max.

Joe stopped.

"Sharp scratch" said Max inserting the needle into Joe's vein in the fold of his arm.

Max slowly pulled the plunger up, and sucked Joe's blood into the syringe.

"Get the plaster ready please Madeline" he said.

Madeline pulled the back off the plaster, and held it ready.

“Now” said Max as he pulled the needle out.

Madeline quickly shoved the plaster onto Joe’s arm.

Max took the syringe, and inserted into Ethel May’s vein in the fold of her arm. He injected Joe’s blood into her. Once the syringe was empty. He grabbed a plaster. He let go of the syringe and left it hanging out of Ethel May’s arm. He pulled the back off, and held it ready in his left hand. He gentle removed the syringe, and shoved a plaster over the needle hole.

Max then repeated the process, and removed the tourniquet.

Max checked Ethel May pulse; it was still very weak. He checked her breathing; it was still very shallow.

“How you doing Joe?” He asked.

“I feel sick, and dizzy, but take more blood if you need it” said Joe sleepily.

“You just relax mate, Ethel May’s vitals are still low, so I’m going to give her a shot of epinephrine,” said Max.

“What’s epinephrine?” Asked Joe.

“Adrenaline” said Max reaching into his bag.

“Just save her man” said Joe very sleepily, closing his eyes.

“Is Joe gonna be, OK?” Asked Madeline.

“He’s fine, he just weak at the moment as I pulled a load of blood out of him really fast, once he eats something, and has a good rest, he’ll be fine,” said Max.

Max found a bottle of epinephrine, and a small syringe. He pushed the needle into the bottle, and sucked up the epinephrine. He removed the needle, and gentle pushed the plunger to expel the air from the syringe.

“We’ll know very quickly if this works,” said Max.

Max inserted the needle into Ethel May’s vein on her forearm. He pushed the plunger slowly, and injected the epinephrine into Ethel May.

He pulled the needle out, Madeline passed him a plaster with the back off. He took the plaster, and put it on Ethel May’s arm.

Suddenly Ethel May sat up headbutting Max.

“Ow” said Max falling back.

Ethel May gasped, and started taking deep breaths to compensate for the shallow breathing.

“What, what, what is going on” she gasped.

“Ethel May” said Joe sleepily.

“Madeline, can you run to the van please, get some water, and a bag of sugar please,” said Max.

Madeline quickly jumped out the wagon.

“Ethel May just keep taking deep breaths please, how are you feeling?” Asked Max.

“I feel great, so alive, I’ve got so much energy, I wanna run” she replied.

“That’s the epinephrine, it’s good stuff. I used it to win the one hundred metre sprint race on sports day at secondary school,” said Max.

“Is she alive?” Said Joe groggily.

“Yes, mate she is,” said Max.

“Oh, Max, I love you man, and you’re a cheat mate,” said Joe.

“Yeah, I know,” said Max smiling.

“What about me?” Said Ethel May.

“I love you as well” said Joe sounding drunk.

“Is he alright?” Asked Ethel May.

“Yeah, he lost a litre of blood, but he’ll be fine after a rest,” said Max.

Madeline climbed back into the wagon. She handed a half full one gallon bottle of water to Max.

“Thanks darling. Here Ethel May have some water” he said holding the bottle up.

Ethel May sipped some water while Max held the bottle for her.

“Joe, wakey, wakey,” said Max.

“No Max, I don’t feel well, I aint going to college today” said Joe sounding drunk.

“Madeline, can you pour some sugar into Joe’s mouth please, he needs to replace the sugar he’s lost,” said Max.

Madeline leaned over, and poured a load of sugar into Joe’s mouth.

“Erk, blah” coughed Joe.

He opened his eyes, and looked around.

“Here mate” said Max holding out the water.

Joe took a swig while Max supported the bottle.

“Oh man, I’ve got a really sweet taste in my mouth” said Joe looking confused.

“That’s cos I just kissed you,” said Max smiling.

“You didn’t, did you?” Said Joe horrified.

“Na, just winding you up,” said Max.

“I’m not feeling well, don’t wind me up” said Joe sheepishly.

“Hey Joe,” said Ethel May.

Joe looked at Ethel May.

“Oh, I’m so glad you’re alright, I love you my beautiful wife” said Joe teary eyed.

Ethel put her right hand on Joe’s shoulder.

“I love you my wonderful husband” she said smiling.

“Right, now what happened to you Ethel May?” Asked Max.

“I don’t know, we saw that grey creature” she replied.

“Yeah, it was Ziggy, he shot Ethel May in the arm with this blue light, a bit like your laser rifle but blue light instead of orange light,” said Madeline.

“I tried to shoot him, but he disappeared,” said Joe.

Max cleaned up the stump that used to be Ethel May’s left arm. The bleeding had stopped. He dressed the stump, and bandaged it up.

"Right, I'm going to pack up the van, and then I'll come back, and we'll all get in the van," said Max.

Max was driving the van away from Wyoming. He wasn't sure where to go, but he didn't want to stay around in case Ziggy was looking for them. Joe, and Ethel May were asleep in the back. Madeline was sat next to Max.

Madeline let out a huge yawn.

"Why don't you go to bed if you're tired?" Said Max.

"I am tired, but I missed you Max, so I want to be with you," said Madeline.

"OK that's fine, I love being near you"

"Max, would Ethel May have died if you did nothing?"

"Most likely, she'd lost too much blood"

"I never thought about how delicate human life is sometimes"

"Well human life may be very fragile, but humans are also tough, and resilient"

"What does resilient mean?"

"It means we have the ability to bounce back after tragedy, and keep going no matter what"

“Oh, I see. That makes sense. Being forced to be a whore for years, I thought about killing myself loads of times, but something inside me stopped me, and I kept going”

Max put his hand on Madeline shoulder.

“Never again will you be forced to do anything you don’t want to do” said Max softly.

“Ah thank you Max, I know, I feel safe with you. Where are we going by the way?”

“I’ve have no idea”

“No idea about what?” Said Joe poking his head through the hole in the partition.

“JOE, you made me jump” said Max annoyed.

“Hey Joe,” said Madeline.

Max started laughing.

“Don’t you dare start that again Maxwell,” said Joe.

“Why are you laughing Max?” Asked Madeline.

“There’s a song in the future called Hey Joe, by Jimmy Hendricks,” said Joe.

“Hey Joe, where you going with that gun in your hand” sang Max.

"Stop it, you used to do this to me every time you got stoned" said Joe annoyed.

"Hey Joe, are you going to shoot your old lady down" sang Max.

"Stop it, cos you always get the words wrong as well, just stop it"

"Is there a reason you are awake Joe?"

"I just couldn't sleep"

"Fair enough, would you like to drive, I'm knackered?"

"I still feel very weak"

"And how is Ethel May?"

"She's asleep"

"Is she still alive?"

"I think so"

"Well can you check please; she is my patient after all"

Joe leant over the bed, and checked Ethel May's pulse. Ethel May let out a small moan as Joe touched her neck.

"She's breathing, and she has a pulse" said Joe looking back through the hole in the partition.

“That’s a good sign then,” said Max.

“You are a wonderful doctor Max,” said Madeline.

“I’m not actually a doctor, but I am probably more qualified than most doctors,” said Max.

“What do you base that on Max?” Asked Joe.

“I have been watching Casualty since it started” said Max seriously.

Joe laughed.

“So, if you want to be doctor, don’t worry about spending years training, just watch Casualty? Is that what you’re saying?” He spoke.

“What is Casualty?” Asked Madeline.

“It’s a TV show in the future, remember I told you about TV, and moving pictures?” Said Max.

“Oh yeah, I can’t wait to see a TV, sounds magical” said Madeline excitedly.

“Depends if there is anything on,” said Joe.

“Any way with my experience, I should have at least eight PHD’s,” said Max.

“What in?” Said Joe.

“Well physics obviously, and chemistry”

“That’s two, and chemistry is a bit debatable”

“Quantum physics, quantum mechanics, and metaphysics”

“OK that’s five, what about the other three?”

“I should get the other three for being a damn good scientist”

“I wish I could live in your world sometimes Max”

“Thank you, Joe, I’ll take that as a compliment”

Max parked the van close to a river that he’d been following for a few hours. It was getting dark now, and Max was getting tired.

“Right think it must be dinner time,” said Max.

Madeline yawned.

“Where are we?” She asked sleepily.

“I have no idea, but I can’t drive any longer. I need some food, and a break,” said Max.

Max, and Madeline got out the van. Max opened the side door.

“Joe, you alright mate?” Said Max.

“Yeah, just a bit a tired mate” replied Joe.

“How’s Ethel May?”

“I’m awake now, and I feel OK, thank you for saving my life Max” said Ethel May sleepily.

“You’re welcome, Ethel May, thank Joe, it was his blood that saved you. Right, we’re going to camp here tonight, so Madeline, and I will get a fire going, then we’ll have some food,” said Max.

“Alright nice one mate,” said Joe.

Max shut the side door.

Madeline, and Max collected up some wood from the ground, and snapped a few branches off a small tree by the river.

Max got the dry fallen twigs alight, and then piled the fresh wood up onto the fire. Soon they had a roaring fire.

Max opened the side door of the van.

“Got the fire going, come, and get some fresh air” he said.

“Joe, I’m sorry to ask, but can you help you go to the toilet?” Asked Ethel May.

“Of course, I can help you with anything you need,” said Joe.

“I’ll start cooking,” said Max.

Max gathered up the cooking stuff, and some tins. He took the stuff to the fire.

“What are we having for dinner?” Asked Madeline.

Max looked at the cans.

“We’ve got baked beans, and beef and onion soup” he said.

“Oh, that sounds nice” said Madeline excitedly.

Max cut the tops off the cans with a can opener he’d found in the house by Fort Laramie. He filled one pot with beans, and the other with beef and onion soup. He then held them over the fire.

Joe came out holding Ethel May who was crying. They sat by the fire.

“What wrong Ethel May?” Asked Madeline concerned.

“She just started crying after I help her use the toilet, she won’t say what’s wrong” said Joe worried.

“It’s just delayed shock, and the realisation that she has lost a limb, perfectly natural” said Max calmly.

Max started shaking the pots gently as the beans, and soup started bubbling. He then poured some soup into each tin bowl, and they poured some beans in.

“Voila, dinner is served, beef, onion, and beans soup,” said Max.

“I’m sorry, I’m upset because I don’t want Joe to help with everything” sobbed Ethel May.

“Don’t worry Ethel May, in the future they can build new arms, prosthetic limbs, and we’ll get you a robotic one that links up with the neural pathways in your brain,” said Max.

“Wow, really? So, I can have a working arm again?” Said Ethel May excitedly.

“Are you sure Max, I know we have prosthetic limbs, but I didn’t know you could get a robotic one that links to your brain,” said Joe.

“Well damn it, if those robotic arms aren’t available yet then I will build one myself,” said Max.

“That’s the thing I love most about you Max, you always want help in any way you can” said Joe smiling.

“Thank you, Joe, I’m so glad to have you as my best friend, I could not ask for anyone better”

Madeline started crying.

“What’s wrong Madeline?” Asked Max worried.

“Nothing, what you two just said was so sweet” said Madeline smiling with tears rolling down her cheeks.

“I feel better now,” said Ethel May.

“Come on let’s eat before it gets cold,” said Max.

Max passed a bowl, and spoon to Madeline, and Joe placed a bowl in front of Ethel May, and passed her a spoon. Soon they were all eating.

“By the way, Madeline, and Ethel May, have you heard of Wyatt Earp?” Asked Max.

“I aint never heard of him,” said Ethel May.

“Me neither,” said Madeline.

“Really?” Said Joe surprised “but he’s the most famous lawman in the west”

“I guess he hasn’t got famous yet,” said Max.

“Why, what year was the gunfight at the OK corral?” Asked Joe.

“Joe, as you know all too well, I am a scientist, not a historian, so ask me science questions rather than history questions please,” said Max.

“OK, have you got any ideas how to get us home?”

“Yes Joe, lightning, I have been thinking about lightning, and I have worked out how to create it”

The next morning Joe woke up next to Ethel May. Ethel May was still asleep. Joe climbed out of bed, and noticed Madeline was still asleep, but Max wasn't with her. Joe popped to the toilet, then he quietly opened the side door, and climbed out of the van.

Max was sat outside by a roaring fire. There was an M16 assault rifle, and a Skorpion sub-machine on the ground next to him. He was holding part of the laser rifle in his hand fiddling with it.

"Hi Max," said Joe.

"Hi Joe" said Max without looking up.

"What you doing?"

"I'm turning the laser rifle into a lightning generator"

"And what's with all the guns on the ground?"

"Protection my friend"

Max started putting the laser rifle back together. Once it was back together, he stood up holding it.

Max looked at Joe.

"You look better mate, now this should produce a forty-gigawatt positive bolt of lightning, of course I've got no way to measure the power output, so we'll just have to measure by eye," said Max.

“This should be interesting,” said Joe.

Max aimed the laser rifle that was now a lightning generator at a small tree by the river. He pulled the trigger. The gun made a huge cracking sound as a huge yellow spark shot out of it, and struck the tree. The tree spilt in half, and caught fire.

Max, and Joe stared open mouthed at the split burning tree.

“That looked like quite a powerful bolt of lightning, didn’t it?” Said Max.

“It sure did” said Joe surprised.

After morning coffee, Max started setting up his experiment. Madeline, Ethel May, and Joe sat, and watched him.

Max piled small rocks together to make a small rocky platform. He placed the spare power supply on top of the rocky platform. He had reactivated the power supply earlier. He stuck some twigs in the ground all around the rocky platform.

Max walked back to the group. He picked up the lightning generator, and looked at Madeline, Ethel May, and Joe.

“Watch this” he said smiling.

Max aimed the lightning generator at the spare power supply, and pulled the trigger.

Madeline, and Ethel May jumped hearing the loud cracking sound.

Max held the trigger down, and lightning streamed from the gun. There was a huge bright flash from where the spare power supply was sat.

Max let go of the trigger, and saw that the power supply, rocky platform, and twigs in the ground had disappeared.

“IT WORKED” he screamed.

“Max that gun is on fire,” said Joe.

“What”

Max looked at the lightning generator, smoke was pouring out of the end. Max put the gun down.

“It’s OK, it just overheated, but it worked, we can go back to future now” said Max excitedly.

“How do you know it worked?” Asked Joe.

“Because it disappeared. If it had gone back in time, it would still be there, but it would look older. As it disappeared it means it must have gone forward in time,” said Max.

Chapter 19
The Pinkerton Detective Agency

“Oh fuck” said Max looking inside the laser rifle.

“What’s up?” Asked Joe.

They sat by the fire outside the van.

“The coil is fucked, and all the wiring is burnt out,” said Max.

“Can you fix it,” said Joe.

“Yes, but I need copper”

“Where can we get copper from?”

“Copper is one of the most common metals in history, if we go to a mining town, we can probably get some”

“A mining town, like Denver?” Asked Ethel May.

“I suppose so. I just wish I knew where Denver is” replied Max.

“Colorado is probably south of us,” said Ethel May.

“Oh of course, you study maps, how do we get to Colorado from Wyoming?” Said Joe.

“I’m not certain, the maps I studied didn’t even have Wyoming on them,” said Ethel May.

“Didn’t we travel north to get Wyoming?” Said Madeline.

“We could check our map, but I’m not sure where we are now” said Max.

Everyone was in the van. Max was driving, and Madeline was sat next to him. Joe, and Ethel May were sat in the back. Max was just about to fire up the engine when he spotted a man on a horse riding towards them.

“Shit” said Max.

“What?” Asked Madeline.

“There’s someone coming towards us,” said Max.

“Where?” Said Joe looking through the hole in the partition.

“At three o’clock,” said Max.

“Oh yeah. It’s only one man though,” said Joe.

“What’s the time got to do with where the man is?” Asked Madeline.

“Imagine we are a clock, twelve o’clock is straight ahead, and slightly to the right is one o’clock, and a bit more to the right is three o’clock where the man is coming from, he’s more one o’clock now,” said Max.

“What are we going to do?” Asked Joe.

“Stay here, I’ll talk to him, he made need help,” said Max.

Max climbed out of the van.

The man was close now. Max could see he was short, and skinny. He had short brown hair, and was clean shaven. He had blue eyes, and looked like he was in his thirties. He wore blue jeans, leather boots, a blue shirt, leather waistcoat, and a black Stetson hat. He had two holstered six shooters on his belt.

“Howdy friend” the man said as he approached Max.

“Hi buddy,” said Max.

The man stopped a few feet away, and got off his horse.

“That’s a strange looking contraption you have there friend,” said the man.

“It’s a horseless carriage, it uses a steam engine to power it,” said Max.

“You sound like an English man”

“Yes, I am thanks, I’m Max”

“I’m William”

“Nice to meet you William”

“Likewise Max”

“Do you need any help, William?”

“No thank you, I’m heading to Fort Laramie to see my uncle, I just spotted you, and thought I’d say hello”

“Oh, that’s nice, do you happen to know the way to Denver?”

“Ha, funny enough my brother lives in Denver”

“Oh, good that where’s we want to go”

“Well, you are in Nebraska at the moment not far from the border with Wyoming. You need to travel about one hundred, and twenty miles southwest”

“That’s great, thank you William”

“My pleasure Max, you have a good day now sir”

“Thanks William, you have a good day too”

It took two days to reach Denver. It was early evening when they arrived. Max parked the van in a quiet spot behind some stables. Joe, and Max covered the van with bushes, and tree branches.

The group made their way to the Silver saloon. The town was really quiet.

They walked into the Silver saloon.

It was empty.

“What the fuck is going on?” Said Max pulling out a Skorpion sub-machine gun.

“Why did you bring that?” Said Joe.

“Because my laser rifle is broken, so I wanted something with more oomph than a handgun,” said Max.

“What shall we do?” Asked Joe.

“Everyone get your guns ready, and let’s get out of here, I have a really bad feeling about this,” said Max.

Joe pulled his Browning out of his shoulder holster, and the ladies got their guns out of their bags.

“OK, let’s move,” said Max.

“YOU ARE SURROUNDED BY PINKERTON AGENTS, COME OUT WITH YOUR HANDS UP” William yelled.

Max peered out the window. He could see William who he’d met two days ago. He was dressed in a black suit, and bowler hat. He had five other guys with him dressed the same. They all carried rifles.

“Motherfucker, that guy I talked to a couple of days ago is a Pinkerton man” said Max annoyed.

“Are we gonna have to fight our way out of this?” Asked Joe.

“Well, we can’t exactly surrender. Right Joe, and Ethel May go, and check the back, and see if we are surrounded. Madeline, you watch the front with me, we’ll let them make the first move, and see what they’ve got,” said Max.

Joe, and Ethel May scurried away to the back. Max, and Madeline peered out the windows.

“WE’LL GIVE YOU ONE MINUTE TO SURRENDER, THEN WE’LL COME IN, AND GET YOU” yelled William.

“Barricade” said Max.

“What?” Said Madeline.

“Help me arrange the tables, so we have cover,” said Max.

Max rushed over, and started laying tables down. Madeline helped. They arranged the tables in a circular formation, so they had cover on all sides. They laid one table on top of another to make the cover higher.

Joe, and Ethel May came back.

“There’s five guys out the back with rifles,” said Joe.

“Right, get inside the barricade, and duck down,” said Max.

They took up position within the barricade. Joe, and Ethel May watched the back, and Max, and Madeline watched the front.

“TIMES UP” yelled William.

They heard the window smashing.

Max looked over the table barricade, and saw a stick of dynamite with a burning fuse.

“Fuck” he said, and dived over the barricade.

He grabbed the dynamite, and ripped the fuse out.

“That was fucking dirty” he said angrily.

Max walked over to the broken window, and held up the Skorpion. He unloaded the clip at the Pinkerton men. The sound of automatic gunfire echoed around the saloon as thirty bullets were released in six seconds. Three of the Pinkerton men were hit. William, and two other men dived for cover.

“WE HAVE SUPERIOR WEAPONS, SO DROP YOUR GUNS, AND REACH FOR THE SKY” yelled Max.

Bullets started breaking through the wooden walls of the saloon.

Max rushed over to the barricade, and dived back over.

“OK we just have seven men left to deal with” said Max reloading the Skorpion.

“How many clips have you got for that?” Asked Joe.

"Just this one in the gun, I only brought one spare clip, I wasn't expecting a battle. I have got four spare clips for my Berettas, so we'll be fine, stay alert everyone, let's see what they do now"

Another lit stick of dynamite was thrown in.

"Fucking piss takers" said Max diving other the barricade again.

Max picked up the dynamite, and held it, watching the fuse burn down.

"Max, fucking chuck it" yelled Joe.

"Just watch the back mate," said Max.

Max strolled over to the window, and peered out. He could see three rifles poking over the top of some barrels, and hats behind them. Max threw the dynamite up in the air in the direction of the barrels.

Max rushed over, and dived over the barricade. They heard a huge explosion outside which shook the ground. The sound of windows smashing, and men screaming could be heard.

"Quick everyone out the front, and back to the van, I'll take point, Joe you take rear guard," said Max.

Everyone got up. Max kicked the tables aside. They rushed over to the front entrance. Max stepped outside, and looked over to the barrels. The barrels were in bits, and two men lay on the ground.

Max started walking out of town. Joe watched the rear.

BANG

"ARRRGH FUCK" screamed Joe as a bullet hit him in the hand making him drop his gun.

Max spun around, and saw William aiming a rifle at them.

BANG

A bullet slammed into Joe's chest bouncing off his kevlar vest.

Max raised the Skorpion, and unloaded it towards William.

William fell to the ground as seventeen bullets ripped his chest apart. He lay on the floor chocking as blood filled his mouth.

He struggled to breathe for a few seconds before dying.

BANG

Madeline screamed as a bullet went through her shoulder.

Max spun round, and saw blood dripping from Madeline's right arm. She dropped her gun. He noticed men with rifles hiding behind some barrels at the edge of the town.

Max dropped the Skorpion, and pulled out his two Berettas, he pulled back the hammers, and walked towards the barrels.

“YOU SHOT MY WIFE; YOU WILL FUCKING PAY FOR THAT” screamed Max.

Max unloaded both Berettas at the same time. The barrels shattered as the forty-five calibre bullets slammed into them. Three men lay on the ground behind the barrels bleeding. Two other men ran round the back of the hardware store where the barrels had been outside.

Max ejected the clips in his Berettas, and crouched down to reload them. He got up, and marched towards the hardware store. He made his way around the back.

BANG, BANG

Two bullets slammed into his chest, and bounced off his kevlar vest. Max fire one of his Berettas, and got one of the Pinkerton agents in the head. The other man started running off. Max fired at him, and hit him in the leg. The man fell onto the dusty ground.

Max walked over to the man on the floor, who was lying face down.

“Turn around, and look at me” Max said menacingly.

The man turned around. He looked like he was in his twenties, with short brown hair, and a clean-shaven face.

"Please, I'm sorry, I have a wife, and two children" sobbed the man.

"Should have thought about them before you shot my fucking wife" said Max angrily.

Max aimed his Beretta, and put a bullets through the man's head. Max watched as blood poured from the man's head onto the dusty ground pooling around where he laid.

The blood looked black in the pale moonlight.

Max marched back around the front of the hardware store.

Max stopped when he got round the front, and looked around. Madeline, Ethel May, and Joe were nowhere to be seen.

"What the fuck?" Said Max looking around.

He heard the wooden sidewalk creak on his right. Max spun round with his pistols raised.

"Don't shoot please," said a woman.

Max looked at her. She had long blonde hair, and looked around thirty. She was wearing a red frilly dress, and was quite tall.

"Did you see some people here, a black man, a black woman, and a white girl?" Asked Max.

“Yes, I saw them, they got rounded up by a group of men in suits, they had the marshal with them, and all his deputies. There was about twenty of them overall. A tall man stepped forward, and told them he was Alan Pinkerton the head of the of the Pinkerton Detective Agency,” said the women.

“Where did they take them?”

“To the marshal’s office”

“Oh fuck. Well thank you for the information, madam”

Max turned, and began walking away.

“What you gonna do mister?” Asked the women.

Max turned to face her.

“I’m gonna rescue my wife, and friends” he said.

“But there’s twenty men guarding them” she said confused.

“Well, I guess twenty men are going to find out what happens when you make Max Walsh angry”

Max turned, and walked away.

Ten minutes later Max arrived back at the van. He opened the side door, and climbed in. Time for a bit of shock, and awe he thought. Max opened the bag up with the weapons in. He grabbed the RPG launcher, and picked up a grenade. There were only two rocket grenades left. Max loaded a rocket grenade into the launcher. He put the RPG down. He grabbed the M16, and picked up a clip which he shoved into the M16. There were three spare clips left for the M16. Max picked up two, and put one in each one of his outside jacket pockets. He slung the M16 over his shoulder, and grabbed the RPG.

Max climbed out of the van, and shut the side door. He opened the driver's door, and climbed inside. He placed the RPG on the passenger seats, then put the M16 down with it. He had two spare clips for his Berettas in his jacket, as well as the two M16 magazines.

Max fired up the engine. He put the headlights on. Max drove the van out of the brush it was in, and headed for the town.

Max drove slowly through the town. He stopped about five hundred feet away from the marshal's office. The marshal's office was a single storey wooden building, with one corner made from adobe bricks where the cells were.

Max surveyed the office. There were three men outside with rifles, and two men on the roof with rifles.

Max put the van into first gear, and held the clutch down. He revved the engine hard, and released the clutch. The front wheels spun, and kicked up dust. The van surged forward. Max slammed the brakes on, stopping about two hundred feet from the marshal's office. The men started firing their rifles at the van. The bullets pinged off the armoured windscreen. Max clicked the full beam headlights on blinding the men on the ground. As the man were shielding their eyes, Max jumped out the van with the RPG.

Max ducked down behind the van as the men on the roof fired at him. Max put the RPG on his shoulder, and placed his hand by the launch button.

Max jumped up, and pressed the launch button. The rocket blasted out of the launcher, and screamed towards the roof of the marshal's office.

A huge explosion shook the whole building. The two men on the roof fell along with lead tiling, and bits of wood. The two bodies, and the front of the roof crashed down crushing the men on the ground.

Max surveyed the scene. There was a twisted pile of bodies, lead tiling, and burning wood on the ground in front of the marshal's office, and what was left of the roof was on fire. The adobe brick work part of the office had a huge crack in it.

Max put the launcher back in the van, and grabbed the M16. He pulled the bolt back locking the weapon ready for use. Max shut the driver's door, and locked the van.

Max slowly walked towards the marshal's office. He climbed over the smouldering mess at the front. He kicked the door in, and stepped inside.

BANG

One of the deputy marshals fired a rifle at him which grazed the side of his head. Max unloaded the M16 singing it from side to side.

The deputy was cut down, and bits of wood flew around the room as the seventy calibre bullets tore up the marshal's office.

Once the rifle was empty Max quickly ejected the clip, and slammed another in. He cocked the gun, and looked around.

There were two dead deputies laying on the floor, and in the corner marshal Daniels lay bleeding from his stomach.

Max walked over to the marshal.

"Howdy marshal" he said calmly.

"Where did you get that gun from?" The marshal asked gasping.

"London. Where is my wife, and my friends?"

"They're gone I'm afraid. Mr Pinkerton took them away in a stagecoach. He said they were going to Chicago to face trial for murders"

"When did they leave?"

"Bout ten minutes ago"

"And they are travelling to Chicago in a stagecoach?"

"No by train, but the train doesn't leave till nine tomorrow morning, Pinkerton said he was gonna take them to another town with a railway station"

“Which one?”

“I don’t know”

“Where is the nearest town with a railway station?”

“Franks town, ten-hour ride south along the railway line”

“Thanks marshal”

Max crouched down, and put his M16 on the ground. He took off his jacket, and removed his shoulder holsters. He took off his shirt which had one sleeve missing. He wrapped his shirt around the marshal’s stomach, and back where the bullets had exited. He removed the marshal’s belt, and put that round his stomach, and back. He pulled the belt tight.

“OOOWW” the marshal screamed in pain.

Max fasted the belt.

“That should stop the bleeding enough until help arrives,” said Max.

“Why don’t you just kill me boy?” Said the marshal looking at Max.

Max smiled.

“Because I’m not a bad guy, I only kill to protect myself, or to protect others” said Max.

Joe pulled at his iron shackles trying to break them as they bounced along in the stagecoach. His hand was bandaged with cloths. Madeline shoulder was also bandaged with cloths.

“Stop trying to break ya shackles” said the Pinkerton agent who was sat in the stagecoach with them.

The Pinkerton agent was tall, and slim. He had short blonde hair, and was clean shaven. He had green eyes, and was thirty five years old.

“You aint gonna escape from us. You are all going to Chicago to stand trial, and you will all be sentences to death for your crimes” said the Pinkerton agent.

“You aint caught our leader though, Mad Max, he is dangerous, and he will be after us” said Joe smiling.

“Well, we got a big head start on Mad Max, and we got five men with Winchesters riding along with us, and the guard at the front of the stagecoach has a shotgun, and a Spencer rifle, so what is Mad Max going do if he catches us?” Said the Pinkerton agent.

“He will kill all you for taking us. I’m Mad Max’s wife, and he will be furious that you have taken me, and his best friends” said Madeline defiantly.

“Oh, I’m mighty scared lady” said the Pinkerton agent.

"You will be when Mad Max makes his move," said Joe.

Max was speeding along in the van, well as fast as he could on the bumpy ground. He was following the railways track south. The ground by the railway was quite flat where the construction work had been done. He was managing to drive at around fifty to sixty miles an hour.

Max started thinking. So, Maxie what are you going to, and what will you do when you catch up to the stagecoach? Good question, well I'll have to run the stagecoach off the road, and deal with the men guarding Madeline, Joe, and Ethel May. Oh, I guess I'll think of something when I catch them.

Max powered along kicking up dust with the headlights on full beam listening to Van Halen.

It wasn't long before Max caught sight of the stagecoach, and five men on horses. Now Max needed to take some action. He didn't want to hurt the horses, but he decided that saving his friends was more important that the well-being of horses.

Max got close to the stagecoach. The men on horses started firing their rifles at the van. The bullets pinged off the van's armoured exterior. Max drew level with the horses. The guard on the stagecoach fired his shotgun at the van. The pellets bounced off. The guard then fired seven shots at the van with his Spencer rifle.

Max picked up his M16 which was locked, and loaded. Max raised the rifle, and pointed it towards the passenger window where the horses were. Four horses pulled the stagecoach.

Max pressed the passenger window button, and the window slid down. The sound of air rushing into the van drowned out Van Halen. Max pulled the trigger, and unloaded on the horses.

The four horses fell to the ground sending a huge cloud of dust up into the air as they fell, and slid along the ground. The stagecoach tipped forward sending the driver, and guard flying forward. They both hit the ground hard face first. They both broke their necks, the guard died, and the driver lay on the ground paralysed.

Inside the stagecoach Joe, Madeline, and Ethel were thrown forward. Joe's head slammed into the Pinkerton agents face. His head contacted just above the Pinkerton agents' nose, Joe hurt his head in the impact, and the Pinkerton agent was knocked unconscious.

Gravity brought the stagecoach back down to Earth with a huge bang. Dust flew up into the air, and the back wheels snapped in half dropping the coach down, so it was laying lopsided on its backside.

Max slammed the brakes on, and the van skidded to halt sending up more dust. Max quickly reloaded the M16, he jumped out the van, and pulled the bolt back on the M16 as he jumped out.

Max ran round the front of the van with the M16 raised. The men on horses came charging towards him. Max unloaded the M16 at them.

All five men were hit Severeal times by seventy calibre bullets. Three men fell from their horses, and the other slumped on their horses.

Max opened the passenger side door of the van, and threw the M16 on the seat. He drew his two Berettas, and made his way over to the stagecoach. Max pulled open the door.

“Max” said Madeline excitedly as he popped his head into the stagecoach.

“Is everyone alright?” Asked Max.

“Well, it would have been nice to have a warning about the emergency stop” said Joe smiling.

Max climbed into the stagecoach, and grabbed the keys from the unconscious Pinkerton agents belt. Max quickly unlocked the shackles on Joe, Madeline, and Ethel May.

“Where are your guns?” Max said.

“No idea, they took them off us,” said Joe.

“Is this Alan Pinkerton?” Said Max looking at the unconscious man.

“No, he didn’t come with us,” said Joe.

“OK, come out now,” said Max.

Max jumped out of the stagecoach. He helped the others to alight the stagecoach. Max climbed up on the roof, and found an iron lock box. He tried to open it, but it was locked. Max climbed back down.

Max handed a one of his Berettas to Joe.

“Keep a look out mate, I’ll see if I can find the key” he said.

Max strolled over to where the dead guard, and the paralysed driver lay. He checked the guard, and found some keys on his belt which he grabbed.

“ARR” moaned the driver in pain.

Max walked over to him.

“I’ll put you out your misery mate” he said.

Max held his pistol over the man’s head, and fired. Blood splattered onto Max’s hand.

“Ew, for fucks sake” he said annoyed.

Max crouched down, and grabbed the driver’s jacket, he used it to wipe his hand.

Max strolled over to the stagecoach, and climbed up onto the roof. He tried a few keys before finding the right one. He opened the lock box, and looked inside. There were three pistols, and a Skorpion sub-machine gun. There were also some silver coins.

“Here” said Max looking over the side of the stagecoach.

He passed the guns down to Joe, and pocketed the silver coins.

Chapter 20
Problems

Everyone was in the van. Joe, and Ethel were in bed together, and Madeline was in the top bunk on her own. Max was driving away from the scene. They were now around ten miles away from the stagecoach where seven dead men, and four dead horses lay. Max was heading north following the railway track back to Denver.

Max stopped the van, and jumped out, he shut the door, and went to back of the van. He opened the side door, and climbed inside, shutting the door behind him.

“How is everyone?” He asked.

“Tired” replied Madeline sleepily.

“Yeah, we’re tired too” said Joe half asleep.

“OK well I need to let you know about a problem we have,” said Max.

Joe sat up.

“What’s up mate?” He asked anxiously.

“Well, we have a quarter of a tank of diesel left, and the diesel is being used faster because of the extra three tons of weight on the roof with the water tank, and the rough terrain we have to drive over,” said Max.

“Shit, what are we gonna do?” Said Joe.

“Well, there isn’t much we can do about the diesel situation, there won’t be any diesel pumps round here for about forty, or fifty years”

“Can you make the diesel stuff?” Asked Madeline.

“Yeah, mister chemistry master, do you know how to make diesel?” Said Joe.

“Of course, I know how to make diesel. You take crude oil, and boil it to separate the gasses from the liquid, the liquid element is then distilled to create diesel, and distilled a few more time to make petrol. It is actually cheaper to make diesel then petrol, so the fact diesel costs more to buy is criminal, but that is the least of our worries. To make our own oil refinery would take lots of time, effectively it would take us six months to a year to fill the tank up. But the main problem with that is we have no protective clothing, and gas masks, crude oil contain hydrocarbons with are highly corrosive, and toxic to humans,” said Max.

“So, the diesel problem is not something you can solve then?” Said Joe.

“No, but with some copper I can get us home, to that end I suggest we go back to Denver to get some copper”

“Are you crazy?”

"That has been suggested to me a few times, by yourself Joe, but there is no other option, we need copper, and we know where Denver is, it is not too far away, so it is the only logical solution"

"And do you not think we would be recognised in Denver?"

"Of course, I do, that's why I have devised a cunning plan"

"OK Baldric, what is your cunning plan?"

"I will cut my hair, and shave my beard off, and walk into Denver alone to collect the copper, no one will recognise me"

"That's actually a very good plan"

"Well don't sound so surprised, I do come up with good plans regularly, I did rescue you all didn't I"

Max, Madeline, Ethel May, and Joe sat by a roaring campfire that Max had started.

"Let me see your hand please Joe," said Max.

Joe unwrapped the bandage, and held his hand out. Max studied it.

"Turn your hand over mate" he said.

Joe did as Max asked.

“OK it’s still oozing blood, and it is showing signs of infection, sorry Joe, only one thing for it”

Max grabbed a frying pan which had been sitting in the fire for a few minutes. He grabbed Joe’s hand, and pressed the frying pan against the wound. It made a hissing sound as it burnt the skin.

“AAARH FUCK” screamed Joe.

Max flipped his hand over, and cauterized the back of his hand.

Max put the frying pan back into the fire. He started unwrapping the bandages on Madeline shoulder.

“Oh no, please Max, don’t burn me” said Madeline nervously.

Max studies Madeline’s wound.

“Right at least the bullet went straight through. Madeline, you know I wouldn’t hurt you unless it was absolutely necessary”

Madeline let out a blood curdling scream as Max cauterized her wound with the hot frying pan.

Max placed the frying pan back into the fire.

Max took some fresh bandages from a packet on the ground. He dressed Madeline’s wound, then he dressed Joe’s wound.

Then Max grabbed a headless rattlesnake from the ground, which he’d caught earlier, and began to skin it with a knife.

“Fried rattlesnake for dinner tonight” he said smiling.

Ethel May smiled back, and Joe, and Madeline gave him dirty looks.

Denver was full of Union soldiers, and federal marshals. Max entered the town clean shaven, with short hair. He walked into the hardware store at the edge of town.

He approached the counter where a young man was stood. He was tall, and skinny with long blonde hair, a huge moustache, and bright blue eyes.

“Howdy fellow, can I help ya?” He asked.

“Sure, can buddy, have you got any copper?” Asked Max putting on an American accent.

“You just looking for raw copper then?”

“I certainly am sir”

“Well, if you want any raw materials from the mines then you need to go to the clearing house down the street”

“OK thank you sir, much obliged”

Max left the store, and wandered along the wooden sidewalk.

As he walked past a boarded up store the door flew open, and someone grabbed him, and pulled him inside. The door shut behind him.

Max was stood inside a bare room with light coming in through cracks in the boarded-up windows.

“Hello Max” said Ziggy stood in front of him.

Max reached for his Berettas.

“No need for that Max, I’m not here to fight,” said Ziggy.

Max pulled his Berettas out, and held them down by his sides.

“Hello Ziggy, what do you want?”

“I want to give you these” said Ziggy holding out his hands.

Max studied Ziggy’s hands. He saw that Ziggy was holding a copper coil in each hand.

“I don’t understand” said Max confused.

“It’s simply Max I like you, you’re one of the bravest humans I have met”

“So, you want to help me get home?”

“Put the guns away, and take the coils, I give you my word no harm will come to you”

Max found himself holstering his guns, even though he didn’t really trust Ziggy. He reached out, and took the coils from Ziggy.

“Here take this as well” said Ziggy holding up a small plastic bag.

“What’s that?”

“It’s some wiring, and a printed circuit board”

Max put the coils in his pocket, and took the bag from Ziggy.

“Why are you helping me, really?”

“Because your actions have altered the timeline. Because of all the people you killed, Franklin Roosevelt, and Dwight Eisenhower will not be born now, that will greatly change the outcome of World War two”

“People will take their places; the world will be fine” said Max in a blasé tone.

“Oh Max, so young, so naive. I want you to get home, so you can see how much the world has changed”

Ziggy disappeared.

“Shit, that may be a real problem” muttered Max.

Max got back to the van. Joe was sat on the foot well at the back of the van panting.

“I take it you finished filling the water tank up?” Said Max.

“Why do you think I’m so knackered, it took thirty trips to the well, and I can only use one hand presently,” said Joe.

“Right, well I’ve got the stuff to fix the lightning generator, so I will do that now”

“Then we can go home?”

“Yes, we just need to head back to our shack near Sherman”

“What! Are you serious?”

“Erm, yeah”

“Why do we need to go back to Sherman?”

“Simple we need to be somewhere we know; we wouldn’t want end up in a wall, or inside a person”

“Oh man, have we got enough fuel?”

“I hope so”

“How long will it take you to fix the lightning generator?”

“About twenty minutes”

“Wow that’s quick”

“Yeah, I bumped into Ziggy in town, and he gave me all the parts I need”

“What”! Said Joe shocked.

“Yeah, he was happy to help, said I may have messed up the timeline a tiny bit. Franklin Roosevelt, and Dwight Eisenhower won’t be born now, so World War two may be a tiny bit different”

“Well, that’s a problem, what if Hitler wins World War two?”

“It won’t come to that, I haven’t stopped Churchill being born have I, everything will be fine”

That evening Max started driving southeast. Madeline sat next to him. Joe, and Ethel May sat in the back. Max drove slowly to save fuel.

“How long do you think this journey will take?” Asked Madeline.

“I have no idea, at least a week I think, I can’t go too fast as it will use all the diesel up” replied Max.

“So, once we get back to Sherman, we can go to the future?”

“Yes, that’s right”

An alarm went off in the van. Max looked at the dashboard. The engine was overheating. The temperature gauge said one hundred, and twenty degrees Celsius. Max stopped the van, and pulled the bonnet release.

“Shit” he said.

“What’s wrong?” Asked Madeline.

“There’s a problem with the engine,” said Max.

“Why have we stopped?” Asked Joe poking his head through the hole in the partition.

“Engines overheated,” said Max.

Max jumped out the van, and walked around to the front. He lifted the bonnet up. He pulled his phone out, and turned the torch on. He looked at the engine with the torch light. The fan belt had snapped.

Max walked around, and climbed back into the van.

“I need a stocking please” he said.

“Why have you decided to take up cross dressing” said Joe sniggering.

“Very funny Joe, the fan belt has snapped, and a silk stocking will strong enough to replace it,” said Max.

“Here” said Ethel May passing a silk stocking through.

“Thanks” said Max taking the stocking.

“Is that a clean one?” Asked Joe.

“Yes, I haven’t worn that one yet” replied Ethel May.

“Sorry Max you’re out of luck no sniffing it” said Joe smiling.

“Thanks Joe, just what I need when I’m stressed, crude remarks from you,” said Max.

Max jumped out of the van. He walked around the front, and began tying the stocking around the fan mechanism. He could feel the heat radiating off the engine. Max closed the bonnet, and got back in the van. He fired up the engine. The gauge was reading one hundred degrees Celsius now. He began driving slowly. The engine temperature started reducing.

“Joe, can you roll a joint?” Asked Max.

“No sorry mate, my hand hurts too much,” said Joe.

“Damn I’m stressed,” said Max.

“Why don’t we stop somewhere, you need to sleep,” said Madeline.

“Yeah Max, when did you last sleep?” Asked Joe.

“The night before last,” said Max.

"Pull over man, we can have you falling asleep at the wheel," said Joe.

Max parked the van by a small group of trees.

Soon they were all in bed. Joe, and Ethel May in the bottom bunk, and Max, and Madeline in the top bunk. They all fell asleep very quickly.

The next morning a train clattered past, close to where the van was parked. The small group of trees shielded the van from the trains view.

Max, and Joe sat on some rocks they had found near to the van smoking a joint together. Madeline was helping Ethel May to shower.

"Oh man, I feel so much better now, I'm not worried at all," said Max.

"Even though we're low on fuel?" Said Joe.

"Don't care mate, we'll be fine, only got one clip left for the M16 as well, and one rocket grenade for the RPG launcher"

"What happens if we run in to trouble?"

"Joseph, we aint gonna have any more trouble mate. We've defeated the Union army twice, we've defeated the Texas Rangers, and the Pinkerton Detective agency, and every lawman that tried to get us. Also lucky for us Wyatt Earp doesn't appear to be around yet"

"I suppose mate, what if they all got together, and tried to get us?"

"No problem, mate, I would show them what a positive four-billion-volts bolt of lightning looks like"

Joe started laughing, which set Max off.

Madeline, and Ethel May climbed out the van wearing white dresses.

"Are we getting married again?" Asked Max sniggering.

Max, and Joe started laughing again.

"You're like a pair of children you two" said Madeline annoyed.

"Don't worry Max rolled one for you two" said Joe holding out a joint.

Madeline took it, and sat down on some rocks that Joe, and Max had placed down for them. Ethel May sat next to her.

Max got up, and climbed into the van. He came back out carrying the AK47, and a Skorpion sub-machine gun.

He placed the Skorpion down by Joe.

“It’s locked, and loaded ready to fire mate, guard the women while I’m gone,” said Max.

Max started wandering off.

“Where are you going?” Asked Joe.

“To find something decent to eat” replied Max.

Max walked towards the horizon in a straight line. As long as he kept walking in a straight line, he would be able to find his way back. The sun was hovering in the east indicating it was still early morning.

After he’d been walking for half an hour Max began to climb a small hill. Once he got to the top he froze in horror.

Below him were the remains of a native American campsite. Max ran down the hill to check it out. Dead native Americans littered the ground. Max immediately recognised them. They were the Comanche tribe who they had run into a couple of times.

Max studied the scene. The muddy ground was stained dark red with blood. Men, women, and children lay dead all around him. The tepees had all been burnt. The sight, and the smell was awful, Max felt sick as he wandered around.

He found what he was looking for. The mighty Chief Rattlesnake was laid on the ground with a large hole through the top of his head. His wife lay next to him with a gaping wound to her neck. It was a very distressing scene. Max felt devastated. He considered these people his friends, and now here they were slaughtered, no butchered. It was clear they had been taken by surprise. These brave, and noble warrior people didn't stand a chance.

Max couldn't believe it, it felt like a bad nightmare. He saw a vulture pecking away at the body of a young boy.

"You fucking bastard" Max said angrily.

He aimed his AK47, and blew the vulture to pieces. The sound of gunfire echoed around him.

Out of the corner of his eye Max noticed some dust. He turned to look at it.

"Oh shit" he said.

You fucking idiot Max he thought. The bodies look fresh, and the tepees were still smouldering. The attack must have happened fairly recently. Only a few miles away from where the van was parked.

The dust began to get closer. Max could see more clearly now. Union soldiers on horses. Hundreds of them, possible thousands.

"Oh fuck"

Max started running up the hill, he charged down the other side.

Fifteen minutes later Max charged up to the van red faced, and sweating. He stopped by Madeline. Ethel May, and Joe, and started panting.

“What’s wrong?” Asked Madeline worried.

“Get in the van, we need to leave now” panted Max.

Everyone stood up.

“Joe grab the M16, and take shotgun please,” said Max.

Joe climbed in the back, and came back out with the M16. He rushed round, and jumped in the passenger seat.

Max picked the Skorpion up off the floor, and passed it to Madeline.

“Be ready just in case” he said.

Ethel May, and Madeline climbed in the back, and Max jumped into the driver’s seat. He put the AK47 on his lap, and fired up the engine.

The front wheels spun as Max floored it. The van surged forward.

“Woe” said Joe being flung back in his seat “what happened to economical driving?”

“Economical driving goes out the window when a thousand Union soldiers start chasing you” replied Max.

“Shit, a thousand soldiers, now that’s a real problem,” said Joe.

“Joe, I have a problem, I’m conflicted”

“What’s up mate?”

“The Comanche people we met have all been slaughtered by the Union soldiers chasing us. I want to kill every last one of those motherfuckers, but the timeline had already been altered, and altering it any more could be disastrous”

“Max when a soldier does something who’s fault is it, you always told me this?”

“Yeah, I know, it’s not the soldiers fault it is the government’s fault, it’s always the government’s fault, the poor soldiers are just following orders, you didn’t see it though Joe, the poor Comanche warrior were caught by surprise, they didn’t even have a chance it was the most horrible thing I’ve ever seen in my life”

“I’m sorry Max, I feel for you, we need to get out of the old west it’s too violent”

Max looked at the fuel gauge it was just below a quarter of a tank. They had been travelling through the wide-open plains for Severeal hours. It was starting to get dark. Max spotted a patch of hills to his right, and headed for them. He parked the van by the foot of the hills. Max cut the engine off.

“Right, we’ll take a break, and then I’ll sleep for a couple of hours, and then start driving again, the sooner we get home the better, I’ve had enough of the old west,” said Max.

“Yeah, I’ve had enough too,” said Joe.

“Have you been travelling south?” Asked Ethel May through the hole in the partition.

“Yes, we’ve covered a hundred, and fifty miles south” replied Max.

“Well after studying your map, I believe we should be close to, or in New Mexico, so we need to start heading south, southeast next,” said Ethel May.

“OK good, now let’s stretch our legs, and get a fire going,” said Max.

They all climbed out the van, and had a good stretch. Max grabbed an axe from the back of the van, and wandered over to a small group of trees about fifty yards away from the van. As the only uninjured member of the group it was his job to do all the grunt work.

Max chopped a small tree down, and dragged it over to the van. After chopping the branches off, and slicing the trunk into smaller logs, he began setting up the campfire.

Ten minutes later the fire was roaring away.

Joe lay on the ground knackered. He watched Max working away doing everything, he wished he could help, but his hand was still very sore. He felt something brush his hand, something smooth, and cold. Joe jumped, and frightened the creature, which bit his good hand.

“AAH something just bit me” he yelped.

Max whipped out his phone, and turned the torch on. He rushed over to Joe, and caught sight of a large lizard scurrying away. Max chased after it, and grabbed it by its tail. He walked back over to the fire dragging the struggling lizard.

“Madeline, can you get me a knife please?” Said Max.

“Sure” replied Madeline.

Madeline got up, and climbed into the back of the van.

“What is that, is massive?” Asked Joe.

“Tonight’s dinner,” said Max.

“No, what sort of lizard, you love reptiles so you must know,” said Joe.

Madeline came out of the van, and handed Max a knife.

Max held the lizard’s head down on the ground. He swung the knife down, and cut into its head, he quickly used a sawing motion to slice through the head, killing the lizard as fast as he could.

“This is a Gila Monster, the second largest lizard in the world, the largest lizard in the USA, and unfortunately for you Joe, it’s venomous,” said Max.

“Do you have antivenom for it?” Asked Joe.

“No, I don’t, but fear not the venom in a Gila Monster is not strong enough to kill a human, it is designed to kill small critters. But when you wake up tomorrow you will feel quite ill, you will throw up, and probably have a spot of diarrhoea for a few days. Oh, and your hand will probably swell up for a while. Just keep washing the wound regularly”

“Ah great, now I have no working hands” said Joe annoyed.

“So, what’s the largest lizard in the world then?” Asked Ethel May.

“That would be the Komodo Dragon found in Indonesia, and you wouldn’t want to get bitten by one of them, they are not venomous, but they contain enough harmful bacteria in their mouths to give you a very Severee case of sepsis, and there’s no way I could pick one of them up, they are massive,” said Max.

Max finished skinning, and filleting the meat. After a good sizzle in the frying pan Max served up dinner.

“Wow it’s hot” said Madeline taking a bite.

“Blow on it first to cool it down,” said Max.

"No, I think she means its spicy" said Joe after taking his first bite.

"Yeah, all venous creatures are spicy, that's why I like eating them," said Max.

"My hand feels like it's on fire" said Joe grimacing.

"That's the gila monster venom," said Max.

Max had been driving south for a few hours, at least he thought it was south. The sun was starting to rise on his left side which told him he was travelling south. He turned the van, so the sun was in front of him, and headed towards it, so he was now travelling east. Madeline was asleep in the top bunk, and Joe, and Ethel May were in the bottom bunk.

Max looked at the fuel gauge. It was now just above an eighth of a tank. The trip computer said one hundred, and thirty miles remaining.

Shit that won't be enough though Max. Drastic action was required. Max stopped the van. He climbed out, and went to side door. He quietly opened the door, and climbed inside. Everyone was snoring away happily.

Max found two plastic one gallon bottles, and climbed out of the van. He walked around the front, and climbed up on the bonnet. He lifted the lid on the water tank, and filled the bottles with water. He climbed down off the roof, and got into the back of the van. He stowed the bottles away, and went to the shower cubicle. He removed the cork on the water pipe, and the water began slowly pouring out. He then went to the toilet, and flushed it.

After ten minutes of running the shower, and flushing the toilet the water ran out. Max found his science bag, and got out his toolkit. He took his tool kit, and climbed up onto the roof. He used an adjustable spanned to undo the bolts holding the water tank to the wooden platform on the roof. Once he'd undone all the bolts, he started sliding the heavy iron tank towards the left-hand side of the van. Eventually after eighteen minutes of slowly sliding the heavy tank it fell off the roof of the van, and hit the ground with a mighty thud, sending up a huge cloud of dust.

"Max what's going on?" Said Joe.

Max looked over the side of the van, and saw a naked Joe standing outside.

"Sorry did I wake you?" Said Max.

"Course you fucking did, I thought someone was firing a cannon at us" said Joe annoyed.

"Sorry mate, just had to ditch the water tank, to save fuel. You can go back to bed now"

Joe started coughing, and threw up.

"Oh God, my stomach hurts" he moaned.

“It’s just the Gila Monster venom mate, go to bed, and rest”

“Hang on a minute, if you got rid of the water tank, how are we meant to wash, and use the toilet?”

“Just imagine we’re camping mate”

“Fine, I’m going back to bed, I’ll tell the girls not to worry”

Joe climbed back in the van, and shut the door behind him.

Max climbed down off the roof, and jumped into the drivers seat. He placed his toolkit on the passenger seat with the AK47 that was laying there. Max closed his door, and fired up the engine. He began to drive eastward slowly. The mileage on the trip computer started increasing as the fuel economy improved.

Chapter 21
Time Benders

Max stopped the van in the wide-open plains of Texas. He was knackered, he'd been driving nonstop for three days. The trip computer said there was one hundred, and twenty miles left of fuel. Hopefully that would be enough to reach Sherman. Max thought he recognised the surroundings from when they left Texas, although wide open plains all looked the same.

He watched a large herd of Buffalo in the distance. He then spotted a man on a horse shooting Buffalo with a rifle. Max had an idea. He looked into the back of the van. Joe, Ethel May, and Madeline were all asleep.

Max climbed out of the van, and shut the door quietly. He started walking towards the herd of Buffalo.

After walking for ten minutes, he got close. The Buffalo were all running about in different directions. Max could see Severeal dead Buffalo laying on the ground. He approached the man on the horse who was riding around. The man spotted him, and stopped his horse. Max walked over to him. As he got close, he could see the man was tall, and slim, with short black hair, and a large moustache. He was dressed like a cowboy with a large black Stetson.

Max approached him.

"Howdy buddy" he said.

"Howdy, are you walking across the plains?" The man asked.

"No, my wagon is parked up, and my friends are asleep"

The man got off his horse, and faced Max.

"I'm Max Walsh"

"Hello Max Walsh, I'm Wyatt Earp"

They shook hands.

"The Wyatt Earp?" Said Max excitedly.

"Oh, heard of me, have you?" Said Wyatt confused.

"Well, I heard there was a famous lawman called Wyatt Earp"

Wyatt started laughing.

"Well, that aint me Max, I'm no lawman, I've been on the wrong side of the law a few times, mainly for horse rustling"

"I see," said Max smiling.

"Can I help you with something Max, or did you just mosey on over to say hi?"

"I was wondering if I could buy a Buffalo off you"

"Sure, you can, you could get one for free if you had a rifle, but if you wanna take one of mine it will cost ya a dollar"

"Here" said Max handing Wyatt a silver coin.

Wyatt took the coin, and looked at it.

“A shiny silver coin, hell you can take two Buffalo for this”

“One will be fine; I can’t drag two Buffalo’s back to my wagon”

“OK, well nice to meet you Max, pick any dead Buffalo you want. I’m going back to work now”

“Thank you, Wyatt Earp, it was a pleasure to meet you”

Wyatt mounted his horse, and rode away. Max pulled his phone out, and snapped a picture of Wyatt Earp riding away. He put his phone back in his pocket, and walked over to a dead Buffalo.

After twenty minutes, he finally arrived back at the van sweating after dragging a large dead Buffalo.

Max, Madeline, Joe, and Ethel May sat by a roaring campfire eating Buffalo meat.

“Are you sure it was the Wyatt Earp you met?” Asked Joe.

“Not a hundred percent sure, but how many Wyatt Earp’s are there in the old west?” Max replied.

“I always though Wyatt Earp was a legendary lawman though,” said Joe.

“Well maybe he was a Buffalo hunter before he was a lawman,” said Max.

“Why was he such a legendary lawman?” Asked Ethel May.

“I don’t know, because of the gunfight at the OK Corral I suppose,” said Max.

“What’s the gunfight at the OK Corral?” Asked Madeline.

“I’m not sure,” said Max.

“I saw it in a film, the Earp brothers, and Doc Holiday faced a gang of criminals, and had a shootout with them, Wyatt Earp was the only one who was uninjured,” said Joe.

“Yeah, that does sound right, but you can’t believe everything in films, they change history all the time,” said Max.

“A bit like you Max,” said Joe.

“Oh God sorry” said Madeline jumping up.

Madeline walked away from the fire, and threw up.

“God, I feel a bit sick too” said Ethel May jumping up.

Ethel May walked away from the fire, and threw up.

“The Buffalo meat was definitely cooked properly, wasn’t it?” Said Joe.

“Red meat doesn’t need to be cooked properly, you can eat it raw, it’s not the meat” said Max.

Madeline, and Ethel May came back over, and sat down.

“Sorry, my stomach feels weird,” said Madeline.

“Yeah, me too, it feels like when I was last pregnant,” said Ethel May.

Max, and Joe looked at each other.

“P, p, p, pregnant” stuttered Max.

“Yes” said Madeline smiling.

“You’re both pregnant at the same time?” Said Joe.

“I don’t understand” said Max bewildered.

“Well, we did have sex the night after you rescued us from Herman, and Ziggy,” said Madeline.

“Yeah, and we had sex the night before when we was locked up,” said Ethel May.

“You had sex in a prison cell?” Said Max looking at Joe.

“Well, we had to do something to pass the time” said Joe with a sly smile on his face.

"So, we're in the old west with two pregnant women?" Said Max.

"Yes, isn't it wonderful" said Madeline excitedly.

"Max will time travel have any effect on an unborn child?" Asked Joe.

"That's a mighty fine questions Joe, I would say no, it didn't do us any harm did it?" Said Max.

"Are you sure Max?" Asked Madeline.

"Yes, I'm sure, the risk of staying in the old west when our wives are pregnant is much greater than the risk of time travel, now I must get some sleep before I do the last part of the journey," said Max.

"Are we close to Sherman then?" Said Joe.

"I bloody hope so," said Max yawning.

After another twenty-four hours of driving Max could see their old shack. The trip computer said fifteen miles. Max was grateful that they had made it. Home was in sight, only about a quarter of a mile left.

Suddenly a large group of Texas Rangers appeared from behind the shack, and blocked the way. Captain Bigfoot Wallace was at the front of them.

Max could see a dust cloud in the corner of his eye. He turned his head, and saw Union calvary soldiers riding towards him in huge numbers, at least a thousand. On his other side he could see a group of lawmen lining up.

They were surrounded by Texas Rangers, lawmen, and soldiers.

Max stopped the van, and cut the engine. He dived through the hole in the partition. Joe was sat down on a seat in the back. Madeline, and Ethel May were asleep.

“What’s up mate?” Asked Joe as Max crashed onto the floor.

“We’re surrounded,” said Max.

“Surrounded by who?”

“Soldiers, Texas Rangers, and lawmen, you had to say it didn’t you Joseph”

“You can’t blame me for this”

“What was that banging sound?” Asked Madeline sleepily.

“Yeah, I heard that too” said Ethel May waking up.

“Don’t worry it was just me diving into the back. We’re surrounded by soldiers, Texas Rangers, and lawmen, we have to go back to the future right now before the soldiers set up their cannons,” said Max.

“Oh, how exiting” said Madeline cheerfully.

Max got the lightning generator out of one of the wooden boxes. He sat on the floor, and aimed it at the power supply.

“I suggest everyone closes their eyes, as this will cause a bright flash” said Max.

Outside the van the Union soldiers were setting up one of their Howitzer cannons. They put the cannon into position. One soldier poured the powder into the cannon, and two soldiers dropped the large iron cannon ball into it. They stood behind the cannon, and manoeuvred it so it was aimed towards the strange white horseless carriage.

“Fire at will,” said the Captain.

A soldier pulled the ignition device, and a spark ignited the powder.

BOOM

The big iron cannon ball exploded out of the Howitzer, and sailed through the air towards the strange white horseless carriage.

Suddenly there was a huge white flash.

The cannon ball slammed down onto the dusty ground embedding itself into the earth, and sending a huge dust cloud.

The horseless carriage had disappeared.

"What the hell," said the Captain.

"Is everyone OK," said Max.

"That felt weird," said Madeline.

"I feel OK," said Ethel May.

"Are we home now?" Asked Joe.

"That's a good question Joe," said Max.

Max stood up, and walked over to the hole in the partition.

"What the fuck" he said shocked.

Max moved backwards, and opened the side door.

Everyone looked outside.

They all saw a green field as far as the eye could see. In the distance there were some hills, and over to the left there was a woodland area.

"That doesn't look like Texas," said Joe.

"No, it doesn't" said Max confused.

"So where are we?" Asked Madeline.

"That's a fine question. Let me think about this logically. We've definitely moved through time, so if this is the twenty first century then we really did screw the timeline up. It is also possible that we could have travelled back in time to when Texas was wild, and green," said Max.

"How can we find out where we are?" Asked Joe.

"Ooh our phones" said Max reaching into his pocket.

Max checked his phone. No signal. Max jumped out the van, and got into the driver's seat. He turned on the radio. No signal.

"Joe, can you shut the side door please," said Max.

"Yeah sure" said Joe sliding the door shut.

Max fired up the engine.

"Where are we going?" Asked Joe.

"Well just in case we are further back in time, I think it would be a good idea to park the van by the trees so we're not so exposed," said Max.

The van struggled over the grassy terrain. The red fuel warning light was flashing. Max parked up by the edge of the woodland. He looked at the trip computer, there was five miles of fuel left.

Max climbed out the van holding the AK47, and shut the door behind him. He opened the side door, and jumped into the back. He rummaged into the weapons bag, and found a couple of extra clips for the AK47. He grabbed a Skorpion, and handed it to Joe.

“OK Joe, you guard the girls, and the van, and I will take a walk, and see what I can find,” said Max.

“Why are you taking the AK with you?” Asked Joe.

“In case I come across a T-Rex,” said Max.

“Fair enough”

“Something is a bit strange though”

“What’s strange?”

“That’s a stinking iris” said Max pointing to a strange plant with red berries.

“What the hell is a stinky iris?” Said Joe confused.

“A wildflower native to Britain”

“You mean, we’re in Britain?”

“Possibly, I need to have a look around. I’ll be back”

“OK Arnie, see you soon”

Max walked over to the bed, and gave Madeline a kiss.

“You stay safe now” she said.

“Don’t worry darling, a T-Rex is no match for a AK47, I think”

Max jumped out the van, and started walking towards the hills in the distance.

The air smelt fresher than Max had ever experienced. Birds chirped happily in the sky. The grass he was walking over was long, and wild. It had grown so long the blades were collapsing under their own weight.

Well, we’re either back in time before lawnmowers existed, or we screwed the timeline so badly lawnmowers were never invented he thought to himself.

A large crow landed near to Max, and stated squawking at him.

“Do you know what year it is?” he said to the crow.

The crow stopped squawking, and stared at Max.

Max strolled past, and carried on towards the hills.

It took half an hour to reach the foot of the hills. The hills weren’t very high. Max clambered up the hill, and peered over.

Below him was a large grassy valley.

Oh, shit he thought to himself as he set eyes on something in the valley.

There was a large camp in the valley. Big white tents. Hundreds of soldiers. Some were sitting down eating, and some were milling around. They wore a distinctive uniform. Red togas with steel armour covering their chests, and their backs. They wore steel helmets with red bristles on the top of them. Max could see black staffs with silvers eagles on them stuck into the ground outside the largest tents. They were definitely Roman soldiers. Max was also fairly certain they were in England back in the Iron age, possible. The stinking iris, a crow, Roman invaders.

Oh, shit Max thought.

Max shuffled back down the hill, and made his way back to the van.

He arrived back at the van with a smile on his face.

Joe, Ethel May, and Madeline were stood by the van.

“Well, you look happy, good news?” Asked Joe.

“Yes Joe, I’m fairly certain we are in England,” said Max.

“Excellent, any idea what year it is?”

“When did the Romans occupy England?”

The End

Not entirely…

Just the end of the first instalment of this epic true story. Find out what happens to the intrepid time travellers in:

Time Benders 2
Fractured Time

Out in the future, or maybe in the past!

Printed in Great Britain
by Amazon